THE ORPHEUS PLOT

CHRISTOPHER SWIEDLER

HARPER
An Imprint of HarperCollinsPublishers

Library of Congress Control Number: 2020950477
ISBN 978-0-06-289444-1

Typography by Michelle Taormina
21 22 23 24 25   PC/LSCH   10 9 8 7 6 5 4 3 2 1
❖
First Edition

For Jack, Andrew, Eleanor, and all of the future pioneers of their generation

1

IF YOU GET caught, I'm going to pretend I don't know who you are.

Lucas stared at the message scrolling across his wrist screen, shielding it with his hand to keep the light from being noticed. He dictated a quick response to his suit's computer, keeping his voice low even though it was physically impossible for anyone else to hear him through the vacuum of space. *This was your idea, remember?*

Tali's response came quickly: *Then do me a favor and don't get caught.*

Lucas poked his head out from his hiding spot behind an empty fuel tank and looked around. The sun had set a little while ago and wouldn't rise again for another nine hours. In the starlight, the surface of the asteroid was a dark, dusty gray, pockmarked with shadowy micro-craters. Off to one side, the skeleton of a ten-person rover that the colony kids used as a play structure glinted silvery white. A small row of blue lamps on the wall ahead of him marked the retractable doors of the naval hangar. It was after midnight, colony time, and if anyone saw him out here they were going to have a lot of questions that Lucas wouldn't want to answer. He needed his sister to stop sending him stupid messages and get down here to let him inside.

Why was she taking so long? *She'd* been the one to message *him*. He couldn't even remember the last time that had happened. Her schedule as a cadet on the teaching ship *Orpheus* meant they only got to see each other every few months. And even when she was here on Ceres at the same time as him, she was usually too busy studying or prepping for the upcoming term to spend much time with him. But then earlier today, out of the blue: *I have a surprise for you. Meet me at the hangar at 0130.* And then, a few seconds later: *You're going to like it.*

Lucas grinned. He could guess exactly what her "surprise" would be.

He felt the low rumble of airlock pumps cycling, and after an agonizingly long wait, the hangar doors slid open wide enough for him to slip inside. He squinted in the sudden brightness of the overhead lights. Military transports, scouts, and cargo haulers were lined in neat rows, all polished to the traditional Navy shine. He ran

2

his hands along the hull of a sleek courier ship. It wasn't much more than a single-seat cockpit strapped to a pair of big engines. What would it be like to fly something like *this*?

He found his adopted sister, Tali, leaning against a desk at the back of the hangar. She was wearing the red-and-white uniform of a naval cadet—the same uniform he'd imagined for himself so many times. A thick bundle of cables ran from a computer screen on the desk to the cockpit of an old patrol ship, where a hand-lettered sign read SIMULATOR TIME LIMITED TO THIRTY MINUTES WHILE OTHERS ARE WAITING.

"Finally," she said, yawning.

"Finally, yourself," he shot back. "I was waiting out there twenty minutes."

She shrugged. "My roommate wouldn't fall asleep."

"So—any suggestions for a packing list?" he asked, abandoning the pretense that he didn't know what her surprise was. He knew he should probably ask her how she was doing or engage in some other kind of small talk, but right now he didn't have the patience.

Two days ago, his news feed monitoring program had alerted him that an outbreak of measles—*measles!*— had forced a transport ship from Earth to turn back. A cross-reference of the passenger manifest had confirmed that a thirteen-year-old girl on board was scheduled to be enrolled on the *Orpheus*. Naval immunization rules meant that she would have to miss the upcoming term, which meant that there was suddenly an open spot with nobody to fill it.

He'd sent in his own application on his thirteenth birthday, and he had nothing to show for it but radio silence. But now, with the recommendation of a senior cadet like Tali . . .

"Packing list?" she asked, frowning.

"I'll get my own uniform, right? But I can't find anything online about whether the Navy provides underwear. You'd think they'd be more clear about details like that."

"Wait," Tali said slowly. "You think the surprise is that I've gotten you onto the *Orpheus*?"

It was well done, he thought. She might have a second career as an actor if the Navy didn't work out. "Stop kidding around. It's not funny."

"Lucas, I'm not kidding. The surprise is that I got you time on the simulator. I thought it would be a fun thing to do before I shipped out."

He suddenly felt as if he'd been dropped into free fall. *This* was why she'd called him down here? So he could practice flying in a stupid video game?

"Lucas, I've told you this over and over," she said. "I can't get you into the academy. It's impossible."

"But there's an empty spot—"

"—which they're *not going to fill with a kid from the Belt*."

"That doesn't make any sense!" Lucas said. "You're from the Belt!"

Tali shook her head. "I was born on Mars. That's totally different."

Totally different? She'd only been six years old when she'd moved here from Port Meridian on Mars. Not long after that, her parents had died, along with Lucas's mother, in the Tannhauser pressure dome accident here on Ceres. Afterward, Lucas's father had adopted her, and she'd lived with them for almost seven years. Most of her life had been spent in space. How was she any less of a Belter than he was?

"You need to stop getting your hopes up," she said. "The Navy has *never* accepted a Belter cadet. Do you think that's an oversight? Or just bad luck?"

Tali's voice had that same I-know-what-I'm-talking-about tone that she'd used to lecture him with when they were growing up on their father's mining ship. She liked to pretend that she was the expert on everything just because she was three years older than him. He'd forgotten how much he hated that tone in her voice.

"Did you even try?" he said, unable to keep the anger out of his voice. "Or were you just lying when you said you'd put in a recommendation for me?"

"I tried," she insisted. "Of course I tried. I talked to anyone who would listen. It was no use."

Was she telling the truth? Or was she just telling him that so he'd shut up and stop asking? Half of him suspected that was exactly what she'd done, while the other half hated himself for not trusting her.

"I know it sounds like it would be great to go to the academy," she said. "But it's hard enough for a kid from Earth or Mars. For you . . ."

Lucas knew that Tali was a lot better at social niceties than he was. Growing up on a mining ship meant spending a few days each month in port with whatever group of kids happened to be there at the time, and so you either got really good at making friends quickly, or you spent a lot of time alone. Lucas was solidly in the second category, and it had only gotten harder once Tali had left and he hadn't been able to rely on attaching himself to her and the friends she made. And sure, it would be even weirder being on a ship where he was the only Belter. But that wasn't going to stop him from joining!

"I'd be okay," he insisted.

"How would you know?" Tali asked. "Literally everything you know about Earthers comes from movies. Trust me—you really don't want to be at that school."

"You sound just like Dad," he muttered.

She stiffened. "Well, he's right. About this, anyway."

Tali and Tomas Adebayo were nothing alike, except for the million ways that they were *exactly* alike. Lucas noticed, and not for the first time, that Tali's reaction when he mentioned her adopted father was almost identical to the way their dad reacted when Lucas talked about *her.*

Suddenly he missed his sister, which was an odd feeling considering she was standing right in front of him. But what he missed wasn't Tali the cadet, but Tali the girl he'd grown up with. The one who had taught him how to use air ducts to sneak from one side of the colony to the other. The one who had taught him to fly *with style,* as she liked to put it. When she'd joined the Navy, it was as if those parts of her had just vanished. Now sometimes it seemed as if the only thing left inside her was anger. Anger at the Navy whenever she ran into some stupid regulation that she didn't agree with. Anger at Belters, especially miners, who she now seemed to think were some kind of primitive culture that she'd managed to escape from. But above all, anger at their father.

"How about we make a deal?" Lucas said suddenly. "I'll never, ever talk to you about joining the Navy again. I won't ask for any more favors or recommendations. I won't bug you about any of it. I just need you to do one thing."

Tali looked at him skeptically. "What's that?"

"Go see him."

He knew exactly how she'd react to *that* suggestion. Which, he supposed, was why he made it.

"You'd do that? Never ask about the Navy again? And all I'd have to do in exchange is go talk to Tomas?"

Lucas nodded. He didn't even have to consider it for a second. The rift between his father and his sister hurt him a hundred times more than not getting into the academy. And the extra, bonus, cherry-on-top stupidity of it all was that he knew it hurt Tali and his dad just as much. They were just too boneheadedly stubborn to admit it.

"Sorry, Lucas. It's not going to happen." She turned and opened up the simulator's canopy. "So are you going to get some practice time in, or what?"

Maybe she and his father were right. Maybe this was all stupid, trying to get accepted as a Navy cadet. He probably ought to just study piloting here on Ceres, like his dad wanted him to do.

Except that wasn't what *he* wanted. Flying little mining trucks was fun, and he was good at it—even Tali had to admit that. But what he dreamed about was piloting the big starliners and cruisers like the *Orpheus*. No apprenticeship in the Belt was going to teach him that. His dad hated the Navy as much as any Belter, but even he agreed that the best capital-ship pilots, hands down, were trained in the Navy.

Lucas turned and looked at the little courier that had caught his attention earlier. It certainly wasn't a cruiser, but it was a lot better than the boats he was used to flying. Maybe there was a way to salvage at least *something* out of tonight.

"Can I sit in it?" he asked Tali, pointing at the courier. "Just for a minute?"

She sighed. "Lucas . . ."

"It can't hurt anything to just *sit*, can it?" he said. "You owe me that much."

Tali frowned, clearly weighing the risks against whatever obligations she still felt toward him. "All right," she said finally. "But if you get caught—"

"You'll pretend you don't know who I am," Lucas finished. "I know."

He ran back to the courier and opened the canopy. Carefully he climbed into the cockpit and settled into the seat. The ship was so new that half of the controls were still covered in plastic wrap. The gauges and controls were all familiar to him from the mining trucks he was used to flying, but at the same time, everything felt completely different. Nothing was scratched up, bolted on, or hanging loose. Everything was in its proper place instead of being jammed in wherever it could fit.

His heart soared just being in a ship like this. It was practically *begging* to be flown. He flipped the main power switches, and the console sprang to life. Diagnostic messages flashed and status lights turned green. He imagined what it would be like to take her out. *If only . . .*

His reverie was shattered by a squawk over his suit's comm system. "Who's turning on my ship?"

Lucas's heart leaped into his throat. *Who . . . what . . . ?* He turned and saw a tall, silvery-haired woman in a blue-and-gold pressure suit striding toward them. Her name tag read Moskowitz. He didn't know who she was, but she was clearly an officer, which meant that he had slightly less than ten seconds of freedom left. Tali looked back and forth between Lucas and the woman, clearly trying to come up with some explanation for what they were doing here.

"Good evening, ma'am," she managed.

The woman stopped and cocked her head at Lucas. She was still a few meters away, and from that distance, the canopy and helmet were probably obscuring his face. Not knowing what else to do, Lucas gave her his best impression of a Navy salute.

"Did you sign up for the night shift?" Moskowitz asked Tali. "I don't remember seeing you on the list."

"Not exactly, ma'am," Tali stammered. "But I thought you might need help."

Moskowitz turned toward Lucas. "You're the new test

pilot? I know I said it was high priority, but I didn't expect you to show up in the middle of the night."

Test pilot? Something perked up in the back of Lucas's mind. Maybe there was a way out of this after all.

"Uh, yes, ma'am," he said, deepening his voice by an octave. What did test pilots sound like, exactly? "Like you said—high priority."

"But we can come back tomorrow," Tali said, giving Lucas an angry glance that he had no difficulty interpreting. "I'm sure now is not a good time for—"

"Oh, I'm not complaining," Moskowitz said. She tapped for a moment at the tablet she was carrying. "This way I won't have to wait until the day shift to get my test results. Push her hard, and do your best to max out the gee forces. I think the hiccup in the starboard engine is fixed, but we won't know until she gets out there."

Lucas grinned. This was even better than he'd hoped. She was actually asking him to *fly* this ship! As if in answer, Moskowitz waved her hand at the hangar doors. "Come on, now. I'm still planning on getting some sleep tonight. Take her out and tell me how that engine does."

Tali turned toward Lucas, her eyes wide, and gave him a tiny but emphatic shake of her head. "Get out now," she mouthed.

He grinned and put his hands on the controls. He

couldn't disobey a direct order from an officer, could he? And anyway, if he opened the canopy, Moskowitz would see that he wasn't even a cadet, much less an actual test pilot.

Ignoring Tali's furious glare, he angled the engines so that they were pointing down and inched the throttle forward. Under his control, the ship lifted off gracefully and hovered a few meters above the hangar floor. He pushed the control stick forward, and the ship soared out through the hangar doors and up toward the stars.

This was flying! Her thrust was only at a few percent of her max and she was already breaking free of the asteroid's gravity. He banked left and flew in a circle above the colony. The main dome glowed a brilliant yellow, with the half-circle of the naval base barely visible around it.

Lucas tilted the ship back until his engines were pointed straight down and jammed the throttle to its limit. Gee forces squeezed him against the seat as the ship leaped up into the night sky. The bright yellow disk of the sun appeared off to his left, and his helmet darkened to compensate for the additional light. He flipped her around quickly and used full thrust to brake to a halt.

"No need to showboat," Moskowitz said over the radio. "How does she feel? Any stutter on that starboard side?"

"She feels fantastic," he answered truthfully. "Smooth as silk."

"All right, then. Put her through a few turns and see how she handles."

He made an experimental S-turn and then rolled the ship onto her back. She responded to every movement of the control stick without a hint of balkiness or lag. He tested rolls, banks, dives, and climbs, momentarily forgetting everything except the joy of flying a ship like this.

As he rose higher and higher above the surface, he caught sight of a gleaming white shape high above: the teaching ship ISS *Orpheus*, where Navy cadets spent their first three years. The cruiser looked both elegant and deadly, with clean lines and polished transplastic windows that made his father's ship, the *Josey Wales*, seem like the back end of a garbage transport.

In less than twenty-four hours, the *Orpheus*, along with Tali and the rest of her students, would be heading out for the next term's cruise. Lucas felt a surge of anger. How many of those first-year cadets from Earth or Mars or Luna knew anything at all about being in space? Half of them were probably sick from free fall and the other half would still be trying to figure out how to brush their teeth in zero gee. It wasn't even the tiniest bit fair.

"All right, that's enough," the officer said. "Come on back in and I'll run some diagnostics."

"Yes, ma'am," Lucas answered, trying to keep the disappointment out of his voice. He flew one more ring around the *Orpheus* and then headed back to the naval base. As soon as he landed, Moskowitz closed the doors and repressurized the hangar.

"Nice flying," she said. "A little flashy, but I got the data I wanted."

Lucas paused. How was he going to get out of the ship without her seeing him? Tali, recognizing his predicament, tightened her jaw and looked around. They needed some kind of distraction. . . .

"Thrust was definitely better," Moskowitz murmured to herself, looking down at her tablet. "Cooling system pressure was a little off, though."

Cooling systems. That gave Lucas an idea. He typed a few commands into the computer console. The screen displayed a warning message, and he jabbed the override button with his thumb. This wasn't something any sane pilot would do, but his situation called for extraordinary measures.

The engines at the back of the ship hissed loudly, and immediately everything outside the canopy was obscured by a thick cloud of water vapor. Moskowitz swore. "What the—"

Lucas popped the canopy and jumped out. Moskowitz was already crouching down behind the engine nozzles, waving her tablet in front of her in an attempt to clear the air. Tali grabbed Lucas's arm with a we'll-talk-about-this-later expression and dragged him to the exit in the back corner of the hangar.

As soon as they were in the corridor outside, Lucas pulled off his helmet. "Clever, huh? I did that once by accident with Aunt Kira's mining-truck racer. It looks bad, but really it's just—"

"Shut. Up."

Tali half guided, half dragged him through the maze-like corridors of the base, her fingers digging painfully into his upper arm. She relaxed her grip a tiny amount as they passed by a sleepy-looking cadet guarding the doors that separated the naval base from the civilian colony, but the guard didn't seem to be the slightest bit interested in them or what they were doing at this hour. Resuming her iron grip, Tali marched Lucas across the courtyard of the main pressure dome. A few recently arrived boys and girls who hadn't adjusted to colony time were playing near the big central fountain. The kids paused their game of tag to watch with curious expressions as Tali led Lucas down a ramp that led to the commercial hangars. Finally she stopped outside hangar three, where the *Josey Wales* was docked, and let him go with a little jerk that made him stumble and almost fall.

"That was the stupidest thing I've ever seen," she fumed. "Do you know what would have happened if she'd gotten a good look at you?"

"What was I supposed to do?" Lucas asked, massaging his arm. "Hop out and say, 'Oops, sorry'?"

"Never again, understand? We're never doing that again."

Did she think she'd actually done him some kind of favor? "Fine. Whatever. It's not like—"

"Is there a problem?" a voice asked.

Lucas turned and saw Tomas Adebayo coming down the gangway of the *Josey Wales*. His long black hair was knotted at the base of his neck, Belter-style. As he walked around the ship toward them, his prosthetic legs clanked loudly on the floor of the hangar. When he saw Tali he stopped, putting his hand on the hull of his ship to help keep his balance.

There was a moment of silence as Tali and Tomas stared at each other. *Well*, Lucas thought. *Here we all are. . . .*

"Hello, Nat," Tomas said finally. "It's good to see you."

"Don't call me that," she snapped.

Tomas nodded as if this was a perfectly reasonable request, but Lucas could see that the words stung. "All right," he said. "It's good to see you, Cadet Natali Chen. That's what you go by now?"

Tali's breath hissed through her nostrils for a moment, and then she whirled around and strode back toward the naval base. Tomas watched her leave, a conflicting set of emotions playing out on his face. When she was gone, he turned to Lucas.

"Do I want to know what happened?"

Lucas swallowed and gave a quick shake of his head.

"Then get into your bunk before I decide to ask."

2

THE NEXT MORNING, Lucas's father seemed to have forgotten all about what had happened the previous night. Except that was almost worse than if he'd brought it up right away, because from long experience, Lucas knew that his dad never forgot anything. At breakfast they talked through the repairs and maintenance work his dad had planned out for the day, using a marker to scrawl out a list on the front of their tiny autopantry. By lunchtime the two of them had disassembled and checked over the entire portside hydraulic system. Tomas had immense patience for work like this. Lucas followed along and helped as best he could, but his mind was on Tali and the *Orpheus*, who would be leaving orbit in just a few hours.

"It was nice seeing Tali, wasn't it?" Lucas asked as his father opened an access panel on the underside of the ship to inspect the control system cabling.

His father's lips tightened almost imperceptibly. After a moment he nodded in that polite way he reserved for people who said something stupid that he didn't think was worth arguing about. "It's good the two of you keep up."

Why do I do that? Lucas wondered. *Why do I bother bringing her up?* It was as if there was some kind of pressure inside him to hear her name spoken, so that the more his dad tried to not talk about her, the more desperately Lucas wanted to.

It was weird to think that Lucas himself was now the same age that Tali had been when she'd broken the news to him that she was leaving for the academy. His first thought had been that at least the fights between her and their father would now be over, but that sense of relief had turned out to be overly optimistic. Even after she left, it was as if the argument between the two of them still hung in the air of the *Josey Wales*. Lucas couldn't even understand what they were angry *about*. His dad had never been fond of the Navy, but he didn't hate it the way a lot of miners did. And though Tali had always been the sort of person to dream about bigger things than a mining ship, she had never despised the life they'd led growing up. But suddenly that summer, it had been as if a switch had been flipped and the two of them had become different people.

When he'd pressed his sister for an explanation—how

had she gotten accepted, and why was their dad so angry about it?—she'd said something vague about her Martian birth certificate and a relative of her mother's who had helped her get into the school. No matter how many times he'd asked, she wouldn't tell him any more than that. His dad wouldn't even let him finish the question before he'd cut Lucas off with a curt "I'm not talking about it."

And then, just like that, she was gone. Not just away from home, but *gone*, as if history had been rewritten and Tali had never been a part of their family. He'd thought that the fights between his father and his sister had been bad, but they were nothing compared to the silence.

"I don't know what she's here for," Tomas said, pulling out a thick strand of multicolored wiring. "But I don't think it's good."

For a moment Lucas thought that his dad was talking about Tali. Then Tomas nodded toward the front of the hangar, where a woman in a naval officer's uniform was standing with her hands behind her back. Lucas sucked in his breath. Why would a Navy officer be here in the civilian wing? Had someone discovered what had happened last night?

"How about you go ask her what she needs?" Tomas said.

"Me?"

"Yes, you," Tomas said crossly. "Seems to me she's either extremely lost or she wants to talk to us about something."

The idea that she was here to talk to them was exactly what Lucas was afraid of. He took a deep breath and walked over to where the woman was standing, giving her what he hoped was a relaxed, natural smile.

"Hello. Can I help you with something?"

"Are you Lucas Adebayo?" the officer asked. Her petite build made her about as physically unintimidating as she could be, but she carried herself with the confidence of many years of authority.

"Yes, ma'am," Lucas said, his voice faint.

"I'd like to speak with you and your father."

His dad was already walking out toward them, wiping his hands on a stained red towel. "What can I do for you?"

"I'm Captain Sanchez," the officer said, reaching out her hand.

"We've got nothing illegal on board," Tomas said. He folded up the towel neatly and put it in his back pocket, ignoring Sanchez's proffered hand. "But I can't stop you from looking."

"I'm not here to search your ship, Mr. Adebayo," Sanchez said, pulling back her hand. "I'm here to talk to you about Lucas."

"Lucas?" Tomas asked, frowning. "What about him?"

About the fact that I'm about to go to jail for stealing a ship, Lucas thought. "Captain Sanchez . . . ma'am—"

"Let the captain answer."

"I understand your son is quite an accomplished pilot," Sanchez said. "And while his schooling has been nontraditional, he's scored very highly on all the standardized tests."

"His schooling has been very traditional," Tomas corrected. "For a boy growing up in the Belt."

"Yes, of course," Sanchez said. She produced a folded piece of paper and handed it to Tomas. "This is a letter to you from the admiralty."

As Tomas read, Lucas craned his neck to try to see the contents of the letter. Was it a warrant for his arrest? A summons?

Tomas frowned and folded the paper. "I'm sure you mean well by this, Ms. Sanchez. But our answer is no."

"Are you sure you don't want to discuss that with Lucas?" she asked, cocking her head to one side.

Tomas pursed his lips and didn't answer.

"Discuss what?" Lucas asked. What was going on?

"They want you to be a cadet," Tomas said. His voice was hoarse, almost a growl. "On the *Orpheus.*"

"A cadet?" Lucas repeated, as if the word were in a

foreign language. His brain struggled to understand what was happening. Sanchez wasn't here to arrest him—she was here to *recruit* him. "But the *Orpheus* leaves tonight!"

"I don't believe she'll leave without me," Sanchez said dryly. "I'm her captain."

The blood rushed to Lucas's head. Was this really happening, or was he in a dream? The captain of the *Orpheus* was here to personally invite him to be a cadet? There was only one explanation: Tali had done it! He mentally took back every angry thought he'd ever had about her.

"Tell me, Ms. Sanchez," Tomas said. "In the whole history of the Navy, how many Belter kids have been invited to that school of yours?"

"None," Sanchez replied, unfazed by Tomas's accusatory tone. "But I believe this change is long overdue. It's the right thing for the Navy and the right thing for the school."

"It might be," Tomas said. "But is it the right thing for him?"

Sanchez looked at Lucas with a curious expression, making him feel as if he were an insect being studied under a microscope. He shifted uncomfortably but kept his eyes locked with hers. Maybe his dad needed convincing that this was the right thing to do, but he didn't.

"All I can promise is that he'll be treated fairly. The

rest is up to him." Sanchez looked at her watch. "But he's right—the *Orpheus* leaves at twenty-two hundred, which means you'll need to decide quickly."

Lucas straightened up. "Of course I'll—"

"Lucas," Tomas said in a warning voice. "You and I will talk about this in a moment—after the captain here takes her leave."

"But—"

"*Lucas.*"

"I hope to see you on board, Lucas," Sanchez said. "But your father isn't wrong. It won't be easy, and I wouldn't blame you for saying no."

She gave them both a polite nod and walked away. Tomas shoved the letter into his pocket and climbed up the gangway into the *Josey Wales*.

"Dad," Lucas said, following along behind him. "You have to let me go. You *have* to!"

His father stopped halfway down the main corridor of the ship and turned toward him. "Didn't you hear her? She said it herself. You don't want this."

Why was everyone trying to tell him what he wanted? Lucas knew *exactly* what he wanted. "But even you say it's the best school—"

"It's the best school for idiot groundhog kids who've never been to space in their life," Tomas said. "But you're a miner. You've been flying since you could walk."

"Not like that," Lucas said, pointing upward in the general direction of the *Orpheus*. "Not in ships like that."

"Ships like *that* go around harassing good people. Impounding their cargo. Throwing them in jail. You were there when that fellow searched your cousin Ivy's ship. Remember what he called her, right to her face? Remember how he tore everything apart, even though he knew there wasn't anything to find? It took the three of us all day to put her cargo hold back together."

"Not everyone in the Navy is like that," Lucas insisted. "And I'm not going to turn out like them."

"That's what I thought about your sister!" his dad shouted.

The word "sister" echoed around the cabin. Tomas's face twisted with anger and pain and regret and a half-dozen other emotions that Lucas couldn't even recognize. His breath hissed through his nostrils, and his eyes were red and glassy.

"And now look at her," Tomas muttered. "Tells everyone that she'd never even *been* to the Belt before she joined up."

What could Lucas say to that? His dad was right. When Tali had left the *Josey Wales*, she'd become a different person. She'd rejected Tomas completely, and on the rare occasions when Lucas got a chance to spend time with her, it felt like there was a million-kilometer gulf between them that he couldn't bridge, no matter how hard he tried. But how was it fair to blame him for that? It seemed like no matter where Lucas stood, he was always in the crossfire between his father and his sister.

"Did anyone talk to you about this?" his dad asked suddenly. "Anyone from the Navy? Anyone from the Belt?"

Lucas looked at him in confusion. What was he talking about? Who else would have talked to him? "No, Dad," he said. "I mean, not other than just now."

His dad stomped down to the engine compartment and stopped. He put his hand on the wall and bent his head down as if he was carrying a great weight.

"If you went, you'd be on the same ship as her." Tomas's voice was flat and emotionless, leaving Lucas to wonder whether this would be a good thing or a bad thing. Lucas knew his dad better than anyone else in the world, but sometimes Tomas Adebayo was still a complete mystery to him.

"Finish the diagnostics on the attitude rockets," his dad said without looking at him. "The transducer will have to keep for now."

"Yes, sir," Lucas mumbled.

His dad took a deep breath. "After that, pack your bags and get yourself cleaned up. You don't want to show up covered in hydraulic fluid."

It took Lucas several seconds to put this together. Pack

his bags? "You mean you're letting me go?"

"Yes, I'm letting you go," Tomas said, sounding as if the words were physically painful for him. "But only because I'm worried that the alternative would be even worse."

Lucas wanted to ask what he meant by "alternative," but he could see that his dad wasn't going to say anything more. What was he afraid of? What was worse, from his point of view, than letting Lucas join the Navy?

Tomas turned back toward Lucas. "Except you have to promise me one thing. Promise that you won't forget where you came from."

Like she did, he didn't need to add. Were those tears in his eyes, or just Lucas's imagination? His dad blinked and looked away.

"I won't," Lucas said. He wrapped his arms around his father and hugged him tightly. "Thank you!"

"Don't thank me yet," Tomas grumbled. "A few days from now, you may wish I'd stuck to my guns."

It took Lucas all of five minutes to change his clothes and pack up a duffel bag containing everything he wanted to take with him to the *Orpheus*. He hardly had any physical possessions on board, since every kilogram of extra mass on the *Josey Wales* meant they burned more fuel and earned less profit. Once he'd packed up a few extra jumpsuits, a small hygiene kit, and a tiny, lightweight photo cube, his corner of the ship's sleeping cabin was practically empty.

"Come on, Dad," he called out, climbing into the cockpit and securing his bag underneath the copilot's seat. He flipped on the nav computer and looked up the orbit of the *Orpheus*. By the time Tomas joined him in the cockpit and settled into his own seat, Lucas had the course mapped out.

"Not leaving much for me to do, are you?" his father said, pulling off his prosthetic legs and strapping himself in. He flipped a switch and the hangar doors opened. "Go ahead, take her up."

With practiced ease, Lucas lifted the *Josey Wales* up off the hangar floor and out through the doors. With the course laid in, he could just let the nav computer do the work, but he liked to fly her by hand and see how close he could come to matching the elegant three-dimensional curve that he'd plotted. He took the *Wales* in a set of slowly widening orbits, increasing his altitude until he'd matched that of the *Orpheus*.

"You know," Tomas said contemplatively, "I've been flying in the Belt for thirty-odd years. I've flown to every part of the solar system a dozen times over. But this is the first time I ever flew *toward* a Navy cruiser."

He pressed a button to open a comm link. "*Orpheus*, this is the *Josey Wales* requesting docking clearance."

There was no response. "*Orpheus*, this is—"

"I heard you the first time," said a man's voice over the radio. "I suppose it was too much to ask you to arrive on schedule?"

Lucas and Tomas exchanged a look. What did he mean about a schedule? "Got here quick as we could," Tomas said.

"Well, watch the docking connector—we just had it painted."

Tomas took over the controls and nudged them toward the *Orpheus* while Lucas kept his eyes on the sensor display. "Lineup good. Touch in three, two, one . . ."

There was a tiny jolt and then a series of clanks as the two docking connectors mated with each other. A light on the control panel flashed green.

"All ashore that's going ashore," Tomas said with a forced smile.

Lucas unstrapped his safety harness and grabbed his duffel bag. He floated after his father down the main corridor of the ship until they reached the airlock.

"Last chance," his father said, putting his hand on the control panel. "You're sure you want to do this?"

Lucas looked around. This had been his home for as long as he could remember. He knew every centimeter of it, from the cramped cockpit to the dingy, oil-stained engine room. But that old familiarity wasn't enough anymore. Already the *Josey Wales* felt too small for him. As much as the ship tugged at him, there was a stronger force pulling him away, toward the *Orpheus*.

"I'm sure."

"All right," Tomas said. "Just remember what we talked about, okay?"

He pulled a wrench from a hook on the wall and banged three times on the airlock door. After a few moments, three quick clanks sounded in response from the other side. Lucas flipped a switch and the door slid open, revealing the interior of the docking connectors. Their half of the small enclosure was dirty and gray, covered with years of scuffs and boot prints and streaks of mining dust.

The *Orpheus*'s docking connector, on the other hand, was so white it almost hurt Lucas's eyes. A Navy officer in a blue uniform floated in the airlock on the opposite side. He was burly and mustached, with arms that were as big around as Lucas's legs. He'd obviously been born on Earth, but he carried himself with the ease of someone who'd been in space for most of their life. The name tag on his chest read Ensign Mendoza.

Mendoza wrinkled his nose and looked them up and down. Lucas was glad he'd taken his father's advice about cleaning up—even with his face washed and wearing his neatest jumpsuit, he was grimy compared with Mendoza.

Among Belters, being dirty was a badge of honor. He could already tell that wasn't true on a Navy cruiser.

"I was told you'd be here two hours ago," Mendoza said. "Can't you bother to read a delivery schedule?"

Tomas tilted his head to one side. "I think there's been some confusion," Tomas said. "If you'll ask your captain—"

"Our *captain*?" Mendoza said, screwing up his face in disbelief. "Our captain has a lot more to worry about than fruit cups and toilet paper."

Fruit cups and toilet paper? Anger boiled up inside Lucas. "But—"

Tomas put his hand on Lucas's shoulder and squeezed. "We aren't here to deliver cargo. My son is here to enroll as a cadet."

Mendoza snorted. "Listen, bud, how about we cut the jokes and you start unloading whatever junk you're here to deliver?"

"I'm not joking," Tomas said. His voice was no louder than before, but now it had a hard edge to it. "Call your captain if you don't believe me."

"I already told you, I'm not bothering our captain right now." Mendoza glanced at the stumps of Tomas's legs. "If this is just a way to get me to help you unload everything—"

"Lucas," came Captain Sanchez's voice from the corridor. "Mr. Adebayo. It's good to have you on board."

Sanchez slid through the inner airlock door and smiled politely at them. Mendoza pulled himself to attention so sharply that he floated toward the ceiling of the airlock and had to reach up awkwardly to keep from hitting his head.

"A pleasure, ma'am," Tomas said, glancing with satisfaction at Mendoza's astonished expression.

"We're due to begin acceleration in less than an hour," Sanchez said. "So we'll have to keep this short. Let's get you to your bunk so you can get some sleep. Classes start tomorrow."

"Yes, ma'am," Lucas said, but suddenly his excitement was gone. What if his dad was right? What if all of this was a gigantic mistake? And how was his dad going to manage on the *Josey Wales* without someone to help? He'd have to do everything himself, from flying the ship to repairs to cooking and cleaning. *Anyone who runs a mining ship by themselves is either crazy or will be soon*, he liked to say. Lucas couldn't leave him like this.

Lucas moved back into the docking connector, pulling his dad with him. "I think we should wait," he whispered.

"Wait?" Tomas asked. "What do you mean?"

"You need a partner," Lucas said, the words coming out in a jumbled rush. "I can't leave you alone. How are you going to do it all by yourself? Let's go back to

Ceres and find a copilot. Then we can meet up with the *Orpheus* and I'll start school. I'm sure they'll let me if we just explain why."

Tomas was silent for a long, long moment. His face was so neutral it was practically expressionless. What was he thinking? Why wouldn't he answer? Lucas dug his fingernails rhythmically into the palms of his hands. He could feel Mendoza and Sanchez watching them from the *Orpheus*'s airlock.

"You're going to be fine," his dad said finally. He kissed Lucas gently on his forehead. "Just keep your head on straight."

Lucas blinked. Had his dad not heard a word he'd said? "It's not me I'm worried about. It's you! How are you—"

"Don't worry about me," his dad said, escorting him gently back into the *Orpheus*'s airlock. "I'll see you when the term is over."

Lucas's mouth fell open in astonishment. He needed to find a way to make his dad understand before it was too late. But everything that was happening felt completely out of his control, as if he was watching it play out on a video screen.

"Your son is in good hands, Mr. Adebayo," Sanchez said.

Tomas nodded. He squeezed Lucas's arm and

disappeared back into the docking connector. Lucas recovered his wits in time to reach out toward the airlock door just as it slid shut with a quiet click, leaving him alone with the two Navy officers.

"This way, Cadet," Sanchez said.

Numbly, Lucas followed Captain Sanchez through the *Orpheus*'s airlock and into a wide corridor. Every surface looked like it had been hand polished, from the control panels on the wall to the handholds on the ceiling and floor. Lucas was almost afraid to touch the walls, worried that his hands would leave dirty fingerprints on the gleaming metal. He paused for a moment and gaped at the curving transplastic windows that ran along the outer wall. Windows, other than the main cockpit canopy, were a luxury that a cargo hauler couldn't afford. Already the *Orpheus* felt completely unlike any ship he'd ever been on.

Lucas watched his father smoothly pivot the *Josey Wales* and nudge her away from the docking connector using only a tiny amount of thrust, a maneuver that was much harder than it looked. It was a subtle display of skill that made Lucas's heart ache. He realized that he'd always thought of his dad as just a miner and not as an accomplished pilot in his own right. Why did it take coming here to the *Orpheus* for him to see that more clearly?

"Ensign Mendoza will escort you to your berth," Sanchez said. "The other cadets in your section will help you get settled."

"Come with me," Mendoza said. He propelled himself down the hallway and then grabbed a handhold to swing into a side passage. Lucas looped his duffel bag over his shoulder and followed after him. They turned down a wide passage marked BROADWAY that ran straight up to the bridge at the very front of the ship, where Lucas could see the dim glow of instrument panels and the faint shimmer of starlight. A ladder ran down the middle of the corridor, passing through six bulkheads that separated the various decks.

Mendoza pointed at a large darkened room behind them. "Rec room. Also the mess room. Past that are classrooms, hangar, and engineering."

He nodded at the ladder. "Decks one through seven, and then the bridge. Do *not* go onto the bridge without permission."

Lucas nodded, trying to absorb everything around him. Mendoza grabbed the ladder and pulled himself along until he reached the third deck from the bottom.

"This is alpha section." He indicated a closed door on one side of the circular deck. "That's the bunkroom for first-years."

"Thank you," Lucas said, uncertain of what else to say.

Mendoza snorted. He started back down the ladder, and then he stopped and looked back up at Lucas.

"Kid," he said, shaking his head, "you have no idea what you've gotten yourself into."

3

LUCAS WRAPPED HIS arms around his chest and stared at the retreating silhouette of Ensign Mendoza. *You have no idea what you've gotten yourself into.* What did he mean by that?

He looked around uneasily. The ship was unbearably quiet. On the *Josey Wales*, there were always background sounds: the hiss of the air recycler, the chugging of coolant pipes, or the rattle of screws in the ventilation ducts. But here on the *Orpheus*, there was almost nothing.

He tapped on the touch panel next to his bunkroom, and the door slid open. The room was dark except for the dim glow of starlight through a large circular window. Sleep sacks were lined up on all three walls. Two of them were occupied, but the third was empty. He floated inside and closed the door.

As his eyes adjusted to the near blackness, he heard a rustling from one of the sleep sacks. He was trying to decide whether to say something or just let everyone keep sleeping when someone grabbed him by his arm.

"Got you!" a voice shouted. Lucas tried to pull away, but the grip on his arm was too tight. The lights came on, and he was suddenly face-to-face with a tall girl with close-cropped blond hair.

"Elena, turn off the lights," a boy moaned from one of the sleep sacks.

"This time I've caught him!" Elena shouted. She shook Lucas by the arm. "Which section are you in?"

"I'm in alpha section," Lucas said. "Let go of me!"

"*This* is alpha section, nummer!"

"I just got here," he said. "Mendoza told me this was where I'm supposed to bunk."

The boy poked his head out of his sleep sack. "That doesn't make sense. The last transport arrived two days ago."

"He's lying," Elena insisted.

"He's got a bag of stuff," the boy observed. "And he's not wearing a uniform. Maybe he did just get here."

Elena poked Lucas in the chest, causing him to drift backward a few centimeters. "So who are you?" she demanded. "Where are you from?"

Lucas sighed. This was *really* not how he'd wanted

to start things off. "My name is Lucas. I flew here from Ceres."

They stared at him in astonished silence. "Ceres is an asteroid," Lucas added helpfully.

"We know what Ceres is," Elena snapped. "Are you saying you're from the *Belt*?"

"Yes," Lucas said, trying to be patient. "I'm from the Belt."

"I heard we were going to have a Belter cadet," the boy said. "But I didn't know it would be in *our* section."

Without leaving his sleep sack, he stretched out and shook Lucas's hand. "I'm Rahul. You've met our resident enforcer, Elena."

"Someone's got to keep watch," Elena grumbled. "Yesterday one of the other sections left a bag of . . . *fecal matter* floating in the middle of our room."

"And you're going to make them pay," Rahul said, yawning. "I know. Lucas, I guess that sleep sack is yours. You've got uniforms there too."

Lucas opened a drawer that was set into the wall next to his sleep sack. Inside, he found a set of four gray jumpsuits and two white uniform jackets with red insignias on the shoulders. He started to take off his own dust-covered jumpsuit, glad that he could wear something that wouldn't make him stick out so much.

Elena cleared her throat. "Shower stalls are across the hall."

39

Lucas stopped with his zipper pulled down to his navel. Did he smell bad? "I took a shower a few days ago."

Rahul and Elena stared at him. He could tell that he'd said something strange, but he couldn't understand what it was. How often did groundside kids take showers? Surely not more than once a week?

"That's good, I guess," Rahul said carefully. "But if you're not going to take a shower, then you should at least change in private."

In private? Was he being serious? From the way the two of them were looking at him, he was pretty sure that he was. Lucas looked around. Where was he supposed to go?

Rahul stretched out his arm and tapped a small button on the wall next to Lucas's sleep sack. Instantly the rest of the cabin disappeared, leaving Lucas in a small area enclosed by blurry gray walls. Rahul pulled his arm back and disappeared completely.

A privacy field, just for his own bunk? That was even more insane than having a shower area on each deck. There wasn't enough room on a Belter ship for any kind of privacy, and there certainly wasn't enough money to install dedicated fields for each bunk. He started pulling on a clean jumpsuit, mentally revising his list of things he was going to have to get used to.

When he was finished, he turned off the privacy field and held up one of the uniform jackets. The cloth was coarse and old-fashioned, and the collar was so stiff it was almost razor sharp. A tingle of excitement ran through him. How many times had he imagined himself wearing one of these? He slid it on and flexed his arms experimentally. The jacket felt tight and constricting. How did anyone *move* while wearing this? He tried rolling up the sleeves a little, but the cuffs were almost as stiff as the collar. He sighed and put the jacket back in the drawer. Apparently even the uniforms here were going to take some time to get used to.

A voice came over the ship's intercom system. "All hands, prepare for acceleration in two minutes. Repeat, acceleration in two minutes."

A girl of around fifteen or sixteen poked her head through the cabin door. "What's going on in here? Why is the door open?"

Rahul and Elena both looked at Lucas. "I'm new. I was just—"

"Never mind. I don't really care. Get in your bunk for acceleration." She paused and wrinkled her nose. "What stinks in here?"

Lucas turned red. He looked down at the civilian jumpsuit he had stuffed into a corner of the drawer. Did it really smell that bad? He quickly shoved the drawer closed. The girl looked at him for a moment as if she was going to say something else, and then she shook her head and closed the cabin door.

"Well, now you've met Maria," Elena said. "She's gamma-section leader."

"She's a little . . . prickly," Rahul added helpfully.

"All hands, acceleration in one minute," the intercom said.

Lucas climbed into his sleep sack and waited. The rumble of the engines was quiet at first but soon grew to a dull roar that he could feel as much as hear. The acceleration pushed him down into his sleep sack like an invisible hand against his chest. He squirmed back and forth, trying to get comfortable. Was this a normal burn, or some kind of emergency maneuver? Back on the *Josey Wales*, his dad had always insisted on the most efficient course changes possible to conserve fuel. Clearly that wasn't an issue in the Navy.

"We're committed now," Rahul said, turning off the lights. "Night, guys."

Through the window on the wall, Lucas could see the cup of the Big Dipper and the tail of Draco. He reached out and touched the cold transplastic window. Had he made the right choice? Or did it even matter at this point? Like Rahul had said, they were all committed now.

He had a sudden memory of a night when he'd woken up from a nightmare back on the *Josey Wales*. He'd been what—five or six years old? In the dream, he was back inside the old pressure dome on Ceres with his mother, right before the accident, and even though he knew what was going to happen, he couldn't tell her, no matter how hard he tried. Then the dome had cracked, and everyone had started running. . . .

He'd woken up screaming. His father had rushed in to comfort him and tell him all the usual things: it was just a dream, it wasn't real, there was nothing to be afraid of. He asked Lucas to tell him what the nightmare was about, but Lucas had just shaken his head. Talking about it made it seem even more real.

When his dad left, though, Tali had come in and climbed into his sleep sack with him. She'd only been around nine years old at the time, but she had seemed so grown-up to him. For a while she'd just held his head against her chest. Then she'd bent her head and whispered in his ear.

I have the same dream sometimes.

Had she really known what his dream was about? Or had she just said that to make him feel better? Somehow he felt that she really did know—after all, her parents had died in the same accident. But either way, it had worked. He'd fallen asleep almost immediately.

That had all been a long time ago. If he had a nightmare tonight, his sister wasn't going to come running. But at least she was here on the same ship—and that was a start. He closed his eyes and tried to sleep.

"Reveille!" a deep voice shouted.

Lucas flipped over in his sleep sack. It couldn't possibly be time to wake up already. He felt sure he'd only fallen asleep a few minutes ago. He opened his eyes and saw Elena and Rahul climbing out of their bunks.

"They've got a thing here about punctuality," Elena said, yawning. "So I recommend you get yourself up before they come looking for you."

As if on cue, a big red-haired boy stuck his head into the room. "Everyone up. Breakfast."

He paused and studied Lucas for a moment. "You're the new cadet?" he asked. "I'm Oliver. Beta-section leader."

He stretched out and shook Lucas's hand. "Uh, nice to meet you," Lucas stammered.

"You too," Oliver said cheerfully. "Now get your butt out of bed."

He disappeared back into the hallway. Lucas slid out of his bunk and stretched his arms. The acceleration had stopped during the night, and they were back in free fall. He squeezed a tube of tooth gel into his mouth, swished it around with some water, and spit it all into a towel.

"Someday I'm going to learn how to do that," Rahul said, watching him wistfully. "But every morning I end up with tooth gel floating everywhere."

Lucas felt guilty as he remembered how angry he'd been at the thought of a ship full of kids who didn't know how to brush their teeth. "I can teach you," he offered.

"Chow time!" Maria shouted from the hallway. "Breakfast in five minutes!"

Rahul worked his way around the room toward the door, moving awkwardly and keeping a grip on a handhold the entire time. Elena waited patiently and then floated after him with graceful, economical movements.

"Have you spent much time in space?" Lucas asked her, grabbing his uniform jacket and hurrying after them.

"No. I'm just a fast learner." She spoke so matter-of-factly that Lucas couldn't tell if she was making a joke, bragging, or just telling the truth.

A line of cadets was already moving along the ladderway toward the back of the ship. Rahul and Elena merged in quickly, but Lucas hung back uncertainly. Several kids gave him odd looks as they passed, and Lucas wondered if word had already gotten around that alpha section had a new Belter cadet.

He followed behind the last cadet until they got to a large cylindrical area at the center of the ship. Long curving tables pointed toward the center of the room like the spokes of a wheel. Some cadets were already floating at the tables, eating and drinking from pouches. The rest were making their way along rows of handholds set into the walls. He picked out the different colorful insignias for alpha, beta, gamma, and delta sections. The first- and second-year kids mostly seemed to stick to their own sections, but some of the tables at the far end of the room had a mixture of colors.

Lucas braced his legs and pushed off toward the other end of the room, where Rahul and Elena were settling in. He snagged the end of their table and swung himself into an empty spot.

"Wow," Rahul said.

"I'm going to have to try that next time," Elena said, which Lucas guessed might be the closest she came to a compliment. He flushed and mumbled a "Thanks."

"Ugh," a short, skinny boy at a nearby table said, looking around with exaggerated concern. "What is that *smell?*"

"Oh, god," a girl next to him said, scrunching up her face dramatically.

Lucas sank down into his seat. Suddenly he *really* wished he'd taken the time to shower last night.

"Don't listen to them," Elena said. "That's just Willem and Katya. A *lovely* pair of people from Luna."

"Oh, hey there, Elena," Willem said, as if he'd just noticed her. "What do *you* think? Does your new section-mate smell awful?"

Elena clenched her jaw angrily. Rahul slid over so that he was in between her and Willem. "Cut it out," he said.

"What?" Willem said in an innocent voice. "I'm just asking her a simple question. Does the new kid smell bad?"

"Yes," Elena muttered, staring down at the table.

"That's what I thought," Willem said, turning back to his friends.

Lucas had never in his life wished for anything more than he wished right now to just disappear. He put his hands on the edge of the table and gathered himself to push off toward the exit. Maybe there was still time to shower before classes started.

"Wait, Lucas," Elena said, putting her hand on his arm. "Let me explain."

"It's okay," Lucas said. "I'll just go—"

"No, you don't understand," Rahul said. "She *had* to say it. She grew up in a truth-sayer commune in Argentina. She's never told a lie in her life."

"It was Peru," Elena said. "But otherwise, yeah."

"Mr. Personality there likes to take advantage of it," Rahul went on, jerking his head toward Willem. "In orientation yesterday, he asked her—"

"Okay, let's *not*," Elena interrupted. "I think Lucas gets the point."

Someone who didn't lie? Like, ever? Lucas was used to finding out about strange Earther customs, but this had to be the weirdest thing he'd ever heard of. He would have been sure they were just trying to trick him, but the earnestness of her expression made it clear they weren't making it up.

"Fortunately they're in delta section," Rahul said. "So we can mostly avoid them."

"If they're not careful, they're not going to make it to second year," Elena said, in a matter-of-fact tone that was slightly terrifying. "So, Lucas, can I ask you something?"

"Uh, sure," he said. Was this a normal Earther thing, asking people whether you could ask them a question? Why not just go ahead and ask it?

"Do people who grow up in space really have fragile bones?"

"I guess so," Lucas said. "I've broken my left arm twice and my right arm once. And I fractured two ribs and my collarbone in an ore loader accident last year."

"I always thought Belters would be really tall," she mused. "Growing up in low gravity and all that. But other than your underdeveloped muscles, you look pretty normal."

"Search for statistics on Belter physiology," Rahul said, staring at the back of the room with an unfocused expression.

"What?" Lucas asked, confused. "Are you asking me to—"

"He's talking to his AI," Elena said. She sighed. "He does this."

"Oh," Lucas said. Curious, he watched the tiny lights flickering in Rahul's eyes as his AI displayed the results of his search. He'd never met someone who had corneal implants.

"The best thing about it," Rahul said, abruptly shifting his attention back to Lucas and Elena, "is that I never have to remember people's names. Like, they're hovering right above everyone's heads right now. I can tell you the name, rank, and blood type of every person in this room."

"Blood type?" Elena said. "You must be a hit at parties."

"It can come in handy," Rahul insisted. "Also, the implants help with astral vertigo. I wouldn't have passed the physical without them."

"Wait," Lucas said. "You really have astral vertigo?"

Rahul clamped his mouth shut suddenly as if he wished he hadn't said anything. "I mean, it's not really *vertigo*. Just a little dizziness."

Lucas had heard of people who became disoriented in

space. Low gravity or weightlessness and a lack of visual cues confused their brain and made them dizzy or nauseated. Sometimes it was bad enough to make people vomit in their suit, and *that* was bad news. But like claustrophobia, it was a problem that didn't affect Belters. At least, not the ones who stayed sane.

He had a thousand questions for his sectionmates, about everything from truth-sayers and astral vertigo to AI implants and growing up on Earth, but at that moment Captain Sanchez called out from the officers' table at the back of the room. "Your attention, please."

Her voice carried a note of authority that made all the cadets fall silent immediately. "Welcome to the *Orpheus*. Each one of you is part of a proud tradition of teaching ships that stretches back hundreds of years. I trust that all of you will do your best to live up to that tradition.

"Whatever specialty of the Navy you're interested in, you'll learn it here better than anywhere. Wherever you come from—Earth, Luna, Mars, or somewhere else—you're a part of this school now."

At the words "somewhere else," a dozen pairs of curious eyes flicked toward Lucas. He hunched his shoulders and sank down a few centimeters, trying to keep himself as inconspicuous as possible.

"If you do your job, I promise we will do ours," Sanchez said. "That is all."

Everyone immediately began chattering and eating again. Rahul elbowed Lucas and pointed to a dispenser at the center of the table. "The French toast isn't French and it isn't toast, but it tastes okay. There's also oatmeal. I strongly suggest you stay away from the one marked 'breakfast protein.'"

"Don't listen to him," Elena said, handing him one of the protein pouches. "You need to put some muscle on your bones."

Lucas opened the pouch and took a sip. It wasn't bad, at least compared with the standard meal pouches on the *Josey Wales*. Looking around at the other cadets, he decided that Elena was right—he did need to build some more muscle. It was easy to pick out the kids who had grown up under Earth gravity just by the size of their shoulders and thighs. Even the Mars and Luna cadets were in better physical condition than he was. He swallowed the rest of the pouch quickly and looked down at his skinny arms and legs. How many protein pouches would it take before he didn't look like a stick figure compared with the other cadets?

"So is this all normal to you?" Lucas asked, waving his hand to indicate the cadets and officers.

"Normal?" Rahul said, blinking his eyes. "Well, no. We're floating in a spaceship somewhere out in the asteroid belt, eating food out of pouches, so I wouldn't call it normal."

Lucas nodded as if this made sense—although to him, the *only* things that felt normal were the parts Rahul had just described.

"I grew up on a communal farm," Elena said. "We had chores, classes, martial arts training. Stuff like that."

"Okay, for the record, that's not normal, even for Earthers," Rahul said.

"Yeah? Look who's talking. You went to a virtual school with the smartest kids on the planet. Your chemistry teacher won a Nobel prize."

"It was physics, but whatever," Rahul said. "I guess the point is that if we were boring and normal, we probably wouldn't be here in the first place. Though to be honest, I think Lucas takes the cake in the weird-background department."

Lucas looked down at the table. As much as it hurt, Rahul was right. Compared to everyone else here, calling him "weird" was an understatement. "I could switch," he offered.

"Switch what?" Elena asked, reaching for another pouch.

"You know—to another section."

Rahul paused in mid-swallow. "Wait, what?" he said, looking aghast. "Why would you do that?"

"Lucas, I think maybe you misunderstood him," Elena said gently. "When he said you had a weird background, that was a compliment."

"Oh, it totally was," Rahul said, relieved. "Did it not sound like that? I can't wait to tell my brother I've made friends with a Belter. He's going to be so jealous."

Lucas felt the blood rush to his face. They were already friends? He'd only met them last night, and that had been under some iffy circumstances. Not that he was objecting!

"Okay, cool," he said, trying to sound as if making friends this easily was completely natural to him. "I, uh, just wanted to check."

"We're going to be like the Three Musketeers, I can already tell," Rahul said, waving his hand expansively. "Or was it four? I can never keep it straight."

Lucas grinned. At least this time he could follow the cultural reference, even though he wasn't really sure what a musketeer was. He pulled a pouch of oatmeal and another of soy milk from the dispenser. He emptied the oatmeal from the pouch and squirted the milk into it until he had a floating, gooey blob. He dabbed away a few loose drops of milk and then started to eat the oatmeal with a pair of chopsticks.

Rahul stared at him. "Okay, forget brushing teeth. Teach me how to do *that*."

"Sure," Lucas said. He wrapped his napkin loosely around his own ball and showed him how to get the milk and oatmeal mixed together into the right consistency.

"The real trick is not letting the little bits float away," he explained.

"Hey—be careful," Elena said, pointing.

Lucas turned and saw that he'd let his own ball of food drift toward the table behind him. He reached out to snag it, but another cadet, apparently in the middle of telling some story, swung his arms out wide and smacked the ball of food with his elbow. Chunks of oatmeal and drops of milk splattered everywhere.

"What the heck?" the cadet said. "Gross!"

Lucas grabbed some napkins from a dispenser and started cleaning up some of the larger globules that were threatening to float away. "It's not my fault," he said. "You should watch where you're swinging your arms."

"My fault?" the cadet said. "Are you kidding? You were the one who left food floating around!"

"What's going on?" someone called. "Who made this mess?"

Lucas looked up and felt a flood of relief as he saw Tali heading quickly toward their table. He was opening his mouth to explain when the other boy pointed at him and spoke up.

"He did. He made a snowball or something with his food."

Tali turned toward Lucas with an angry scowl. "You must be our new cadet."

Lucas looked at her, dumbfounded. New cadet? Did she not recognize him in his uniform?

"I don't know how you eat out in the Belt, but here we keep food in the pouches." She turned toward the tables with the older kids. "Hanako, does your section have kitchen patrol today?"

"Yeah," replied a girl with long black hair that floated around her like a halo. "Delta third-years."

"Well, they're off the hook," Tali said. She jerked her head at Lucas's table. "You three will have the pleasure."

Rahul groaned. "We just had KP yesterday!"

"Do you want it for the rest of the week?" Tali snapped.

"No, ma'am," Rahul mumbled.

Lucas was still struggling to understand what was going on, but he knew that the last thing he needed was to get his own bunkmates mad at him. "They didn't have anything to do with it. I'll clean it up myself."

"Suit yourself," Tali said. She pulled a trash bag from the wall and thrust it at him. "I want this room spotless.

If I end up with oatmeal in my hair at lunchtime, you'll be scrubbing waste-disposal tanks for the rest of the term."

She pushed off toward the front of the room without waiting for him to reply. Lucas looked down at the trash bag in his hands. How had everything gone so wrong so quickly?

"That's so unfair," Rahul said to Lucas. "It wasn't your fault."

"Well, it was his food," Elena said. "And he did let it float away." When Rahul shot her an exasperated look, she amended, ". . . but the punishment does seem much harsher than necessary."

A bell chimed three times. "First period in five minutes," a tall woman called from the officer's table. Her head was shaved clean and her scalp was dyed a shimmering blue.

"That's Ensign Weber," Rahul whispered as everyone began clamoring for the doors. "As far as I can tell, her only job is shouting at us."

"Clean up your pouches!" Weber yelled at one of the tables. "This isn't your kitchen back home!"

Elena and Rahul stuffed their pouches into the trash bag that Lucas was holding, then headed off after the others with apologetic looks. Despite Weber's admonishments, napkins and empty food pouches floated all over the room. Weber herded the last few stragglers toward the hallway at the front of the room, and then the door swung closed with an echoing clang.

Lucas gritted his teeth and stuffed a few napkins in the trash bag. This wasn't fair. He was supposed to be here learning how to be a pilot, not picking up after Earther cadets' breakfast. After ten minutes he'd only managed to clean up about a third of the room. *Fantastic,* he thought. First period would be over before he finished. And nobody had even told him where he was supposed to go after this.

A door on the side of the room opened up. Tali slipped inside and quickly closed it behind her.

"Lucas," she said in a low, furious voice. "What the heck are you *doing* here?"

4

"I TOLD YOU not to come, didn't I?" Tali said, more to herself than to him. "I told you it would be a mistake. But somehow, here you are."

Without waiting for him to respond, she grabbed a second trash bag and started picking up empty pouches. "The autovacs will get anything smaller than your fist. You just have to get the big stuff."

"They invited me," Lucas protested. "And you put in a recommendation!"

Tali paused for a moment, then tied up her trash bag and slung it into a garbage receptacle on the wall. Something was odd about her expression. . . .

Realization dawned on him. "You *didn't* recommend me, did you?"

She didn't respond, but she didn't need to. He could tell he was right. "How could you lie to me like that?"

"Because I wanted to protect you," she said simply.

"Protect me? From all of this?" he asked, waving his hand to indicate the *Orpheus*.

"Yes, actually."

"What about how you're pretending you don't even know me—is that to 'protect' me too? Or is that because you're too embarrassed to admit that you're from the Belt, just like me?"

"Keep your voice down," she snapped.

"That's it, isn't it? That's the whole reason you've tried to talk me out of coming here? Because you don't want anyone here to find out your little secret?"

She was silent for a moment. "It's more complicated than that, Lucas."

"It seems pretty simple to me."

"Everything seems simple to you," she said. "Which is exactly why I wanted you to stay away."

"Well, I'm here now," he said. "So you're going to have to get used to seeing me."

"Just get one thing straight," she said, tapping him on the chest. "As far as anyone else on this ship is concerned, *you and I have never met*. Understand?"

"Whatever," he said.

"Promise me, Lucas. It's important."

He snorted. "I promise. But you ought to hope that I'm better at keeping my promises than you are."

The door at the front of the room opened, and Maria stuck her head in. "Tali? I'm supposed to take Lucas to his first class. Is he ready?"

"No," Tali said with a sigh. "He's not. But there's no point in waiting."

Lucas glared at her and pushed off toward Maria. He snagged a handhold and followed her into a corridor that ran toward the back of the ship. They passed the airlock and docking connector and turned onto a ladderway that was identical to the one at the front of the ship, except that this one was labeled PARK PLACE instead of BROADWAY. They followed the ladder down to the third deck and stopped outside a closed door.

"What do I do?" Lucas asked.

Maria handed him a tablet-sized screen. "You go inside."

She launched herself back up the ladderway and out of sight. Lucas looked at the screen, which was displaying a schedule for the day. The first item listed was Introductory Calculus with Commander Novak. He took a deep breath and rapped on the door with his knuckles.

"Come in," a faint voice said.

He opened the door and straightened himself up as best he could. "Lucas Adebayo reporting, sir."

He realized too late that Commander Novak wasn't a man, but a woman in her mid-sixties with short-cropped gray hair and a thin, angular face. She was floating in front of a small group of kids seated at desks. Behind them on the wall, a recruiting poster showed a trio of smiling officers with Jupiter rising in the background.

Every eye turned toward him. "I mean, Lucas Adebayo reporting, *ma'am.*"

Novak motioned toward an open desk. "Take a seat. I don't have all day."

Lucas sat down behind Elena, who gave him a tiny nod. A few seats over, Willem and Katya smirked and whispered something to each other. Novak glared at them irritably.

"As I was saying, please do not misunderstand the term 'introductory' to mean that this will be an easy course. We will be going over a broad set of topics at a rapid pace. Has everyone studied calculus before?"

Everyone but Lucas raised their hand. A dozen pairs of eyes turned toward him, and his heart sank. Of *course* he would be the only one.

"Ah," Novak said, looking at him thoughtfully. "We'll need to do an evaluation, then."

"An evaluation for all of us?" Katya asked. "Or just *him?*"

"All of you," Novak said, typing something into her screen. "Which is for the best, since it will give me a chance to find out where the class stands."

There was a collective groan as a test popped up on everyone's screens. Several kids glared openly at Lucas. He hung his head and looked down at the first problem. This was definitely *not* how he wanted to start things off with his classmates.

The test wasn't too hard at first, but the questions quickly became more difficult. When he got to the third section, he stopped and raised his hand tentatively.

"Do you have a question?" Novak asked, coming over to him.

He pointed to his screen. "I don't know what this word means," he said in an embarrassed voice.

"You've never worked with logarithms before?"

Willem and Katya tittered simultaneously. Lucas turned red and shook his head.

"Skip that section, then."

The last part of the test was algebra, which was at least something he'd studied before. But abstract math had never been his strong suit, and it took him a while to work out each answer. Eventually Novak checked her watch. "Five minutes left."

Lucas looked around and noticed that everyone was finished except for him. He scanned through the remaining pages of the test. There was no way he was going to finish in time. He moved on quickly, jotting down his best guesses at the answers, since surely putting *something* down was better than nothing. When the bell chimed to end the period, everyone else in the class burst from their desks and headed for the door.

"Time is up, Cadet Adebayo."

Lucas nodded and pressed submit. A score flashed up at the top of his screen: 45%. He hadn't even gotten half of the answers correct.

He made his way out into the hallway. His heart felt like it had fallen into a black hole. Was this really what school here would be like? He half expected Tali to show up and say "I told you so."

"So how did you do, Aaron?" Willem asked in a loud voice, turning to a burly Earther boy wearing delta section's colors.

"Eighty-nine percent," Aaron said, shrugging.

"That's not too bad. I got ninety-four. Katya?"

"Ninety-one."

Willem turned toward Lucas with an innocent look. "How about you, Lucas?"

"It's none of your business," Elena said.

Willem grinned. "That's about what I thought." The three delta-section kids headed up toward the rec room, passing Rahul as he came down from the deck above.

"Oh, no—what's got them so happy?" Rahul said, looking back at the delta-section kids.

"Nothing," Lucas mumbled.

"How was your class?" Elena asked.

Rahul made a face. "It was *awful.*"

"It couldn't have been that bad," Elena said. "Aren't you some kind of math genius?"

"Sure, linear algebra is easy. But the homework is insane! And Hofstra says I can't use my AI implant for *anything.* He wants us to type it all up on our screens." Rahul waggled his fingers at them. "I can already feel the blisters starting to form!"

"Looks like I've got orbital mechanics with him next," Lucas said, looking at his own screen. Which at least sounded like something more interesting than stupid *logarithms.*

Rahul pointed upward. "One deck up. I wish you luck."

Lieutenant-Commander Hofstra was short and heavy-set, with a patchy reddish-brown beard. There were no desks in his room, and every wall was covered with large whiteboards. This time, at least, Lucas managed to get there early. After a few minutes, there were five cadets in a semicircle. Except for Lucas, all of them looked like second- or third-years. As soon as the last cadet arrived, Hofstra closed the door and turned toward them.

"Three laws," he said in a deep, resonant voice. "That's it. Three laws. Everything we do here comes from Sir Isaac Newton and his three laws. Now, let's begin with some simple problems."

Hofstra began drawing a problem on the board. His handwriting was difficult to read, but Lucas soon recognized the diagram.

"The Jovian moons!" he blurted out.

Hofstra frowned and glanced back at Lucas. "You're familiar with this?"

Lucas froze. Had he done something wrong? "Uh . . . yes, sir. A little."

"I see," Hofstra said, peering at him with an odd expression. "You're our new Belter cadet, I assume. Please stay quiet for the rest of the class."

One of the other cadets snickered loudly. Lucas's face turned bright red. What had he done wrong? Was it his fault he'd seen that diagram before? It was one of the first navigation problems any Belter kid studied.

He took a little satisfaction in noting that by the end of the class, all the other cadets looked overwhelmed by Hofstra's rapid pace. When the period ended, Hofstra opened the door and waved them out.

"Read the first three chapters of Stuttgart," he said. "We meet three times a week. Homework assignments have been sent out. Office hours are posted and I suggest you make use of them if you have any trouble. Cadet Adebayo, please stay behind."

Hofstra said this last bit in such a casual way that it took Lucas a moment to realize what he'd said. The other kids exchanged looks and slipped out through the door quickly.

"Since the problem I presented was apparently too elementary, let's dive a little deeper," Hofstra said, handing Lucas a stylus.

Lucas began to explain that he hadn't meant to be rude, but Hofstra had already launched into his first question. Lucas closed his mouth and dutifully went through the various calculations step-by-step. Hofstra seemed less interested in the actual answer than in the reasoning that went into it. What's the logic behind that part there? What's the meaning of that variable? Every time he saw that Lucas understood a particular concept, he would wave his hand and move on to something else. Soon they were calculating interplanetary rendezvous trajectories, which was an area where Lucas had always just relied on the computer to do the hard work. Eventually Hofstra grew impatient.

"Yes, that's *what* you do," he said, smacking the whiteboard, "but *why?*"

"I don't know," Lucas admitted.

"Ah," Hofstra said, sounding satisfied. "Perhaps one day that hole in your education will be remedied. But not today. You are dismissed."

"I don't understand—"

"I can *see* that you don't understand, cadet. Which is

why you are now dismissed. It's time for lunch, and I've got a ravenous appetite."

Hofstra pointed toward the door with an expectant look. Lucas mumbled a "Yes, sir," and headed out to the ladderway. Glumly he followed the sounds of cadets eating lunch until he'd reached the rec room again. By the time he got there, Elena and Rahul were already halfway finished with their lunch.

"Hofstra is a bowl of cherries, isn't he?" Rahul said, seeing Lucas's expression.

"I don't want to talk about it," Lucas said. He didn't have any appetite at all, but he pulled a food pouch out of a dispenser and squirted the contents into his mouth. He grimaced and read the label. Tofu and vegetable stew, and heavy on the cauliflower.

"We've got physical education next," Elena said. "That'll be fun."

Rahul and Elena soon began talking excitedly about an Earther martial-arts series that Lucas had never heard of, doing slow-motion demonstrations of their favorite sequences. Lucas watched silently and drank a water bulb.

Why had he come here? What had made him think that this was a good idea? He'd always known that people from the inner planets were different. But until now he'd never realized *how* different. Was he ever going to fit in, or was he always going to be a complete outsider?

A chime sounded throughout the ship. "All first-year cadets, fold up the tables and meet in the back of the rec room for physical education," a burly officer called out. Everyone immediately began tossing food and water pouches into trash bags.

Rahul sighed. "Who schedules phys ed right after lunch?"

When they'd folded up their table and put away their trash bags, the officer herded them toward the other end of the room. "My name is Lieutenant-Commander Palmer," he said. "This is your exercise and combat class."

At the word "combat," Elena perked up. Several of the other kids groaned in dismay.

"First up is gravity simulation in the centrifuge," Palmer said. "You should all be familiar with this from your trips out here. Sort yourselves by planet—Earth, Mars, and Luna."

Lucas had seen pictures of centrifuges, but he'd never encountered one in person. This one took up the entire back wall of the rec room. It was basically just a ring-shaped padded floor that could spin around its axis. Anyone standing inside would be pushed outward, against the floor. The faster it spun, the stronger the simulated gravity would be.

Elena and Rahul looked at Lucas uncertainly as the

other kids formed three groups. "Does he know who you are?" Rahul whispered.

"Maybe he wants you to join the Luna group?" Elena suggested.

Palmer looked over at them and frowned. Lucas had the uncomfortable feeling that, with his skinny arms and legs, he looked exactly like Palmer expected a kid who'd grown up in space to look.

"You're our new Belter kid, aren't you? Get on a bike and start pedaling."

Willem and his friends grinned and whispered to each other. Lucas did his best to keep his face neutral. Why wouldn't Palmer let him try the centrifuge? He'd spent time on all the bigger asteroids, where there was at least a little gravity, and his dad had always insisted that he keep up with his strength exercises on the *Josey Wales*. Did Palmer really think that Belters were just weak and frail?

He looked enviously at the other cadets. Compared to the Earthers, he *was* weak and frail. Even the Mars and Luna kids had more muscle mass.

"Hey, don't listen to them," Rahul said. "It's not like this is going to be any fun."

He and Elena lined up with the other Earther kids inside the centrifuge. "This time, all we're going to do is a few squats," Palmer called out. "By the end of the term we'll be doing push-ups, burpees, and devil stands."

Lucas didn't know what a devil stand was, but it was clear from Palmer's tone that they weren't going to be fun for anyone involved. He started pedaling on one of the bikes and watched as the centrifuge started to turn, pressing everyone inside against the outer ring. After a moment he had to look away—the sight of everyone spinning around like that made his stomach churn.

"Don't over*do* it," Willem called to him in a singsong voice.

Lucas focused on the bike and kept pedaling. He had the difficulty setting turned down low, but it still didn't take long before his legs started to ache from the effort. He could feel the other cadets watching him. *Don't slow down*, he told himself. *Whatever you do, don't slow down.*

The centrifuge spun to a halt. Palmer led the Earthers out and escorted the Mars kids inside. "Oh, man," Rahul said, rubbing his legs. "Was that really just five minutes?"

"If you'd kept up with your exercises on the transport ship, it wouldn't be so bad," Elena said.

"Nobody did their exercises on the transport ship." Before she could respond, he amended, "Nobody but you, anyway."

"Maybe you should take a break," Elena said to Lucas. "You look pretty frazzled."

Lucas shook his head. Tiny beads of sweat flew off his forehead. "Not yet."

"Remind me to spend some extra time in there," Willem said loudly. "I don't want to turn into some weak pile of jelly who can't support his own weight."

"Stuff it," Elena snapped.

"I'm just saying, it's a lot of work keeping up muscle mass. It would be nice to be a Belter and not have to worry about it."

Lucas stopped pedaling and wiped sweat out of his eyes. "I could do it. Palmer just won't let me."

"He won't let you because he knows you can't," Aaron said.

"Luna cadets, line up!" Palmer called as the centrifuge stopped and the Mars kids climbed out. Lucas watched Willem and the other kids from Earth's moon file into the centrifuge. Luna's gravity was only a sixth of a gee. He could do that for five minutes. He switched off the bike and launched himself toward the centrifuge.

"Sir," he said to Palmer. "I'd like to try."

"Keep pedaling, cadet."

"Please, sir," Lucas said. "Give me a chance."

Palmer studied him for a moment. Finally he shrugged. "Fine. Go ahead."

Lucas headed inside and positioned himself with his feet on the padded floor and one hand on the handrail. Willem grinned with delight from the other side of the centrifuge.

"How long do you think he'll last?" he said to Aaron.

"Three minutes," Aaron said. *"Maybe."*

Willem shook his head. "Two, tops. Look at those legs."

Lucas ignored them and adjusted his grip on the handrail. From outside the centrifuge Elena waved and gave him a cheerful thumbs-up. A signal chimed, and lights on the ceiling turned from green to red. The centrifuge began to spin, and the faint tug of pseudo-gravity pulled Lucas's feet against the floor. He adjusted his stance and flexed his legs.

"Make that ninety seconds," Aaron said, eyeing Lucas.

A nearby gauge climbed to 0.09 gee. Already this was higher than the gravity on Ceres or any of the other asteroids, and his legs were rubbery from the exercise bike. He could do it, he reminded himself. The *Josey Wales* accelerated at a sixth of a gee all the time, didn't it?

Yes—but he was always in an acceleration couch when that happened, not trying to stand up. He put both hands on the railing to steady himself.

At 0.12 gee, his knees threatened to buckle. "How's it going?" Willem shouted.

"Fine," Lucas gasped.

When the display leveled out at a Luna-normal 0.17 gee, he let go of the handrail. "One," Willem called out. "Two. Three . . ."

Lucas's head was starting to swim, and his stomach

felt as if it were turning in slow circles. He fixed his eyes on the floor in front of him and concentrated on staying upright. By the time Willem got to sixty, Lucas knew he wasn't going to make it. The muscles in his legs felt like jelly and his vision was turning blurry. He locked his knees and clenched his fists. *Just a little longer . . .*

"Sixty-three . . . sixty-four . . ."

Just a little longer . . .

"Sixty-eight . . . sixty-nine . . . seventy . . ."

Lucas's legs buckled and he toppled backward. He reached out frantically toward the railing, but it slipped through his fingers and he crumpled to the floor.

"That's it, ladies and gentlemen," Willem called out. "Poor Lucas here couldn't make it past seventy seconds."

Lucas barely heard him. His head was ringing, and everything around him felt distant and foggy. After what seemed like forever, the centrifuge spun to a halt and he floated up off the floor.

Palmer sighed and floated over to Lucas. "I told you, didn't I?"

"You did, sir," Willem said, nodding.

"Cadet," Palmer growled, "mind your own business. Lucas, get back on the bike."

Lucas pulled himself upright and grabbed onto the centrifuge railing. His stomach contracted, and bile surged up into his mouth. He clenched his jaw and tried to swallow it back down, but his body was suddenly doing everything it could to separate itself from the contents of his stomach.

"Are you okay?" Rahul asked, watching him with concern.

Lucas opened his mouth to reply, and as if taking this as a cue, his stomach lurched one last time, and vomit sprayed everywhere like a wet cloud.

Not *everywhere*. Mostly in front of him. Mostly all over Lieutenant-Commander Palmer.

5

AT LEAST THE Navy had excellent showers, Lucas told himself a few hours later, as he floated in a spray of hot, soapy water. It had taken a while to convince the ship's medbay team that he was okay, but they'd finally let him go with a diagnosis of "mild concussion," a shot of perithental, and a warning to take it easy. The chief medical officer, Dr. Voorhaus, had been particularly reluctant, but in the end he hadn't found any reason to keep Lucas for observation.

"Your bones are *extremely* fragile," Voorhaus had said, peering at Lucas as if he were a specimen on a lab table. "You must be cautious. I do not want to see you in here again anytime soon."

Lucas turned off the shower and got dressed in a clean uniform. After a quick check of the ship's map, he headed down to deck nineteen to drop off his vomit-covered jumpsuit at the ship's laundry. As he was studying the various bags and receptacles, trying to figure out which one he should put his uniform in, a babble of voices caught his attention. He turned and saw Maria leading the first-year cadets down the Park Place ladder toward the hangar. Willem paused briefly on the ladderway to stare at Lucas and his stained jumpsuit. Willem's eyebrows shot up and he started to laugh.

"Oh, shut up," Elena said tiredly, pushing him to keep going.

Embarrassed, Lucas shoved his uniform into the nearest bag and headed over to the doorway. Willem raced down the ladderway toward Aaron and Katya and gleefully began explaining what he'd seen. Katya's shrill giggle echoed through the lower decks as they disappeared into the hangar.

"Don't pay any attention to them," Elena said.

Lucas nodded. How many times was someone going to have to tell him that? "Is suit training about to start?" he asked.

"Yes," Rahul said mournfully. "I already feel sick to my stomach, and we're not even outside yet."

"Well, if you puke on your uniform, I can help you out," Lucas said, smiling half-heartedly. "I'm kind of an expert."

"Gee, thanks," Rahul said.

"Cadets!" Maria snapped, sticking her head out of the hatchway that led to the hangar. "We're waiting."

Lucas followed Elena and Rahul down the ladder, but Maria shook her head. "Not you."

"It was on the schedule you gave me," Lucas protested.

"You were scratched off," Maria said, shrugging. "Captain's orders."

She ushered Elena and Rahul down into the hangar. Lucas watched dejectedly as the first-year cadets assembled down on the hangar deck. Why was he being excluded? Suit training was his chance to demonstrate that he actually knew something.

"Hey," Tali said, coming down the ladderway behind him. "Shouldn't you be down there with the others?"

"Apparently not," Lucas said. He jerked the hatch upward, and it closed with a loud clang that reverberated through the lower decks.

She frowned. "Did they tell you why?"

"Well, I pretty much flunked every other class today," Lucas said, clenching his jaw. "So I'm guessing Sanchez decided she made a mistake and is trying to cut her losses."

"It was that bad?"

"Yeah," he said. "That bad."

Tali paused. "I'm sorry, Lucas."

"Why? You're getting what you wanted, right? I'm leaving."

To his surprise, his sister didn't launch into one of her I-told-you-so lectures. Instead she squeezed his arm. "Maybe you're wrong. Maybe they're not going to send you away."

"And what if I'm *not* wrong?"

Tali thought for a moment. "Then I guess you should make the most of the time you've got left. Follow me."

She opened the hatch and headed inside. He paused for a moment, and then shrugged and followed her through.

After the tight confines of the rest of the ship, the hangar seemed enormous. The ladderway emerged from the hatch in the ceiling and ran straight down through an opening in the floor, which Lucas guessed led to the engine room. The main hangar doors had been rolled back, and the faint shimmer of an airfield stretched across the opening. The first-year cadets were clustered in a small group near the hangar doors, listening to a lecture from one of the junior officers. Toward the back of the room, a pair of medium-sized patrol ships were lashed to the deck. The engine assembly on one of the patrollers had been pulled out, and two officers were clearly in the middle of a major overhaul.

Lucas stopped on the ladderway. He recognized one of the officers—a tall woman with silvery-white hair. "That's the engineer from Ceres," he whispered to Tali.

"Come on," Tali said, pulling him forward. "She

doesn't know it was you who flew that ship."

"How do you know?"

"Because I haven't been expelled," Tali said impatiently. "Now are you coming, or not?"

Reluctantly he followed her down to the two ships, ignoring the curious looks from his fellow cadets. "Chief Moskowitz?" Tali said. "I'd like to introduce you to one of our new cadets. This is Lucas Adebayo."

Unable to decide whether it would be better to look Moskowitz in the eye or avoid her completely, Lucas managed the worst of both, shifting his gaze back and forth between her and Tali.

"Welcome to the *Orpheus*," Moskowitz said, giving him a polite nod.

The man next to Moskowitz stuck out his hand. "I'm Randall Clarke. You're our new Belter cadet?"

"Yes, sir," Lucas said, shaking his hand.

"The 'sir' isn't necessary," he said. "Technically I'm an adjunct adviser, which is a long-winded way of saying I'm just a teacher here. You're a miner, is that right? I've done a few stints on Vesta and Ceres."

"Yes, sir."

"Iron and nickel?"

Lucas nodded. "And uranium, when we could find it."

"That's honest work," Randall said.

Lucas felt a surge of pride. At least here was *someone*

who didn't see a miner from the Belt as either a freak or a threat. He felt sure that Randall and his father would get along very well.

"Ma'am, you might be interested to hear that Cadet Adebayo has some experience working on smaller ships," Tali said.

"Now *that's* good to hear," Moskowitz said. She paused and frowned. "Have we met before? Something about you looks familiar."

"No, ma'am, I don't believe so," Lucas said, trying not to sound nervous. With curiosity that was only partly feigned, he bent down and inspected the engine assembly. "Looks like you've got a leak in the pressure lines?"

"What makes you say that?" Moskowitz asked.

"Well, you're taking apart the manifold. That's what my dad starts with any time he thinks there's a pressure leak."

Randall chuckled. "Logical."

"I've never worked on anything with redundant fuel pumps, though," Lucas said, running his fingers along one of the lines.

"That's standard Navy design," Moskowitz said, nodding.

Lucas squinted into the guts of the engine. "Stupid that you don't back it up with high-pressure valves, though. I'd bet that's why you get these leaks."

There was a moment of silence. "That's *also* standard Navy design," Moskowitz said.

Something in her voice made Lucas straighten up. Belatedly, he realized that what he'd said was probably extremely rude. Was he really going to mess everything up with these officers too? "I'm sorry, ma'am. I didn't mean it like that."

Moskowitz chuckled. "Yes, you did. But don't worry about it. I spend half my time fixing leaks and the rest complaining about those valves."

"If you need another pair of hands, maybe Lucas could help you out," Tali said.

"Sure," Lucas said. "I'd love to work on an engine like this."

"I wish my own cadets were that enthusiastic," Moskowitz said wryly. "Somehow they always seem to disappear when work like this comes up. If you've got the time—"

She was interrupted by a call over the intercom. "Cadet Adebayo to Captain Sanchez's quarters. Repeat, Cadet Adebayo to Captain Sanchez's quarters."

Lucas's heart sank. This was it—the call he'd been half expecting all afternoon. Apparently he wasn't even going to make it through an entire day before being sent home.

"Sounds like you don't," Moskowitz said, sighing. "Next time, maybe."

"Yeah," Lucas said hoarsely. If he was right about why the captain was summoning him, then there wasn't going to *be* a next time. He looked around the hangar at the patrol ships, the disassembled engine, the racks of suits on the wall. He could spend weeks in here and still not learn everything he wanted to learn—and this was only one little part of the ship.

"You'd better get going," Randall said. "Not good to keep a captain waiting."

"Remember that we've got a section meeting at nineteen hundred hours tonight," Tali added.

It was a good touch, Lucas thought, pretending that he would actually still be a cadet here by tonight. He nodded glumly and pushed off toward the ladderway. As he headed up toward the front of the ship, he passed a group of older cadets from gamma section going to the hangar. They moved aside almost without looking at him. It was probably out of politeness, but it made him feel as if he was untouchable, like a drop of oil drifting through a current of water.

He wanted to punch himself for being so stupid and clueless. Why couldn't someone back on Ceres have taught him about logarithms? Was this really how it was all going to end? As he floated through the rec room toward the upper decks, he tried as hard as he could to keep his face neutral. If he really was getting bounced out, then this might be the last time anyone saw him, and he didn't want anyone to remember him as a teary-eyed brat.

He hurried up the Broadway ladder and stopped at Sanchez's cabin on deck two. The bridge, just above him, was close enough to touch. The hatchway was open, and he could see the big transplastic canopy and a vast swath of the Milky Way. A junior officer sat at the pilot's console, her fingers brushing idly against the screen. Lucas's anger rose. He belonged in there. He belonged on this ship. How did no one else understand that? He rapped his knuckles on Sanchez's door.

The door slid open and Sanchez waved him in. Her cabin was the same size as the alpha-section bunkroom, though it felt much larger. There were framed paintings on the wall and actual, real-life books on a small wooden shelf. Lucas was astonished—the books alone must have weighed more than all the personal possessions he'd ever owned, combined.

"Good to see you, Lucas," she said. "So—how do you feel about the school, after your first day of classes?"

Was that a genuine question, or one of those times when an adult asked you something but didn't want to hear the actual answer? He came up with a few polite responses—*It was fine, I enjoyed it a lot, I'm excited to be here*—and threw them all away. If he wasn't going to be sticking around here for very long, there wasn't any reason to hide the truth.

"Honestly, I think it was all pretty stupid," he said. "I believe that if I were given a fair shot, I could do well here. But Commander Novak wants me to know logarithms and Lieutenant-Commander Hofstra thinks I ought to already know the theoretical parts of navigation, and as far as Lieutenant-Commander Palmer is concerned, I'm completely useless. Mr. Clarke is the only person who seems to like me, and he's not even an officer."

Sanchez cocked her head to one side and looked at him with an expression he couldn't read. Lucas knew he should probably stop, but his anger was still boiling over and the words tumbled out anyway.

"I mean, why did you bring me here if you're just going to send me away after one day? I didn't even get to go to suit training. What sort of officers are you training for? People who can actually fly ships, or people who can sit in classrooms reciting stupid facts and theory that nobody needs to know?"

"I see," Sanchez said, rubbing her thumb and forefinger together contemplatively. "Apparently there are a few misconceptions that we ought to clear up."

"I don't think—"

"Cadet Adebayo," she interrupted. "Your argument, if I understand correctly, is that you're capable of learning and following orders. I suggest that you demonstrate that fact by shutting up and listening. Ideally before that temper of yours digs you even deeper into the remarkably deep hole you've just gotten yourself into."

Even though she had hardly raised her voice more than a fraction of a decibel, her words seemed to physically reverberate around the room. Lucas closed his mouth with an audible click.

"First, despite what you seem to think, my staff was quite happy with your first day here. Novak has reported that your math background is weak but that your aptitude was a very pleasant surprise. Hofstra has already made it very clear to me that his only frustration is with whoever put you into a beginning orbital mechanics course when you already know more than most of his third-year students. He's positively ecstatic at the idea of teaching theory to a cadet who already knows the practical side of navigation. And not thirty seconds before you arrived, I received a request from Chief Engineer Moskowitz to have you assigned to her cadet repair team so that she can have, quote, 'Someone who actually cares about what they're doing.' She clearly agreed with my decision that there are much better uses for your time than making you sit through basic suit training."

A pleasant surprise? Ecstatic? Novak and Hofstra had made it seem as if he'd failed completely. He desperately wanted to ask for more information, but instead he kept his mouth shut and waited for her to continue.

Sanchez watched him for a moment, and then she nodded. "It gives me some hope to see that you're capable of staying quiet when necessary. Let me ask you a question: after today, do you think you belong at this school?"

What was she asking, exactly? Whether he fit in with the other students? Or whether he thought he was competent to be here? Or just whether he even *wanted* to be here after how everything had gone so far?

"Yes, ma'am," he said, hoping he sounded more convincing than he felt. "I think I do."

"I told you before you arrived that this school will be challenging," she said, a little more gently. "You will need to adapt. But in the same way, your presence here will be a challenge for the Navy. Which means we will need to adapt to *you*."

Lucas tried to picture someone like Ensign Mendoza or Lieutenant-Commander Palmer adapting to him. "Somehow that doesn't seem very likely."

"Give it some time." She looked at him curiously for a moment, and Lucas had the same under-the-microscope feeling he'd had the first time they'd met. "I understand you want to be a pilot. Is that right?"

"Yes, ma'am."

"I imagine you'd be quite a good pilot," she said,

drumming her fingers on her desk. "In fact, I imagine you're *already* quite a good pilot, and it's not our habit to try to teach cadets things they already know. But more than that, I think you might be selling yourself short."

"Flying is all I've ever wanted to do," Lucas said, a little confused.

"Perhaps that's only because you've never been given the opportunity to do something more," Sanchez said. "You have remarkable self-confidence and intuition. I think you could make an excellent captain."

This was something Lucas had never really considered. Belter ships were usually too small to dedicate precious life-support capacity to a person whose only job was to give orders.

"To be clear, you have a lot to learn," Sanchez went on. "Like anything else, leadership is a hard skill to master. You'll meet with me regularly, in addition to your usual classes. It will take some effort, but I trust that you'll be able to keep up with your academics."

"Yes, ma'am," he mumbled, not at all sure that this was true. From his point of view, the last thing he needed was another class on top of everything else.

"In fact," Sanchez said, "now would be a good time for you to learn your first lesson. Which is that in the Navy, accusing your captain of unfair treatment will at best get you thrown out of their cabin, and at worst will get you thrown off of the ship. Possibly without a suit. Is that clear?"

He flinched. Her voice was casual, but from the look in her eye, she wasn't entirely kidding. "Yes, ma'am. I'm, uh, sorry about that."

"One of the nicer things about the Navy is that personal apologies to a commanding officer are rarely necessary." Sanchez looked thoughtful for a moment. "However, this might be an exception. Apology accepted."

6

WHEN LUCAS GOT back to his cabin, Elena and Rahul were watching a news broadcast on the wall screen. He was about to launch into an explanation of how his first day hadn't gone quite as badly as he'd thought when he read the text scrolling across the bottom of the screen. *Hijacking of passenger liner leaves at least two dead. Six Belter miners believed to be in standoff with ship security.* A shaky handheld video playing on a loop showed a pan-icked crowd being herded into a large dining room by a man and a woman holding mining lasers.

He stared at the screen in shock. "Is that real?" he asked.

"No," Rahul said irritably. "We're watching a *fake* news broadcast."

"It's all over the nets," Elena said. "Nobody knows

how it happened. Apparently they almost made it to the bridge."

"I can't believe—" Lucas said, and then stopped. "I mean, I don't understand—"

"Believe it," Rahul said. "They put out a manifesto and everything. Some crap about tariffs and the 'hegemony of the oppressor planets.'"

"Maybe we should stop watching now?" Elena said. "They're just showing the same information over and over. If anything changes, someone will let us know."

She reached out toward the wall screen, but Rahul grabbed her arm. "Leave it on."

Elena pursed her lips. "He's pretty sure his parents are on that liner," she explained to Lucas.

"What?" Lucas asked. "Are you serious?"

"Yes, she's serious," Rahul snapped. "They flew out with me so they could take a vacation on Mars. Now they're on their way back. Or they were, until *this* happened."

"Are they okay?"

"Most of the passengers are safe," Elena said. "But some are still hostages."

"And they're not saying who," Rahul added bitterly.

Lucas watched Rahul for a moment, his heart aching. Maybe Tali would know what to say in a situation like this. She was good with people. His own main talent seemed to be putting his foot in his mouth.

But maybe there really just wasn't anything to say. Maybe Rahul just needed to know his friends were with him. He settled down on the floor next to Rahul and Elena and watched the broadcast. It was the last thing he wanted to do right now, but if it helped Rahul a little, then it was worth it.

Elena was right—the news feed wasn't much more than an endless loop of repeated information and analysis by people back on Earth who clearly didn't know the first thing about the Belt. As he watched, one thought kept running through his head: who would possibly do something like this? He'd heard his share of complaints from miners about tariffs and Earther jurisdiction. But attacking a passenger ship and taking hostages? It was insane. What did they think it was going to accomplish?

A reporter on the news feed gave a summary of the situation for the thousandth time, adding one new bit of information at the end. "According to authorities, six passengers have sustained serious injuries and are being treated in the ship's medical bay."

"Who?" Rahul shouted at the screen. "Why won't you say who?"

"Maybe you could try calling them from the comm room?" Elena suggested.

Rahul shook his head. "I tried. They're directly

sunward of us. There's too much interference right now."

An idea popped into Lucas's head. "What if you had a relay to route the signal through?"

"Well, sure," Rahul said. "As long as they were in a good position. But who—"

"Come on," Lucas said, grabbing Rahul and pulling him toward the door. "I think I know how to make it work."

They headed quickly down the Broadway ladder and around the rec room to the lower decks. When they got to the comm room, Lucas swung himself inside, nearly colliding with Ensign Mendoza.

"I'd like to make a call," Lucas said, out of breath.

Mendoza frowned. "Right now?"

"Yes," Lucas said. "It's important."

"Okay," Mendoza said, sighing. He jabbed his thumb at one of the comm cubicles. "Booth one."

The three of them crammed into the little comm cubicle, and Lucas activated the privacy field. He looked at the screen and frowned. He could call his father on the *Josey Wales* and ask him to patch through a call. But his dad would want to talk about school and the *Orpheus* and a thousand other things, and right now Lucas just didn't want to do that. Feeling a little guilty, he typed in the comm code for the *Josey* and added a password that would let him access the ship's computers directly.

"Is this legal?" Elena asked, watching over his shoulder.

"Well—it's not *illegal*," Lucas answered. He pulled up the *Josey Wales*'s communications interface and turned to Rahul. "What's your parents' comm code?"

Rahul typed in the code quickly. "Will this really work?"

"I guess we'll see," Lucas said.

The screen flashed a dark blue for close to a minute, and then a woman's face appeared on the screen. There was a crowd of people around her, and for a moment all they could hear was the chatter of overlapping voices. She looked exhausted, but her face brightened as soon as she saw them.

"Rahul!"

"Mom!" Rahul said frantically. "Are you okay? Is Dad okay?"

There was a maddening delay of almost twenty seconds before her response arrived. "We're fine—really, we're fine. Some excitement this afternoon. But we're both okay."

She smiled reassuringly, but it was clear that whatever had happened had been a lot more than just "some excitement."

"Where is Dad?" Rahul asked.

"He's getting something to eat," his mother said. "He broke his arm, if you can believe that. I promised that I'd let him tell you the story. He'd be furious if I spoiled it."

"Okay, but—"

"Who are these kids with you?" she asked. "Are these your friends?"

"Yes, ma'am," Elena said, giving her a little wave. "We're his sectionmates."

"This is Elena and that's Lucas," Rahul said impatiently. "Are you sure you're all right? Can I talk to Dad?"

His mother looked around. "Of course. Let me see if I can find him."

"We'll give you some time," Elena said, nudging Lucas toward the cubicle exit. When they were outside the privacy field, she gave him a quick hug. "You're a good friend. He was getting so worried he didn't know what to do with himself."

Lucas was feeling an almost overwhelming sense of relief that Rahul's parents were safe, so he could only imagine what Rahul himself must be feeling right now. It felt good to be able to help.

"Sorry to break the bad news," Mendoza said from his spot near the door. He flipped around his tablet screen and showed Lucas the headline: *Miners in custody, all hostages safe.* "Must be disappointing."

It took Lucas a moment to realize what Mendoza was saying. Disappointing? That everyone was safe? He opened his mouth to reply, but no words came out.

"Are you trying to say that Lucas *wanted* this to happen?" Elena demanded.

Mendoza shrugged. "It was his people who did this, wasn't it? They always say it's a fringe group, but I don't buy it. Every ore miner I've ever met was ready to snap. You spend that much time out there on your own, you're going to get a few screws loose."

"I wouldn't—" Lucas sputtered. "There's no way—"

"Come on," Elena said, pulling him out through the doorway. "I think it's against regulations to punch an officer, and the longer I stay here, the more tempted I am to find out."

All of Lucas's relief at finding out that Rahul's parents and the other hostages were okay had suddenly been replaced by a burning fury at Mendoza's accusation. How could anyone think that Lucas would be disappointed that the hijacking hadn't been a success?

"Let's get back to our cabin," Elena said.

Lucas shook his head. "I just want to be alone right now."

"Are you sure?"

"I'm sure," he said, already moving down the ladderway toward the rear of the ship. He didn't know where he was going, exactly. All he wanted was to be away from everyone else.

He reached the hangar and floated down toward the

floor. Chief Engineer Moskowitz was nowhere in sight, but Randall was still tinkering with the engine on one of the patrol ships.

"Hey," Randall said. "You okay?"

"Yeah," Lucas said, though "okay" wasn't anywhere near an accurate description of how he felt right now. "Can I go outside?"

Randall raised his eyebrows. "Like, outside the ship?"

Lucas nodded. Randall watched him for a moment, and then he shrugged. "Technically first-years aren't allowed. But I don't think you were quite what people were thinking when they made that rule. Be careful."

Lucas gave him a grateful smile and hurried into the prep room at the back of the hangar. He put on a suit quickly and headed back out to the main hangar doors, which were still open to the blackness of space. He looked at the shimmering barrier hesitantly. He'd heard of airfields, but he'd never actually encountered one. They were similar to privacy fields, except that they were designed to keep air from leaking out instead of just blocking light and sound.

"I just go through?" he asked Randall. "That's it?"

"That's it."

Lucas stuck out his hand and reached through the field. His glove expanded a little as it adjusted to the

96

vacuum of space. He took a deep breath and floated out through the field.

Randall was right—that was it. No airlock, no waiting for pressure to equalize. It was like magic. One second he was inside, the next he was out in space, surrounded by the reassuring glow of the Milky Way.

How long had it been since he'd been outside? Just a few days? It seemed like so much longer.

He used his suit's thruster pack to skim along the hull of the ship. Right now he just wanted a quiet place to relax. He found a sunny spot away from any windows and tethered himself to the hull so he wouldn't drift away. He turned off the light filter on his helmet and closed his eyes, basking in the faint warmth of sunlight on his face.

At least there was this, he thought. Space was the same everywhere. Out here it didn't matter if you were a Navy cadet or a miner or some kid from Earth. There was just a reassuring, infinite emptiness and the warm glow of the sun.

"Guess I'm not too surprised I'd find you out here," Tali said over the radio.

Lucas opened his eyes and turned around to see his sister pulling herself hand over hand along the hull toward him. He shrugged. "At least out here nobody thinks I'm the enemy."

"At least you won't have to put up with them for much longer, right?"

"Actually, I talked to Captain Sanchez," Lucas said. "It was all a big misunderstanding. I'm not getting sent home after all."

"You're staying?" Her jaw twitched slightly. "Lucas, I know you think that's a good thing. But I'm going to say it again: you'd be better off withdrawing."

For a moment Lucas wondered if maybe she was right. Nothing at the school had gone the way he'd expected. Everything was twice as hard as it ought to be, and after the news reports about the attempted hijacking, he was pretty sure almost nobody actually wanted him to stay.

But this was his only chance. If he left now, he'd never be able to come back. He hadn't even been here for a whole day yet. Was he really going to run away just because it wasn't as easy as he'd expected?

He shook his head. "I'm staying."

"You always were stubborn," she said, sighing. "Even when we were kids, we spent more time arguing about the rules for games than we did actually playing. I remember being jealous of how my friends bossed around their younger siblings."

"You bossed me around plenty," Lucas protested.

"Yeah, I guess eventually I learned," she said. "Maybe

that's why I'm here now, bossing around a bunch of groundhog kids."

He punched her lightly in the arm. "You're welcome."

In response, she just looked away. What was weighing on her so heavily, Lucas wondered, that she couldn't relax even when it was just the two of them? It was like she was always playing the part of Tali Chen, senior cadet from Mars, and couldn't break out of it even for a second.

There was something she was keeping from him—something big. He wanted to ask her, but he knew she wasn't going to tell him until she was ready. He wasn't the only stubborn one in their family.

"I'm going back in," she said. "You coming?"

He supposed it wasn't all that much of an invitation, but it was something. He nodded and followed her back along the hull. Instead of going through the hangar doors, though, she led him all the way down to the engine room's maintenance hatch.

"Isn't this area off-limits to cadets?" Lucas asked as she cycled the airlock.

Tali smiled wryly. "Don't worry. If we get caught, I'm going to pretend I don't know who you are."

The main engine room was a place Lucas could have spent a hundred years exploring. He'd seen pictures of fusion rockets, and he had a reasonable idea of how they worked, but he'd never been up close to one. He wandered around the main engine assembly, tracing the feeder lines in his mind. It was almost enough to make him want to give up piloting and become an engineer.

"So, did you see it?" a man said from the other side of the engine. "There's a spot. . . ."

The voice trailed off. A moment later, an arm shot out from around a coolant tank and grabbed Lucas roughly by the arm. Lucas was suddenly brought face-to-face with a tall man with a silver-flecked beard. The man glowered angrily at him.

"Eavesdropping?" he growled. "That's not polite, son."

Lucas jerked his arm away. "I wasn't eavesdropping. I was just—"

"This is our new cadet," Tali interrupted, coming around from the other side of the engine. "Lucas Adebayo."

The man blinked in surprise. "The Belter kid?"

Lucas nodded. How many times was he going to go through this?

"And here I was accusing you of spying on us! Sometimes this ship makes a fellow too suspicious for his own good. What I *ought* to have said is how it's a genuine pleasure to meet you. I'm Abbott McKinley, born and raised on Pallas."

McKinley grabbed his hand and pumped it up and down vigorously. Lucas stared at him in astonishment. He couldn't have been more surprised if the man had just told him that he was Charles Darwin. "You're actually from the Belt? I thought I was the only one!"

"You're the only Belter *cadet* in the Navy. But there are a few dozen of us as enlisted mates in the fleet."

"Oh, wow. I was starting to think . . . ," Lucas said, and stopped.

"You were starting to think you were the only sane person on this crazy ship?" McKinley clapped Lucas on the back and bellowed with laughter.

A warm feeling of relief flooded over Lucas. He wasn't as alone as he thought—there was someone else on this ship he could talk to! Someone who would understand him. It wasn't like being back home, but it was light-years better than nothing.

"Hey," McKinley said, suddenly looking a little more serious. "Nobody has been giving you any trouble, have they? About all the nastiness on that passenger liner?"

"A little," Lucas admitted. "Ensign Mendoza."

McKinley grimaced. "I should have guessed. Don't listen to him, eh? He just likes to stir people up."

"We should get back," Tali said, tugging on Lucas's arm. "It's almost dinnertime."

"You'll be fine, though, won't you?" McKinley went on, escorting the two of them toward the ladderway. "Tough kid. I can see it written on your face. And you've got a friend now. Belters stick together. Right?"

"Yeah," Lucas said, smiling. "Belters stick together."

7

ONCE LUCAS FIGURED out the basic rhythm of the ship, he started to feel a little more comfortable. Hofstra's advanced class on orbital mechanics was fascinating, and with a little tutoring from Rahul, Lucas even stopped dreading Novak's calculus lectures.

Rahul insisted repeatedly that he was okay now that he knew his parents were safe. But Lucas noticed that he spent nearly all his free time sitting in their bunkroom staring at the wall and talking to his AI corneal implant.

"Tell me about the power generation systems on Ceres," he said one afternoon before dinner. Confused, Lucas had been about to tell him that he didn't know much about that side of the colony, but then he'd realized that Rahul had just been running a query through his AI. Elena gave Lucas a concerned, inquisitive look. She was clearly thinking the same thing—why was Rahul researching Belter colony power systems? Lucas just shrugged. It was just Rahul being Rahul, he figured. And if it was his way of getting over the stress of being worried about his parents, well, it was certainly better than a lot of things he might be doing.

Surprisingly, the one-on-one sessions with Captain Sanchez turned out to be Lucas's favorite part of the day, though he wasn't sure what most of it had to do with commanding a ship in the Navy. They mainly talked about ancient Earth history, some of which, Lucas was surprised to discover, was fascinating. He'd heard about some of these places—America, South Africa, Hong Kong—but he knew almost nothing about them or how they had formed. At the end of the first week, Sanchez asked him to write an essay on a historical period that had parallels to the current day. It was a fun project, and he turned it in with a feeling of pride and excitement.

Sanchez had read through it—twice—and cleared her throat. "It's a very . . . *interesting* comparison, linking England's tariffs on tea to the taxes on soy milk in the Belt."

Lucas didn't understand what she was saying. Interesting? Was that good? Why did she have such an odd expression?

"So what do you think that implies?" Sanchez asked.

"Ma'am?"

"We study history because of what it can teach us about today. What was the end result of the taxes on tea in the American colonies?"

This was actually something Lucas hadn't considered. He thought for a moment, and then his eyes went wide. Did she think that he'd written that essay to argue for a revolutionary war here in the Belt? "I wasn't suggesting . . . I didn't mean to say—"

"I didn't read it that way," Sanchez said reassuringly. "But it's something for you to keep in mind. And let's pray that nobody on Ceres decides to sneak into a hangar and throw a hundred tons of soy milk out into space."

On his way back to his cabin that afternoon, he stopped outside the comm room. He'd been here for seven days and he hadn't called his dad yet—at least, not unless you counted the first day, when he'd used the *Josey*'s comm systems to let Rahul call his parents. He slipped inside, where fortunately the on-duty officer was Lieutenant Feinman and not Mendoza.

"Can I make a call?" Lucas asked her.

"Sure," she said. "Booth two."

He settled into the cubicle and turned on the privacy field. It took him a moment to remember the comm code for the *Josey*, even though it was a number he'd had memorized since he was four years old. After a brief delay, his father's face appeared on the screen.

"Hi, Dad!" Lucas said, grinning broadly. "How are you doing?"

"I'm doing well," Tomas replied. "It's good to see you."

Alarm bells went off in Lucas's head. They hadn't seen each other in a week, and this was how his dad responded? He was upset about something. Was it the hijacking of the passenger liner? Or something else? It was hard to tell over a video call.

"Classes are going well," Lucas said. "The teachers are all really smart. I got moved up to an advanced navigation class."

"I'm glad to hear it. You must be very busy."

Maybe his dad was mad because he hadn't called before this? "Yeah," he said, nodding vigorously. "They keep us moving—it's a super-busy schedule. And they have a special room where you have to go to make calls. High security, I guess."

"I see," Tomas said. "So it's been hard to find time to talk, I guess?"

"Exactly."

"Then I'm curious how you managed to find time in that busy schedule to route a call through my comm systems—without bothering to ask, or even say hello."

Lucas froze. How had his dad found out about the call to Rahul's parents? He'd been careful to cover his tracks—a fact that only made the whole thing look even

106

worse. And how long had his dad known? A horrible guilty feeling settled over him.

"Right," he said. "Uh . . . sorry about that. A friend of mine needed to talk to his parents. They were on that hijacked passenger liner, and I thought I could help them out without bothering you."

"Well, it was good of you to help out your friend," Tomas said, sighing. "Is his family okay?"

Lucas nodded. His dad was trying to make him feel less guilty, but somehow that only made it worse. Why hadn't he called before now? He couldn't even put his finger on the reason. The night he'd boarded, the thought of being here by himself and leaving his dad all alone on the *Josey* had seemed almost impossible. Had he really gotten so wrapped up in everything here that he hadn't even wanted to talk to his father?

Promise you won't forget where you came from, his dad had said. *Well done*, Lucas thought glumly. It had taken him less than a week to break that promise.

"I'm sorry," he mumbled.

His dad was silent for a few moments. "It happens," he said finally, in a gruff voice. "I'm glad everything is going well there. Tell me more about your classes. Advanced navigation, eh?"

Was it going well? Lucas supposed that it was—at least since that awful first day. He talked for a while about the officers and cadets and the general routine of the ship. At first it felt strange, describing the *Orpheus* to his father, but gradually it started to feel more comfortable. His favorite part, he discovered, was talking about Elena and Rahul and how they'd already become friends. His dad listened carefully, nodding along or adding little encouraging comments.

"How is everything on the *Josey*?" Lucas asked. "Are you doing okay by yourself?"

"Oh, it's all good," Tomas said.

But Lucas could see that wasn't entirely true. His dad was trying to hide it, but he was haggard and exhausted. Running a mining ship by yourself wasn't easy, either psychologically or physically. Lucas's guilt deepened. He'd gotten his chance to come to the *Orpheus*, the place he wanted to be more than any other. And as a result, he'd left his father alone.

"Any news on a copilot?" he asked hopefully.

Tomas shook his head. "Got a few recommendations, but none of them are what I'm looking for. I'm picky, I guess."

Well, that was the truth. Lucas wondered if anyone would be able to live up to—or put up with—his finicky repairs and mind-numbing maintenance routines.

"Well, make sure you find someone, okay?"

"Sure, sure," Tomas said. "All right, I'll let you get back

to your friends. I've got a clog in the starboard plumbing I'm going to try to fish out."

"Okay," Lucas said, feeling a little disappointed. "I'll call you soon."

Tomas smiled faintly. He started to say something and then stopped himself. "Take care of yourself, son," he said finally.

"I will," Lucas promised, but his dad had already closed the link.

He sat back in his seat. No matter what happened, he wasn't going to let himself drift away from his life back on the *Josey Wales*. He wasn't going to forget where he came from.

No matter what happened, he wasn't going to turn into his sister.

"Of *course* we get the same airlock as them," Rahul muttered, glaring at Willem, Katya, and Aaron as they waited with their helmets on the other side of the prep room.

"Don't get too dizzy out there!" Willem called, jabbing his thumb at the airlock at the far end of the room. A tiny patch of stars was visible through the transplastic window in the airlock doors.

"I'll be fine," Rahul shot back. "Just make sure *you* don't get lost. It'd be a real shame if we had to leave you behind."

For the entire fourth week of the term, classes for first-year cadets had been canceled so that they could practice basic spacesuit maneuvers. According to Elena, Rahul had done well and mostly managed to keep his vertigo in check. Inevitably, though, word had gotten out, and naturally Willem and his friends had made the most of it every chance they'd gotten.

To his dismay, Lucas hadn't been allowed to join them for any of the previous training drills. Sanchez had helpfully pointed out that his time would be better spent in tutoring sessions to help him catch up in his academic subjects. As a result, after many hours huddled in a room with Novak, he finally had a decent understanding of logarithms and had moved on to matrices and linear equations. Today the first-year cadets were graduating from simple maneuvering drills to what the Navy called "full-scale exercises." Lucas wasn't exactly clear on what that meant, but the only thing that mattered was that he would be there with the other cadets instead of being locked inside. The whole thing made him feel like a prisoner released on parole for good behavior.

"Have you ever been to Volkov Station before?" Elena asked him.

Lucas shook his head. "It's off-limits except to the Navy."

He craned his neck to peer through the airlock

window at the steel latticework floating a few hundred meters from the *Orpheus*. Most of what he'd heard about Volkov had been from older kids back on Ceres, most of whom had insisted it was filled with either mutant experiments or alien life forms from another dimension. It was slightly disappointing to discover that it was really just an abandoned monitoring station that was used for training by the Navy.

Randall floated into the room with an armload of thruster backpacks. He passed one out to each cadet, pausing in front of Rahul. "If you need to come back inside, let me know. Star vertigo gets better the more time you spend outside, but for god's sake please don't puke in your suit."

"Yes, sir," Rahul mumbled.

Willem opened his mouth to say something, but Randall snapped his fingers and pointed at him. "No comments, cadet."

Willem's eyes widened innocently. "I wasn't going to—"

"Yes, you were," Randall said. "Now, everyone listen up. The other cadets are already in the station. We're going to meet them at the tactical sphere for a game of capture the flag."

Randall tapped on a comm panel on the wall and spoke briefly with Ensign Weber, who was serving as the officer of the watch on the bridge. When Randall had gotten the go-ahead, he turned back to the cadets. "Helmets on, everyone. Let's get going."

They crowded into the airlock and Randall closed the door behind them. "Anyone familiar with explosive decompression?"

Nobody spoke up. Lucas cleared his throat. "Are you really going to—"

"Yes," Randall said. "Everyone hold on."

He flipped a large red handle, and the outer doors shot open. There was a teeth-rattling bang as all the air vented out into space. Willem, who had apparently not listened to Randall's warning, was jerked out through the outer doors. Randall grabbed his leg to keep him from drifting too far away from the ship.

"Next time, pay attention," he said over the radio.

There was a beep in Lucas's headset as they were hailed from the bridge of the *Orpheus*. "Gee, thanks," Weber said, her voice dripping with sarcasm. "Do you know how long it took me to get us perfectly lined up?"

Randall grinned. "I'm just demonstrating the principle of equal and opposite reaction for our young cadets," he called back.

"What's she upset about?" Katya asked.

"The force of all that air venting out may not seem like much," Randall explained. "But in space, it's enough to push the *Orpheus* a few millimeters per second the other way. Which, in turn, is enough to drive a perfectionist like Weber up the wall."

Lucas noticed Rahul floating behind them in the doorway of the airlock. His face, lit from below by the light in his helmet, was looking a bit green. "You okay?" Lucas asked over the alpha section's private channel.

Rahul shook his head. "I can't stop thinking about how far away everything is. If I started drifting . . ."

"Keep your eyes focused on something," Elena suggested. "And don't think about it."

"Have you ever tried to *not* think about something? It's harder than it sounds."

"All right," Randall said, pointing at the flag sphere, which was floating inside one of the rings of the station. "There's your target. There's a beacon if you get too far off course."

One by one they pushed themselves away from the ship and kicked in the thrust on their backpacks. Aaron's aim was a little off, and he had to be rescued by the beacon, which overrode the manual controls and brought him back on course when he had strayed too far. Willem arrived only a few meters from the beacon itself, though Lucas would have called it more of a low-speed collision than a landing. Unsurprisingly, Elena did beautifully, following along behind Lucas and imitating the way he pivoted around to decelerate using the main thrusters on his back rather than the weaker ones on his chest. Rahul followed after her, doing surprisingly well considering how miserable he looked.

"I didn't puke," he said weakly when they were all gathered together again. "At least I didn't puke."

"Nicely done," Willem said sarcastically. "Quite an accomplishment."

"We're about to play a game of capture the flag, right?" Rahul asked Randall. "Am I allowed to hurt him?"

"No," Randall said. After a moment, he added, "Not deliberately, anyway."

He passed out flags to each of them. Each had a little sensor on it that would detect when it had been pulled from the wearer's belt.

"I don't care whether we win or lose," Rahul said to Lucas and Elena as they attached the flags to their waists. "I'm going after Willem."

"I need to go collect the older cadets and get the game ready," Randall said. "Wait here. I'll be back in a few minutes."

Randall tapped a button on his wrist screen, and a large circular hatchway slid open. He grabbed the edge of the opening and swung himself inside. Curious, Lucas peered through the hatchway, but all he could see were some hand-welded pieces of metal forming

114

what looked like an obstacle course.

Willem stretched his arms and looked at Lucas mischievously. "So this is where you shine, right? I mean, as opposed to gravity. Or centrifuges."

"I guess," Lucas said.

"Well, I bet I can still beat you."

"I guess we'll see," Elena said.

"I was thinking more of a race," Willem said. "From here to the ship and back."

"You're dreaming," Rahul said. "Lucas was born in space. *Literally.*"

Lucas resisted the urge to point out that he'd actually been born in the medical center on Ceres. He wasn't sure what made Willem think he could maneuver out here better than Lucas could, but he wasn't about to pass up the chance to show him he was wrong. "Sure, I'll race you."

"Okay, but no help from our friends back here," Willem said. "So radios off. And no transponders, either, or else everyone will see us."

Lucas shrugged. "Whatever. To the ship and back, no radios or transponders."

"I don't like this," Elena said over their private channel. "He's planning something."

"He ought to be planning to lose," Lucas said. "I'll see you back here in less than a minute."

He turned off his radio and transponder via his wrist screen and watched Willem do the same. He detached his thruster pack's control stick and positioned his fingers on the controls. When they were both ready, Katya floated out a little ways in front of them and raised her hands.

"On your marks," she mouthed. "Get set. Go!"

She dropped her arms, and Lucas pressed his thumb down on the control stick. The thrusters on his backpack fired, pushing against the small of his back like an invisible hand. As he accelerated away from the sphere, he stole a glance over his shoulder. Willem was nowhere to be seen. Lucas grinned. This was going to be a piece of cake.

With his radio off, the silence of space was soothing. All Lucas could hear was the low growl of his thruster pack and a faint hiss from his air unit. For a few moments, he felt more at home than he had since he had arrived on the *Orpheus*. *See*, he told himself. *Not everything here is studying and classes.*

He passed by the hull of the *Orpheus* near its midpoint, just behind the bulge of the rec room. He skimmed past the arm of the centrifuge and kicked in the attitude thrusters to bring him around and back toward the tactical sphere. The sun winked out behind the hull of the ship, leaving him briefly in shadow. As he curled around and came out into the light again, something caught his eye. Someone was crouched against the *Orpheus*'s hull, just behind the main sensor array.

Repairs? It seemed an odd time for that. And there was something else—whoever was down there had turned off their suit's transponder, so that there was no indicator on Lucas's heads-up display. If he hadn't happened to glance down, he might not have seen them at all.

As Lucas swung around the ship and headed back toward the station, the suited figure next to the sensor array straightened up. The person was facing away from Lucas, so he couldn't see the face. But even though Lucas only had a brief glimpse of the silhouette before he disappeared back around to the other side of the ship, Lucas was sure it was his sister, Tali.

What was she doing there? As a cadet, even a senior one, it wouldn't be her job to make any kind of repairs. Especially not now, and not with her transponder off. If something happened to her, nobody would be able to track her down and bring her back in.

Which reminded him of what *he* was doing flying around out here, and how it was probably not the smartest decision he'd ever made. He looked around for Willem, expecting him to come out around the far side of the *Orpheus*. Why was it taking so long? There was no way Willem was *this* slow. And why had he been so insistent on turning off their radios? On an impulse, Lucas flipped his comm unit back on.

"—*back right now!*" Elena was shouting over the alpha-section channel. "Are you listening? Willem never left! He's floating right here."

Lucas banged his fist against his helmet. He'd been a complete idiot. Of course Willem hadn't thought that he could beat him. All he'd wanted to do was get Lucas in trouble.

"Lucas, get back here!" Rahul called. "Randall will be back any minute!"

Lucas triggered another big burst from the rockets in his backpack. He had to get back as quickly as he could, even if it made for an unpleasant landing. When he was a few dozen meters from the sphere, he flipped around and kicked the thrust to its maximum. His head snapped back and hit the rear of his helmet, and pain shot through his legs as his knees suddenly bent ninety degrees. With a bone-jarring thud, he landed against the surface of the sphere a little ways from the other cadets.

"Are you okay?" Rahul asked, helping him up.

"I think so," Lucas muttered, glaring at Willem. Like the alpha cadets, he was on his section's private channel, but he was laughing so hard Lucas could practically hear it without audio.

"Okay, I'm with you," Elena said to Rahul. "Win or lose, we take him out."

Randall poked his head out of the opening of the sphere. "All right, we're ready."

Lucas and the others followed him inside. The interior of the sphere was a jumble of randomly placed struts, fuel tanks, and cargo containers. Bright floodlights glowed all around the inner surface of the sphere, but the obstacles inside still made for lots of shadowy places to hide. The rest of the cadets were already there, gathered into a few groups.

"All right, listen up," Randall called out. "We're going to play capture the flag—alpha and beta versus gamma and delta. Section leaders, gather everyone up and make sure they know the rules."

Oliver, the beta-section leader, shepherded their team into a clump near one wall while Hanako and Maria gathered up the gamma and delta cadets. "Where is Tali?" an older girl from alpha section asked.

"She had to go back to the ship because of a problem with her air unit," Oliver said. "She should be back any minute."

A problem with her air unit? Tali had certainly seemed fine when Lucas had seen her. An uncomfortable feeling settled in his stomach. What had she been doing out there on the hull of the ship?

The more senior cadets gathered together and started discussing strategy. The girl who had asked about Tali floated over to Lucas and his friends. Lucas recognized her from Hofstra's class, though they'd never spoken. "Hi, I'm Britta, and this is Kai and Samir. We're alpha-section second-years."

"Any advice for us?" Rahul asked.

"Stay out of the way and don't try to do too much," Samir suggested.

"If you see someone who looks like they know what they're doing, run away," Kai added.

"Great," Rahul said. "This is going to be fun."

Tali appeared through an entrance on the other side of the sphere and pushed off toward the alpha cadets. "All right, everyone. Are you ready for this?" she asked as she landed next to them.

"Everything good with your suit?" Britta asked.

"All better now," Tali said. "Let's get this game started."

Lucas watched his sister as she talked casually with the other cadets. When had she gotten so good at lying? There was a time she couldn't hide anything from him. But if he hadn't seen her outside the ship, he would never have guessed that she wasn't telling the truth.

"The rules are simple," Tali said. She held up one of the flags that Randall had passed out. "If someone from the other team grabs this, you're out for sixty seconds.

Head over to the neutral area there to wait it out."

She attached a large red flag to a buoy and placed it just outside the opening they'd come through. "This is our base. If they get this flag, they win. So don't let that happen."

"How do you capture it?" Rahul asked. "All the other team has to do is play a little defense, and it's impossible to get to."

"As far as I know, nobody has *ever* captured the team flag," Oliver said. "But your team gets a point each time you get someone's personal flag. If nobody wins outright, then the side with the most points when time runs out is the winner."

"It's true that nobody has ever captured the team flag," Randall said. "But that doesn't mean it's impossible."

Lucas had to agree with Rahul: the opening in the sphere was small enough that even a single person could guard it easily. Why was the game set up like that? It seemed odd.

"First-year kids, stay near our flag," Tali said. "The rest of you are on offense. Keep together and don't let them isolate you."

Randall verified that both teams were ready and headed over to the marked-off neutral area on one side of the sphere. "Three. Two. One. Go!"

The next fifteen minutes were complete chaos. The

score racked up quickly as kids from each side tackled one another and wrestled away their opponent's flag. Tali, Oliver, and the other fourth-year kids played offense, and each scored a half-dozen points. But it soon became clear that their second- and third-year groups were outmatched by their rivals on the other team. Repeated attacks took out the alpha and beta kids' midfield guard, forcing Tali and the others to fall back to help.

The only bright side of the match, as far as Lucas could tell, was that their plan of focusing on the delta-section first-years worked beautifully. Most of this was due to Elena and Lucas, who racked up multiple points each on Willem, Aaron, and Katya. Rahul only managed to score one point, but it was a satisfying one: he ambushed Willem from behind a fuel tank, tackling him hard and ripping the flag off his waist with exaggerated delight. But it wasn't enough, and with five minutes left, Lucas's team was down by eleven points.

"They're playing conservative," Tali said as alpha section regrouped near the flag. She leaned her head against a fuel tank, breathing hard. "They know there's no way we can catch up if they just defend."

"Cowards!" Oliver shouted over the general channel.

"Just playing smart," Maria called back, floating near the center of the sphere.

In response, Oliver banged his hand against the inner

surface of the sphere. The force caused him to drift away gently toward the center of the playing area.

It was another demonstration of equal and opposite reaction. Just like Randall had said: in zero gravity, any force pushed both sides away from each other. Which meant that even though it was far more massive, the sphere would have just moved a tiny amount in the opposite direction. Something about that idea tugged at Lucas. He was sure it was important, but he couldn't put his finger on why.

Suddenly it clicked in his mind, and he had answers to all the questions that had been nagging him. Why was this game designed to be so difficult to win? Why were the flags kept *outside* the sphere? And why had Randall chosen today to demonstrate the effect of decompression on the *Orpheus*?

"I know how to beat them," Lucas said, grabbing Tali's arm.

Tali squinted dubiously at him. "What are you talking about?"

"The sphere isn't attached to anything, right?" Lucas said. "It's just floating. Which means we can move it."

"Okay, *maybe*," Britta said. "But how would that help us?"

Lucas pointed to the other team's flag, floating just outside the other side of the sphere. "Because the flags aren't attached to the sphere. Which means that they'll stay right where they are."

"You're not talking about *moving* the sphere," Tali said. "You're talking about *rotating* it."

"I've got no idea whether that will actually work," Oliver said, looking thoughtful. "But we're not going to win this game any other way."

Tali nodded. "First- and second-years, stay here and help Lucas. That'll attract the least amount of attention. The rest of us go wild in the center and try to keep them distracted. We can't let them figure out what we're doing."

Tali led the older alpha-section kids toward the other team's base, waving their arms aggressively. The other team froze for a moment and then fanned out, still playing defensively.

"Now's our chance," Lucas said. "Find a good spot. Something secure."

He and the other cadets positioned themselves against some of the stronger-looking tanks that were welded to the inside of the sphere. Britta found a spot next to Lucas and gave him a little nod. "One, two, three!" Lucas said.

Each of them flicked on their thruster packs, ratcheting the throttles up slowly. "Ow," Rahul said, shifting his weight. "I'm being smushed."

Lucas had to agree: it wasn't a pleasant feeling. As far

as he could tell, all he was doing was crushing himself against the fuel tank in front of him. "Keep going," he gasped. "Make sure the thrust is aimed at a right angle."

"How's it going back there?" Tali called from the sixty-second waiting area. "We're getting killed."

Lucas glanced over his shoulder at the opening they'd come through. Their flag had already disappeared, and the stars outside were gently drifting past. But it was going to take a while to rotate the entire sphere one hundred and eighty degrees. Would they have enough time?

Sensing an advantage, the other team stopped playing defensively and started pushing back into alpha and beta's territory. Britta led Elena and some of the other cadets to where Oliver was waging a defensive battle against Hanako and a group of delta kids, leaving Rahul and Lucas as the only ones still pushing back at their base. Lucas turned and focused on applying as much force to the sphere as he could. He had to trust that his teammates could give him enough time.

Elena and Britta were soon taken down by a trio of delta cadets, though they managed to grab two of their flags in the process. One by one, their teammates were captured and sent to the waiting area, until only Tali was left. She danced around, delaying the inevitable for as long as she could, but finally lost to a concerted rush by Maria and another cadet.

"Looks like this is my chance," Rahul said. He switched his radio to the general channel and let out a bloodthirsty scream as he leaped toward Willem, Katya, and Aaron. He somehow managed to tackle all three at once, losing his flag in the process but knocking them all back away from the edge of the sphere.

"Heroic of them, I guess," Maria said, approaching Lucas.

"I guess," Lucas agreed. He shut off his thrust and slid over toward the opening in the sphere. All he needed was a few more seconds.

"But now we're going to capture all of you *and* get your team flag," Maria said. "First time ever."

"Maybe," Lucas said, looking through the hatchway. Almost there . . .

He lunged forward and stretched out his arm through the opening. Startled, Maria grabbed his leg and pulled him back inside.

"Got you!" she shouted, grabbing his flag and holding it triumphantly above her head.

"Maybe," Lucas agreed. He opened his clenched fist, revealing the gamma-and-delta team flag.

"But *we* won."

8

"I'M JUST GOING to say it one more time," Rahul crowed as the three of them climbed into their sleep sacks that night. "That was *brilliant*."

"Yes, it was," Elena said tiredly. "But regular classes start again tomorrow, so—"

"Rotating the entire sphere!" Rahul went on, twisting his fist to demonstrate. "Genius! And the looks on their faces when they found out they'd lost were *priceless*."

The subject of the "stolen" victory had led to a dozen heated arguments over dinner. Despite Randall's assurances that Lucas's strategy broke no rules, half of the cadets on the ship were clearly convinced that he'd cheated. Even an official announcement from Captain Sanchez that alpha and beta sections were the winners of the match didn't clear up the controversy. At least four times, a cadet from delta or gamma section angrily told

Lucas that tricks like that weren't going to work the next time they faced off.

But as Lucas lay in his sleep sack, his mind wasn't on any of that. He wasn't reveling in his victory or worried about what the other cadets thought. Instead, all he could think about was his sister.

He desperately wanted there to be some reasonable explanation for why she'd been outside on the hull of the *Orpheus*. If there was a problem with her suit, then what had she been doing near the sensor array? Why had her transponder been turned off? And could it possibly be a coincidence that this had happened during the one time when all the cadets would be off the ship?

No matter how hard he tried, he couldn't come up with answers to any of these questions. Or at least, not any *good* answers.

An hour after lights-out, still wide awake, he decided that he had two options. The first was to ask his sister outright what she had been doing out on the hull. He could imagine how that would go: denial, anger, dismissiveness. After going through all that trouble to hide her actions, Tali wasn't going to suddenly admit to what she'd been doing—not even to him. Maybe *especially* not to him.

Which left him with the second option.

Quietly he slipped out of his bunk and got dressed in his uniform. He reached for the control to open the door, but in the darkness his fingers accidentally brushed against the touchpad for the lights instead. The light bars in the ceiling flashed on to full brightness, momentarily blinding him. He turned them off again quickly, but it was too late.

"What's going on?" Rahul asked blearily.

Elena sat up in her sleep sack. "Lucas is going somewhere."

Fortunately Lucas had thought ahead. He remembered how Tali had always told him that the best lies were as close to the truth as possible. "I'm going outside."

"Like, outside the ship?" she asked. "In the middle of the night?"

"Back on my dad's ship, if I had trouble sleeping, I'd go out and look at the stars," Lucas explained, doing his best to sound matter-of-fact. "It's beautiful. Very relaxing."

"So it's like some kind of Belter cure for insomnia?" Rahul asked.

Lucas shrugged. "Something like that."

"You're going out by yourself?" Elena asked doubtfully. "That really doesn't seem like a good idea."

"He's not," Rahul said, swinging out of his bunk. "Because I'm coming too."

Lucas's mouth fell open. This was something he definitely hadn't expected. "Seriously? What about your vertigo?"

"That's exactly why I'm coming," Rahul said. "You heard Randall. I need more time out there."

Lucas tried to think of an argument for why Rahul shouldn't come, but he was trapped by his own lie. Maybe he shouldn't have made it sound so appealing? Of course, who could have predicted that a kid with astral vertigo would want to come along?

"What about you?" Rahul asked Elena. "You're not really going to stay behind, are you?"

"That's exactly what I'm going to do," Elena said, rolling over in her sleep sack.

"Oh, come on," Rahul said, pulling on his uniform. "It'll be fun. Didn't you ever sneak out back home? To tip over cows, or whatever?"

From his spot near the door, Lucas saw a flash of raw emotion on her face. Was it anger? Pain? He couldn't tell, but it was clear that Rahul's words stung her.

"No," she growled. "I never snuck out to tip over cows, or whatever."

Rahul grinned as he zipped up his uniform jacket, clearly oblivious to how upset Elena was getting. "Wow. Talk about a missed opportunity."

"It's okay," Lucas put in. "If she doesn't want to come—"

"Fine!" Elena snapped, sitting up suddenly. "I'll go out on your stupid little mission. Are you happy?"

"The Three Musketeers!" Rahul crowed, and then put

his hand over his mouth. "Sorry. Forgot how late it was."

Lucas sighed. This was getting worse and worse. How was he going to search the spot on the hull where he'd seen Tali if Rahul and Elena were with him? He might as well bring along Captain Sanchez herself.

"Everyone ready?" Rahul said cheerfully when they all had their uniforms on.

"Ready," Lucas and Elena mumbled in unison.

They floated quietly out into the hallway and looked around. It was 0320 ship's time, and with any luck, nobody would be awake except for the night crew on the bridge. Lucas led them down the Broadway ladder, barely touching the rungs, and then headed down a corridor on deck nine until he reached the main airlock and prep room.

Rahul peered through the window of the airlock. "Looks quiet out there, at least."

"It's space," Elena said. "It's always quiet."

They put on suits and helmets and found backpacks that had full charges of oxygen and propellant. Lucas was about to open the airlock when Rahul grabbed his arm. "Whoa, are you crazy?"

"What?"

"If you open that door, an alert is going to go off on the bridge," Rahul whispered. "The duty officer will be down here before you can say 'court-martial.'"

This was something Lucas hadn't considered. The Belter ships he'd been on weren't exactly security conscious. "If you knew we can't go outside, why did you let us come down here and get suited up?"

"I didn't say we can't go outside," Rahul countered. "I just said you can't go opening doors like Alice in Wonderland."

He pulled out a handheld screen and turned it over. The back cover had been removed, exposing a dense web of circuitry. Rahul knelt down and opened up a panel next to the airlock door.

"Green goes to green, red goes to black," he said in a singsong voice, though from what Lucas could tell, none of the connections he was making had any relation to the colors he was reciting.

"How long is this going to take?" Elena asked, looking over her shoulder at the corridor behind them.

"Patience," Rahul said. "Nothing worth doing is easy. Though to be honest, this is script-kiddie stuff. I don't think whoever designed this was super worried about people going *out*."

He stood up, bowed dramatically, and pushed a button on his handheld screen. There was a brief pause, and the airlock doors slid open.

"You're the best," Lucas said as they crowded into the airlock. "How hard is that to learn?"

"Nothing to it," Rahul said, preening. "At least, not if you're a founding member of the Mumbai Chaos Computing Club."

Lucas cycled the airlock, wincing at the sound of the air pumps. Hopefully there were no light-sleeping officers on nearby decks. The outer door slid open, revealing the brightly glowing disk of the sun. Lucas squinted and looked around, trying to find the spot where he'd seen Tali.

"This is something I probably should have checked on before," Rahul said. "But does anyone know the penalty for sneaking outside like this? I mean, is it a 'Go to your room without dinner' kind of thing, or more of a 'Hey, thanks, you're expelled'?"

"I don't know," Elena said. "And no point worrying about it now."

Lucas craned his neck and made out the top of the big antenna dish a little ways around the other side of the hull. "Let's head that way," he suggested, as if he'd just thought of it. "It'll be nicer once we're out of the sun."

Getting there turned out to be a bit harder than he'd anticipated. Not only did they have to avoid all windows to make sure they weren't noticed by any officers who happened to be awake at this hour, they also had to make sure they didn't bang against the hull and wake anyone up. Sound wouldn't carry out here in the vacuum of space, but Lucas knew from experience on the *Josey Wales* that it would be easily heard inside the ship.

Finally he stopped next to the cluster of sensors where he'd seen Tali earlier that day. He stretched his arms and looked around, trying not to look too curious. From up close, this area was much larger than it had seemed when he was flying past at high speed. How many different antennas did a ship like this need? In addition to the big high-gain antenna, there were two smaller dishes and one that looked like a folded-up umbrella.

What was he expecting to find, exactly? Some kind of intentional sabotage? Now that he was out here, it seemed crazy. Maybe Tali had a good reason to be out on the hull when everyone was away from the ship. Lucas, Rahul, and Elena would sure look suspicious to anyone who happened to notice them.

"You're right," Rahul said, yawning. "It is pretty relaxing being out here. I could totally find myself dozing off."

"I *was* dozing off," Elena said. "Back in my bunk, before the two of you dragged me out here."

Lucas made his way around to the other side of the big antenna. As the sun disappeared behind the curve of the big dish, something caught his eye. A panel next to one of the antennas had scratches on it, and a thin wire led out to a tiny box. He bent down and looked more closely. Something about the box didn't look like it belonged. He pulled at it experimentally and it came off in his hand. Turning it over, he found a small magnet on the other side, but there were no markings or indications of any kind. He peered inside the small hole and saw what looked like hand-assembled circuits.

Lucas was suddenly sure of two things. First, whatever this device was, it wasn't Navy-made. And second, Tali had put it here. He jerked the wire out through the gap in the panel and shoved the little box in his pocket.

"Everything okay?" Elena asked, coming around the back of the high-gain antenna.

"Sure," Lucas said defensively. "Why wouldn't it be?"

"You tell me," she said. "You've been acting weird ever since we got back to the ship."

"Well, Lucas is always a little weird," Rahul said. "And just to be clear, I consider that a compliment."

"Okay," she said. "*Tense*, then."

Lucas shrugged. "I'm ready to get back to regular classes, I guess."

He regretted the words immediately. Get back to regular classes? Whatever happened to lies that were somewhere close to the truth? Clearly he wasn't any good in the deception department.

Elena raised her eyebrows skeptically. "If you say so.

Does that mean we can go back to bed now?"

"Sounds good to me," Rahul said. "I'm starting to feel a little—"

He was interrupted by an announcement over the general radio channel. "Course correction in thirty seconds," a tired voice said from the bridge. "Repeat for all hands, course correction in thirty seconds."

Rahul looked at Lucas. "Please tell me that doesn't mean what I think it means."

Lucas didn't understand. He'd checked the nightly announcements before going to bed. There'd been nothing about a course change. And why were they only giving thirty seconds of warning?

He pushed the thoughts aside. *Why* didn't matter—all that mattered was that they got back inside before the engines fired. "Go!" he shouted.

Why had he agreed to let them come? By himself, he could have been back to the airlock in plenty of time. He and Elena helped Rahul along as best they could, but they were moving far too slowly. Lucas looked back over his shoulder. How much time did they have?

An answer came in the form of an orange glow from the back of the ship. The engines were powering up. Whoever was making this course change, they were in a hurry to do it. Lucas found a set of handholds and pulled Elena and Rahul toward him. "Grab on and don't let go!"

The three of them laced their fingers around the rungs just as the thrust from the engines kicked in, nearly jerking Lucas's handhold out of his grasp. A moment later an attitude rocket fired, close enough that he could feel the heat through his suit.

"Climb!" he shouted, pointing up toward the airlock.

In response, Rahul just moaned something unintelligible and clung to the hull of the ship. Lucas grabbed him under his shoulders with one arm and tried to pull him upward.

"I can't . . . ," Rahul said, scrunching his eyes closed. "I can't move—everything is spinning."

Elena reached the airlock and looked down at them. "You have to climb!" she yelled.

"I can't," Rahul said. "I can't!"

The acceleration was increasing. Soon they would be struggling to hang on, and climbing might be impossible. Lucas craned his neck and tried to judge the distance to the airlock. How much force would it take to get both of them there?

"Let go!" he said to Rahul. "I'm going to fly us up!"

"What?" Rahul said, opening his eyes. "Are you crazy?"

Lucas gathered his feet underneath him and pushed away from the hull. Rahul clutched at the handhold and gave out a strangled cry as he lost his grip. Immediately, the two of them started to fall backward, toward the tail of the ship. Lucas straightened himself out and ignited his thruster pack. Rahul grabbed on to him reflexively as the force pushed them back upward. Lucas craned his neck, trying to see past Rahul's helmet. Where was the airlock? Where was Elena?

A second later, they collided with the hull next to the airlock. Disoriented, Lucas reached out and snagged the edge of the doorframe entirely by accident. His fingers scrabbled against the smooth metal for a moment before a hand grabbed his arm. Lucas tightened his grip on Rahul as Elena dragged them both into the airlock, where they collapsed in a heap on the cold metal floor.

"Oh, god," Rahul moaned. "Oh, god. I'm never doing that again."

"Well, that's good," Elena said. "Because neither am I. Now please, get off me."

Lucas rolled away and pushed himself to his hands and knees. Rahul stood up shakily and reached down to help Elena to her feet. "Thank you," he said. "I thought we were goners."

"We almost were," she pointed out, straightening out her spacesuit.

Lucas suddenly remembered the little device. What had happened to it? He put his hand into the pocket of his suit, but there was nothing there. It must have fallen out when they'd collided with the hull of the ship.

"Come on," Elena said. "We need to get back to our bunks."

As Rahul and Elena headed back, Lucas paused and put his hand on the window of the airlock. Tonight had been a complete disaster. They'd almost gotten killed, and he had nothing to show for it.

Which meant that all he had left was a suspicion—and every sign was still pointing toward his sister.

9

THE NEXT MORNING, the ship was still under acceleration. Lucas swung his legs out of his sleep sack and jumped down to the deck. It was around a sixth of a gee, he guessed, about as much as Earth's moon. It wasn't much by planetary standards, but it was a lot for a ship. And only one month ago, it had been a lot for Lucas—apparently Palmer's phys ed regimen was doing its trick.

The existence of gravity made Lucas feel as if he was on an entirely new ship. In free fall, the interior of the *Orpheus* felt like a horizontal tube, with the bridge at one end and the engine room at the other. Now that they were under acceleration, the front of the ship was clearly 'up' and the back was 'down.' The circular bulkheads that separated the decks suddenly became floors, and you had to climb up and down the ladderways instead of just pulling yourself along. The big cylindrical rec room was perfectly safe and usable in free fall, but under gravity it had to be split into three levels by retractable floors, since a fall from one end to the other would be bad news, even at a sixth of a gee.

Breakfast for the alpha-section cadets was unusually quiet. Lucas was bleary-eyed from lack of sleep and Rahul stared blankly at the wall, lost in some interaction with his AI implant. Elena, though, seemed more tense than tired. Sometimes it seemed like she was on the verge of saying something, but each time she just ended up sitting back in her seat. Other times she would look at Lucas as if there was something she expected *him* to say.

Rahul suddenly gave a low whistle. "It's true!" he said under his breath. "There really was a second attack."

"Second attack?" Elena asked. "What are you talking about?"

Rahul focused his eyes and turned toward them. "Apparently some people tried to shut down the power on Pallas. Officially it was just an attempted prank. But some people are putting together the eyewitness reports and security camera footage, and it was definitely a serious attack."

"On Pallas?" Lucas asked. An uneasy feeling settled inside his chest. He and his dad visited Pallas at least a few times per year. The colony there was famous for its underground fish farms and sushi restaurants. Why would anyone try to shut down the power systems?

"That's crazy," Elena said.

"It gets crazier," Rahul said. "The attack happened at the *exact same time* as the hijacking of my parents' ship."

Lucas's uneasiness was now full-blown anxiety. After weeks of constant news broadcasts, the story of the hijacking was finally starting to die down. But if Rahul was right, then soon everyone would be talking about it again. "Maybe it's a coincidence?" he offered.

"No way," Rahul said, shaking his head. "This was coordinated."

"If it's being kept so quiet, how did you find it?" Elena asked.

Rahul glanced around and leaned toward them. "I'm part of a citizen-action team," he said in a low voice. "It's a group of people who put these sorts of things together. We're going to find whoever was responsible and make sure they pay."

"You mean like those crazy people who post about the Loch Ness monster and Bigfoot?" Elena said doubtfully.

"No—*not* like that. This is all based on real evidence. I'm telling you, there's something big going on."

To Lucas's relief, their wrist screens all buzzed simultaneously. He tapped at his and read the notification. "Apparently we just got a new assignment for this afternoon."

"Please tell me we're not flushing out engine coolant again," Elena said. "My uniform still smells like a used-car lot."

Rahul pulled out his pocket screen and scrolled through the message. "Wow. Bridge training!"

This news brought Elena out of whatever funk she was in. She grabbed his screen and double-checked it as if she thought someone might be playing a trick on her. "I thought our turn wasn't till next month."

"Delta section got hit with demerits or something, so *they're* the ones stuck on engine-room duty. Which means we get their bridge slot."

"Is it on the actual bridge?" Lucas asked.

"Well, no," Elena said. "It's on the backup bridge. But still, it's fully functional."

"I wish I'd known," Rahul said mournfully. "I would have studied up. This might be my chance to impress Hofstra."

"Don't worry about it," Elena said. "This is our first training session. I doubt Hofstra will even be there."

Elena's prediction turned out to be correct. When they got to the backup bridge, they were greeted by Ensign Weber, who waved tiredly at the crew stations. "Sit down, shut up, and don't touch anything."

The readouts on the consoles showed them their spots. Rahul was assigned to the engineering station, which made sense. But the pilot's console was listed as ELENA PRUITT, and Lucas's name was displayed on the commander's station.

"Hey, I don't think this is right," Lucas said. "Shouldn't I be piloting?"

"Apparently not," Weber said. "Sanchez picked these assignments herself."

A little disappointed, Lucas settled into the commander's seat. The pilot was the one who actually flew the ship, and the engineer ran all the sensors and navigation. He liked Sanchez's command training well enough, but he would still rather do the flying himself instead of sitting back here and giving orders. And so far all she'd taught him was history and theory—not a single thing about actually commanding a ship. He inspected his control panel and discovered that he could *see* everything that the pilot and engineer saw, but he couldn't control any of it. Fantastic. Only the Navy could make a job this boring.

He looked around, wondering how often this room was used to actually fly the ship, instead of just being used for training. Not often, he guessed—it would have to be a major emergency for the captain to divert control like that. Out of habit, Lucas adjusted the captain's console so that it was positioned over his lap.

"Before we get started, a few notes," Weber said. "Right

now we're in observation mode, so we have full access to sensors, but no actual controls. In a moment I'll switch us to training mode. First, though, some basics."

When Weber said basics, she certainly meant it. She started with a long-winded explanation of the responsibilities of the commander, pilot, and engineer. While she talked, Lucas stared at the giant wraparound video screen in front of them, which showed a replica of what the main bridge was seeing. It seemed silly to waste time with lectures in here when they could be learning how to actually operate the ship.

"Contact bearing two-two-five," a voice over a comm link said.

"Well, looks like we'll get to follow along with the main bridge," Weber said. "That's Lieutenant Feinman, the on-shift engineer. Apparently we've just detected another ship."

"Any identification?" Sanchez asked.

"Negative," said Feinman.

"Well, this is interesting," Weber said. "Our new friend isn't advertising his presence."

She reached over Rahul's shoulder and tapped at his console. The main view screen switched to a blurry view of a small gray dot. From this distance it was impossible to tell what sort of ship it was.

"How often does this happen?" Rahul asked.

"Every few weeks," Weber said. "Usually it's just miners operating illegally. This one's pretty far off, though. It'll be up to Sanchez whether we turn and chase or just let them be."

"Stay on course," Sanchez said, as if on cue. "No intercept."

"Too bad. Would have been fun," Weber said. She snapped her fingers as if she'd just had an idea. "Of course, we can still *simulate* an intercept."

Weber switched the bridge to training mode and set up a program with a ship at a similar distance. When everything was ready, she showed them how the navigator would plot an intercept course. Lucas was excited to see that there really wasn't a lot of difference between navigation on the *Josey Wales* and here on the *Orpheus*. Despite all of Hofstra's admonitions about needing to have a "deep understanding" of orbital mechanics, the computers still did all the hard work.

"While all this was happening, the engineer would be keeping close tabs on the target," Weber said, nodding at Rahul. "And the pilot would be reviewing the course to make sure she's happy with it."

"What about the commander?" Lucas asked.

"The commander is watching everything, because nothing's going to happen until they say so."

"Don't we have to warn the crew about the new

course?" Lucas pressed.

Weber nodded. "Unless it's an absolute life-or-death emergency, the commander needs to confirm that everyone on board is ready for a change in acceleration."

Weber showed Elena how to initiate the course that had been plotted on Rahul's station. Lucas watched with idle interest. When Elena ramped up the engines, it would only be a simulation. But it was supposed to be authentic, right? Lucas pressed the shipwide intercom button on the commander's console and leaned toward the microphone.

"Crew, prepare for emergency acceleration," he said in a deep voice.

Immediately, Weber whirled around and jerked Lucas's hand away from the intercom button. She leaned forward and jabbed it with her own finger. "Belay that! No course change. Repeat, no course change."

"What's the matter?" Lucas asked, staring at her in shock. "It's just a simulation, right?"

"Who gave that order?" Sanchez asked. "What's going on?"

"Just an overeager cadet on bridge training," Weber growled. "Sorry about that, Captain."

"Bridge, this is hangar," Moskowitz's voice said. "Confirm no acceleration?"

"All hands, that call for emergency acceleration was

a mistake," Weber said over the intercom. "No course change planned. As you were."

"Copy that," Sanchez said. "Get me an incident report, please."

"Didn't I tell you not to touch anything?" Weber demanded, stabbing her finger at Lucas.

Lucas fumed silently for a moment. He'd done exactly what a commander was supposed to do. How could he have known that the intercom wasn't part of the simulation? "I know what I'm doing," he muttered.

Weber put up her hands in mock deference. "Well, if that's the case, then maybe I should step aside and let you run the mission like an actual commander?"

"Sure," Lucas said, much more confidently than he felt. But everything he'd seen so far was familiar to him. How hard could it be?

"Then please, be my guest." Weber moved to the back of the room and folded her arms across her chest.

Lucas cleared his throat. "Elena, is that course ready?"

"Yes," she said, and then paused. "I think so."

"Initiate, please."

She slid her fingers over the control panel, and the simulated thrust began to increase. Lucas settled back in the commander's chair. *See?* This wasn't so hard. Out of the corner of his eye he saw a flashing light on the engineering console. "Rahul, what's that reading?"

Rahul looked at his screen and studied it for a moment. "I'm not sure—dust particles?"

"How big?"

"A few kilometers across, it looks like."

"No," Lucas said impatiently, "how big are the particles? Is it safe to fly through, or do we have to route around?"

"How do I tell?" Rahul asked.

"It's right there on your screen—average diameter or average mass, something like that."

"I don't see anything like that."

"Elena, cut thrust," Lucas said. He unbuckled himself from his seat and peered over Rahul's shoulder. "Why don't you have the high-frequency radar turned on? We're not going to see anything small with this sensor setup."

"You didn't tell me to," Rahul said defensively. "And anyway, I activated all of the—"

"Here," Lucas said, elbowing past him. "It's on another screen."

Rahul sat back and glowered while Lucas searched for the right settings. Finally he found the sensors he was looking for and flipped them on. As soon as they were active, Elena's console blared an alarm.

"Collision warning," she said. "Though I can't tell what it thinks we're going to hit."

"It's the dust cloud," Lucas said, looking up at the main

bridge wall display. "Wait—why are we still accelerating? I told you to cut thrust!"

"You didn't say how much to cut it by," Elena said. "So I reduced it to fifty percent."

"Cut thrust means *turn it off.*"

"Oh," she said. She started to slide the thrust level back down, but Lucas grabbed her wrist.

"It's too late. We have to adjust course. Rahul, can you give us an evasion plan?"

"Um, sure," Rahul said. He tapped at his screen, slowly giving it the commands to plot a course that avoided the dust cloud.

"It's an emergency," Lucas said. "Just tell the computer to avoid collision!"

"I'm trying," Rahul snapped.

Lucas clenched his jaw in frustration. Rahul was going through the niceties of working out an actual course that bypassed the cloud and then returned them to an intercept with the Belter ship, when all they needed was an emergency evasion.

"Elena," Lucas barked. "Four seconds of yaw, and then full thrust."

In response, Elena frowned and began to search through the commands on her display. Lucas pointed at the manual controls on the side of the console. "Right there!"

"*Collision imminent!*" a computerized voice blared.

Elena flexed her fingers and put her hands on the manual control stick. "Four seconds of yaw in five, four—"

"Just do it!"

She pulled back on the stick and then pushed the thrust controls all the way forward. There was a flash on the main screen and the overhead lights flipped to a dim red. Every console on the bridge began beeping damage warnings.

"And I think that will end our simulation," Weber said dryly. She entered a few commands at the captain's station and the lights returned to normal. "And I have to say, eighty percent casualties is a new record for that particular mission."

Lucas fumed. There shouldn't have been *any* casualties. All they'd needed to do was vector around a stupid dust cloud. He could have done it in his sleep.

The bell chimed to end the class period. "I think that's enough for today," Weber said.

Rahul looked at Lucas with a furious expression and then headed out into the hallway. Elena unbuckled herself from the pilot's station and stretched her arms.

"Well, *that* was a disaster," she said, sighing.

"I can't believe we messed that up," Lucas said, heading out after Rahul. "All we had to do—"

"All we had to do was not have *you* commanding!"

Rahul snapped. "Why couldn't you just leave well enough alone?"

"My orders weren't the problem," Lucas shot back.

"You're right—it was your stupid cocky attitude!" Rahul said, shoving Lucas hard in the chest. "I'd never even *been* on a bridge before today. So while I'm trying to learn, you're acting like I ought to know everything already."

"We should have just let Weber keep teaching us," Elena said crossly.

"There's practically nothing to teach!" Lucas shouted. Why were they acting like *he* was the one who had made the mistakes? "If you'd just listened to me—"

Lucas was interrupted by Captain Sanchez's voice over the intercom. "Attention. All cadets are restricted to their bunkrooms until further notice. Afternoon classes and training sessions are canceled. All off-duty officers report to the wardroom."

"Seriously?" Rahul groaned. "Now we're going to be locked in our bunkroom for the rest of the day?"

Weber pushed past them and headed down the ladderway toward the rear of the ship. "You heard the captain," she said. "Get to your cabin."

The climb up to the alpha-section deck was much more difficult than heading down, Lucas discovered. By the time they got to their bunkroom, his arms were starting to feel rubbery. He sat down in his sleep sack and massaged his shoulders. The sudden flurry of activity that had followed the captain's announcement soon faded into silence. After a little while, Tali opened the door to their cabin.

"We're in lockdown," she said curtly. "Don't leave this room."

"What about food?" Rahul asked. "We're not going to miss dinner, are we?"

Tali looked at him for a moment with a disbelieving expression and turned to go. Lucas jumped up and started to follow her out onto the deck, but she stopped suddenly. "What part of 'Don't leave this room' don't you understand, cadet?"

"What's going on?" he asked. "Is there something—"

"There's a shipwide search," she said, heading into her own cabin. "That's all I know. Now get back to your room."

Lucas's anxiety, which had been mounting ever since the first announcement, suddenly went into overdrive. A lockdown might mean anything, from a mechanical problem to an imminent attack. But there was only one explanation for a shipwide search—someone had found out about the device Tali had planted. And now they were trying to find out who had done it.

As soon as Lucas came inside and closed their door,

Rahul sat up in his sleep sack. "Do you think this has anything to do with last night? It couldn't, right?"

"I don't know," Elena said, folding her arms. "But just so we're clear, if anyone asks me about it—"

"I know, I know," Rahul said. "You're not going to lie. I guess this is what I get for dragging you along."

"And this is what *I* get for agreeing to such a stupid idea," Elena said angrily. "Wasn't it enough we failed our first simulator run? If we get kicked out of this school—"

"We're not going to get kicked out," Rahul said. "We don't even know what they're searching for. Maybe it has nothing to do with us."

Lucas, lost in his own thoughts, barely heard them. Did Tali suspect that they were searching for the device he had found? Probably, he guessed. But he still didn't know what it was or why she had put it there.

"Acceleration ending in thirty seconds," Palmer said over the intercom.

"I was just getting used to gravity," Rahul mourned. "But maybe this means—"

"All cadets should remain in their cabins until explicitly instructed to leave."

Rahul sighed. "Or maybe not."

The distant roar of the engines died away, and weightlessness returned. Even to Lucas, who had gone through this hundreds of times, the transition always felt disturbingly like falling into a hole with no bottom. He floated in his sleep sack for a few minutes, then pulled out his screen and opened up the chapter Hofstra had assigned in his last class. But his mind wouldn't focus, and after a little while he stuffed the screen back into its cubby and closed his eyes. Sleep was probably even less likely than studying, but maybe he could relax a little.

He'd finally managed to get his thoughts into a slightly less agitated state when he was distracted by an odd thumping sound. He opened his eyes again and saw Elena punching and kicking an overstuffed laundry bag.

"Really, Elena?" Rahul asked wearily.

Elena answered by unleashing a flurry of punches that made her drift back against her bunk. She reset herself and started practicing a lunging side kick.

"Have you ever done zero-gee combat before?" Lucas said.

"No. But I did karate back on Earth. And tae kwon do. And jujitsu." She punctuated each word with a jab.

"You might want to try—"

"Oh, are you some kind of expert at this too?" Elena said, grabbing the bag to keep it from floating away.

"No," Lucas admitted. "But I've seen some fights."

"Well then, Mr. I've Seen Some Fights, maybe we should spar." She used the sleeve of her shirt to wipe sweat from her forehead.

"Elena, stop," Rahul said.

"It's not really my thing," Lucas said, shrugging.

"Wow—I thought *everything* about space was 'your thing,'" Elena said. "I mean, really, why are you even here?"

Lucas sat up and glared at her. "What's your problem? I'm here so I can learn, same as you."

"You want to learn? Then maybe I can teach you something. Show me how you punch."

"I know how to punch." Of course he'd never actually punched anyone, but everyone knew how, didn't they?

"Show me, then. One punch."

Lucas floated out of his bunk and grabbed the punching bag, but Elena shook her head. "No, I mean punch *me*."

"You want me to hit you?"

"I want you to *try* to hit me."

"This is not a good idea," Rahul warned.

Lucas glared at her. He couldn't get in trouble for punching her, right? After all, she was *asking* him to do it. And right now it would feel wonderful to wipe that smug expression off her face. . . .

He drew his arm back and swung at her. He thought he'd moved quickly enough to catch her off guard, but she was much faster than he expected. She slid to the side and swung her right arm upward. The back of her wrist caught his forearm with a loud crack.

"That's about what I thought," she said.

Lucas grabbed his arm and grimaced in pain. He closed his eyes and took a few deep breaths. His forearm was fractured in at least one place, maybe two.

"What's the matter?" Elena asked. "That couldn't have really hurt."

"You broke my arm," he said through gritted teeth.

"What are you talking about? All I did was a simple outside block." She was still glaring at him belligerently, but a note of uncertainty had crept into her voice.

"Yeah, well, this didn't just happen on its own." He held out his arm as straight as he could, trying not to wince.

"Oh my god," Elena said, staring at the jagged-Z shape of his forearm. "Oh god."

Rahul's eyes went wide and he swung himself out of his bunk. "We need to get you down to medbay."

"We're in lockdown," Lucas protested weakly. The pain in his arm was making him a little dizzy.

"They'll make an exception," Rahul said, opening the door. He helped Lucas float out into the hallway.

"I can take him," Elena said, following after them.

"Seriously?" Rahul asked. "You don't think you've done enough for one day?"

She looked at Lucas with a pleading, distraught expression. "Please."

He could tell her not to come, but why? Just to make

her feel more guilty? "Fine," he gasped. "Whatever."

Rahul sighed and helped him put his good arm around her shoulder. Lucas and Elena slid over to the ladderway and made their way toward the back of the ship, moving in awkward, jerky motions. When they reached the medical bay they found Dr. Voorhaus, a thin, bald man with round glasses, floating cross-legged in front of a large wall screen that appeared to be showing a three-dimensional model of a blood vessel. In an adjacent supply room, a red-haired woman in her twenties was inspecting the contents of a large cabinet.

"Well," Voorhaus said, eyeing Lucas's arm. "I see that you're back. Lieutenant Travis, if you please?"

The woman took Lucas's good hand and gently helped him over to an examination area. "How did this happen?"

Elena started to answer, but Lucas cut her off. "It was my fault. She was teaching me some martial arts moves, and I took a bad swing."

"Mmm," Voorhaus said. He ran a scanner over Lucas's arm. "Your bone density barely registers. You've broken it before, I see."

Lucas nodded. Voorhaus put away the scanner and put his hands gently on Lucas's shoulder. "This is going to hurt, I'm afraid. Though I suppose you already know that."

With a quick motion he slid the broken pieces into

158

proper alignment. Lucas bit his tongue to keep from crying out. When his arm was straight, Voorhaus injected it with a hypospray and wrapped it in a thin plastic cast.

"Come back in three days and I'll remove this cast. In the meantime, no more martial arts or strenuous activity."

Lucas nodded. Elena helped him out of the chair and into the hallway. From the anxious and miserable expression on her face, anyone passing by would have guessed that she was the one who'd gotten injured.

"You didn't have to lie to him," she said. "Not for me, anyway."

"Well, it's none of his business."

"Mmm," she said, leading him to the ladderway. "Just like it's not my business why you needed to go out onto the hull last night?"

He paused. "What do you mean?" he asked carefully.

"Well, it's pretty obvious that we didn't go outside last night just to cure your insomnia. And the fact that the captain is searching the entire ship isn't just a coincidence, is it?"

Lucas sighed. He should have known that he wasn't going to be able to fool her. "You're right. It's not a coincidence."

"You know, for some reason I thought you were going to be the one person around here who would always tell me the truth," she said, jabbing her finger at him. "I thought maybe you would know what it was like to feel different. Guess I was just being stupid."

Her words were like a knife in his chest. She was right. Not only had he deceived his friends, he'd almost gotten them killed. But Tali was his sister, and he had to find some way to protect her. What was he supposed to do?

"This is exactly why my parents told me not to come here," Elena said. "Maybe I should have listened."

Lucas tried to imagine what it would feel like to spend your entire life with people who always tell the truth and then come to a place where your own sectionmate lied. Ever since he'd arrived here, he'd been keenly aware of how different he was. He hadn't even thought about how Elena might feel just as much like an outsider, even though she came from Earth.

"I'm sorry for lying to you."

"Well, I'm sorry for breaking your arm," she said. "Though somehow it doesn't feel like that makes us quite even."

Lucas wanted to ask whether she meant that breaking an arm was worse than a lie, or whether it was the other way around. But right now probably wasn't the time.

"So what did you do when we were out there?" Elena asked. "Did you sabotage the ship or something?"

"No!" he said quickly. "I swear. I was *looking* for something. The same thing the captain is searching for, I think.

But I can't tell you any more than that. I promised . . ."

"You promised someone else," she finished for him. "You're protecting them."

He nodded.

"At least you're being honest with me," she said. "That's a start. But you're asking me to trust you, even though you don't trust *me* enough to tell me what's actually going on."

Lucas was silent. What could he say in response? Everything she was saying was true.

Elena turned and stared out a nearby window. "I just can't get used to it. *Everyone* lies, here. All the time, about everything. It's insane."

"We don't lie *all* the time."

She snorted and nodded at his cast. "Does your arm hurt?"

"No." Lucas flexed his arm gingerly. "Well, yeah, a little."

"See what I mean?"

"Okay, but that doesn't count," he protested. "I was just trying to not make you feel bad for snapping my arm in half."

"Once you start telling little lies, you start telling big ones too," Elena said, as if she were quoting from something.

She had a point, he decided. He thought for a moment

and then stuck out his hand. "Let's start over. My name is Lucas Adebayo. I'm a new cadet here."

She raised her eyebrows and shook his hand. "Elena Pruitt. Nice to meet you."

"You look like you need a friend you can trust," he said. "So I hereby promise not to ever lie to you about anything, ever. Big or small."

The corners of her mouth twitched into a smile. "Thank you, Lucas Adebayo," she said. "Maybe nobody here would understand, but—it means a lot."

"So, Elena Pruitt . . . does this mean we're going to be friends?"

"Of course," she said, taking him by his good arm and helping him to the ladderway. "And just wait till you meet Rahul. He's a little odd, but I think the two of you will hit it off *beautifully*."

10

THE NEXT MORNING, Captain Sanchez announced over the intercom that all cadets were free to leave their cabins and classes would proceed as normal. When she finished, a faint combination of cheers and groans could be heard from the other bunkrooms.

"That's it?" Rahul asked. "Just, 'Hey, we searched the ship for something, but now we're all good'?"

"Well, what do you expect her to say?" Elena said, floating out of her sleep sack. "'We suspect sabotage, and here's what we found'?"

"We don't know it was sabotage," Lucas pointed out. "Maybe it was nothing."

Of course, if he hadn't been so stupid as to lose the device he'd removed, he would know the answer to that. Though on the other hand, he wasn't completely sure whether he *wanted* to know.

His tablet flashed another schedule change notification. He sighed and scrolled down to read the full text. "Hey, I just got a message that I'm supposed to go to the officers' wardroom instead of to my morning classes. Did any of you get that?"

Rahul, who was in the middle of brushing his teeth, grabbed his own screen and peered at it. He spit the tooth gel out into a paper towel and shook his head. "Not me."

"Me neither," Elena said. "There's no explanation? Just go to the wardroom?"

"It says the change was requested by the captain herself."

"Ooh, that sounds fun," Rahul said. "I didn't think we were even allowed in there. Maybe the captain is rewarding you. Though on the other hand, she might be punishing you. Hard to tell."

Elena looked over Lucas's shoulder at his screen. "I guess you'll just have to go and find out. You'll need to hurry, though—it says you're supposed to be there five minutes from now."

With his arm in a cast, Lucas ended up using most of that time just getting his uniform on. He took a quick detour through the rec room and grabbed a bulb of breakfast protein before heading down to the wardroom. Why couldn't they have warned him earlier so he'd at least have a chance to eat properly? Though, he decided, maybe it was for the best, since if he'd known, he might have spent a sleepless night trying to figure out what this was all about. Surely it couldn't be related to their trip outside the ship two nights ago, could it? If Sanchez knew about that, she'd probably send armed guards, not a schedule change.

The officers' wardroom was on deck eleven, just behind the rec room. It was a large, curving room with an outer wall made entirely of transplastic, making for a beautiful view of the Milky Way. The only furniture was a long table with comfortable-looking chairs. Lucas's nervousness tripled when he saw that the only two people in the room were Sanchez and his sister, Tali.

He cleared his throat. "Cadet Adebayo reporting, ma'am."

"Come in, Cadet," Sanchez said. "Have a seat, if you'd like."

Lucas glanced at Tali, trying to figure out if this situation was as bad as it seemed, but her expression was unreadable.

"You know Cadet Chen, of course?"

Lucas nodded, feeling slightly relieved to discover that Sanchez hadn't found out that Tali was his stepsister.

"She tells me that you were the one behind the strategy that won alpha and beta sections' capture-the-flag game. That was very well done."

165

"Uh—thank you, ma'am."

"According to Ensign Weber, yesterday's bridge training was slightly *less* well done." She glanced down at a report on her screen. "I'm interested, however, in hearing your take."

Lucas was now thoroughly confused. Why did Sanchez want to talk about capture-the-flag games and their bridge-training session? "Well, Ensign Weber is right. The simulation went terribly. Nobody seemed to understand my orders, and if they did, they didn't act on them properly. The result was that we failed what should have been an easy mission."

"I see," Sanchez said. "So the problem was with your crew?"

Lucas opened his mouth to say yes, but then he stopped. Something about her tone made him suspect that blaming them wouldn't be the right answer. He thought back to the training session. He'd been furious with them at the time, but was it really their fault? They'd done their best. They just hadn't understood what he wanted them to do.

"I guess not. I was the commander, so it was my responsibility."

"That is the first lesson of leadership," Sanchez agreed. "The historical figures we've been studying—what did they do well?"

Lucas thought for a moment. "They understood people, I guess. Even the ones they didn't like."

"And that's the second lesson. Leadership is fundamentally about persuasion, but before you can persuade someone, you have to know how they see things."

"I thought commanders just gave orders," Lucas said with a frown.

"Sometimes they do," Sanchez agreed. "But if *all* you do is give orders, the results are going to come out like you saw in bridge training. If you want to be an effective leader, you have to have empathy—the ability to understand another person's feelings and point of view."

"That doesn't sound easy," Lucas said. "As far as I can tell, I don't see things the same way as *anyone* on this ship."

"That does present a challenge," Sanchez said, smiling slightly. "But it's one I feel you can overcome. In fact, it's why I've called you down here. Cadet Chen has been studying the finer points of command, and she now leads training cruises on our patrol ships. I've asked her to bring you along so that you can learn."

Lucas perked up. Sanchez wanted him to go along on one of Tali's training missions? "This stuff about commanding is interesting. But I still want to be a pilot, ma'am."

Sanchez smiled. "And I still have some time to persuade

you. Speaking of time, the mission is scheduled to leave shortly. So the two of you should get down to the hangar."

"Yes, ma'am," Lucas said. "Thank you."

Tali gave Captain Sanchez a salute and headed out to the ladderway. Lucas chased after her. "I'm really coming with you?" he asked when the wardroom door slid shut behind them.

"Apparently." Tali sped down the ladder to the hangar and pushed off toward one of the patrol ships. "Suit up and get on board. And whatever you do, don't screw this up."

She was halfway across the hangar before he could think of a reply to *that*. He glared at her for a moment and then ducked into the prep room and slid on a pressure suit. When he arrived at the ship, he found Oliver and Maria already inside, with Tali settling into the commander's seat.

"So," Oliver said from the pilot's station. "You're our new junior officer?"

"He's just an observer," Tali corrected. "Let's not get ahead of ourselves."

"Well, whatever you are, have a seat," Maria said, glancing up from the engineering console. "We need to get going."

Lucas climbed in and sat down behind Tali. Oliver

closed the hatch and Maria powered the ship up. Everyone began going through their preflight checks. "So what should I be doing?" Lucas asked Tali.

"Absolutely nothing."

What was the point of being here if there was nothing for him to do? Shouldn't Tali be explaining something, at least? *You have to know how other people see things,* Sanchez had said. The frustrating thing was that sometimes he had more trouble understanding his own sister than anyone else on the *Orpheus.*

"Engines ready," Maria called out.

"Ignition," Tali said. The patrol ship trembled as its main engines powered on. Carefully—too carefully, in Lucas's opinion—Oliver piloted them out of the hangar and through the atmosphere containment field.

"Course laid in," Maria said, typing at the navigator's console. "Nothing unusual on the sensors."

"Should I—" Lucas began.

"No," Tali snapped.

Oliver caught his eye and gave him a little apologetic shrug, as if to say, "That's Tali." At least he wasn't the only one thinking she was acting crazy.

Training missions, as it turned out, were pretty boring, especially when you were a useless supercargo trainee. Not that Tali bothered to train him in anything; she mostly just sat cross-legged in the commander's seat, flipping between the different sensor readings on her console. As much as he was irritated by the way she was acting, it made him homesick to think about how she used to sit just like that in the copilot's spot in the *Josey Wales*. Sometimes she seemed so different from what he remembered that he wasn't sure she was the same person. But then something subtle would change, and all he could see was the old Tali, dressed up in a Navy pressure suit and trying to learn how to be a cadet, just like him.

"Hey—I think I've got something," Maria said, tapping at her console.

"Pull it up," Tali said. A moment later, a radar signature appeared on the main screen. At first all Lucas could see was the irregular blob of a small asteroid, but then Maria overlaid a false-color pattern from the spectrographic sensor, and the clear image of a mining ship appeared in the noise.

"Contact," Moskowitz said from the bridge of the *Orpheus*.

"We see it," Tali replied over the radio.

"I don't think they see us," Moskowitz said. "They may all be out on the surface."

"Kind of dumb, don't you think?" said Mendoza. "If I were mining illegally, I'd keep someone on lookout."

Mendoza's tone irritated Lucas. Maybe the miners had

a valid permit, and so they didn't need to keep any kind of watch. Or maybe they just figured that there wasn't any chance they'd escape from a Navy cruiser. He'd met a lot of miners in his life, and he hadn't known a single one that could be described as dumb, especially when it came to their job.

"They're getting ready to move," Maria said. The false-color image bloomed as the ship's engines ignited.

"I guess they're not so dumb after all," Lucas said under his breath. Tali gave him a half-amused, half-disapproving glance.

"Are they repositioning? Or running?" Sanchez asked.

"Not sure," Mendoza replied.

Tali increased the magnification on the main display. "Looks like they're headed for the other side of the asteroid."

Lucas watched the blip that represented the mining ship as it accelerated. Whoever they were, they were moving fast and staying low. But why? He'd never seen a Belter ship do anything like this. Did they think that their radar signature would get lost in the reflection from the asteroid? So far it didn't seem to be working.

The ship arced around the edge of the asteroid and disappeared from sight. "Contact lost," Maria announced.

"Requesting permission to make an intercept," Tali said.

"No intercept," Sanchez said. "But get a little closer."

"Aye aye."

Oliver and Maria worked to produce a flight plan that would take them nearer to the asteroid. Maria, especially, seemed a little uncertain of what she needed to do, which surprised Lucas. Apparently mid-flight course corrections weren't something she was used to.

"Captain, I'd like to point out that we have a cadet on that training flight who—" Mendoza said.

"I'm well aware of who's on board, Ensign."

Lucas stiffened. Was Mendoza really suggesting that because he was a Belter he didn't belong on a training ship during an intercept? What did he think Lucas was going to do—signal to the miners so they could get away?

"Contact!" Maria called out. A bright dot appeared on the display, heading away from the asteroid.

"They're running," Moskowitz confirmed from the bridge of the *Orpheus*.

"Belay current course," Sanchez said calmly. "Plot an intercept. Cadet Chen, stay close to her."

As Oliver and Maria adjusted their recalculated course, a second dot bloomed on the screen, heading out from the asteroid in the opposite direction. "Another contact!"

"Two ships?" Sanchez asked.

"Appears to be," said Moskowitz.

A third dot appeared, and then a fourth, fifth, and

sixth, all in quick succession, until the sensor display looked like a kid's drawing of a sun, with rays of light leading off in all directions.

"What the hell?" said Mendoza.

"It's some kind of decoy system," said Moskowitz. "One of them is the real ship. The others are fakes."

"Then get me the right signal," Sanchez said. "We don't have time to chase them all down."

Oliver glanced at Lucas. "Have you ever seen anything like this?"

Lucas shook his head. His dad, like every Belter, would skirt a regulation or two if he thought he could get away with it. He might not correct the duty officer on Ceres if they underestimated the mix of uranium to iron-nickel in a load of ore, and once in a while he'd buy a third-hand mining permit at a don't-ask-where-this-came-from price. But Lucas couldn't imagine him ever trying to run away from a Navy ship.

"We're running out of time," Sanchez said. "Chief Moskowitz?"

"All the signals look identical," Moskowitz said, clearly frustrated. "If I gave you one, it would just be a guess."

"Cadet Chen?"

Tali glanced at Maria, who shook her head. "We don't see anything unusual about any of them."

Lucas stared at the fast-moving blips. If he were the

captain of that Belter ship, what would he be doing right now? Which of those radar signals would he be?

Suddenly he realized the answer. His eyes locked on the craggy outline of the asteroid at the center of the radar display.

"For god's sake, someone please tell me which one is the damn ship!" Sanchez bellowed.

"None of them!" Lucas blurted out.

Tali, Maria, and Oliver turned toward him in astonishment. For a moment the radio link was silent. "What do you mean, Cadet?" Sanchez asked.

"If they have decoys that can fool our sensors, why risk getting caught at all?" Lucas said excitedly. "Why use five decoys when you can use six?"

"You're saying they're still behind the asteroid?"

"Yes, ma'am."

"Anyone have a better theory?" Sanchez asked. "All right, then. Cadet Chen, see what's on the other side of that rock."

Tali watched Oliver and Maria confer about yet another course change. Finally she sighed. "Lucas, switch places with me."

"What?" Lucas asked, blinking.

She unfastened her harness and motioned toward her console. "Use the commander's manual-control overrides and fly us in. We don't have much time."

Oliver frowned in annoyance at the implied insult to his navigational skills, but he didn't object. Lucas tried to keep his face neutral and professional as he settled into the commander's seat, but he couldn't keep a tiny grin off his face at the thought of showing Ensign Mendoza what happened when you had a Belter cadet on a training flight. He strapped himself in and put his hands on the manual controls.

"Acceleration in three, two, one . . ."

He slid the main throttle forward a few notches, and the patroller's engines kicked in. With a practiced eye he used the small control sticks to get them on a course for a flyby. As they approached the asteroid, he kept his eyes on the radar display, nudging the controls to make sure they didn't approach too closely. An egg-shaped gray blob appeared in the cockpit window, growing larger and larger until it suddenly flashed past. With a quick motion he flipped the ship around one hundred and eighty degrees and braked to a halt.

"Maria?" Tali said.

"Contact!" Maria said excitedly. "This side of the asteroid. She's powered off and laying low."

"Interesting," Sanchez said over the radio. "Cadet Chen, if you please?"

Tali tapped a button to open a general ship-to-ship channel. "This is a patrol ship from the ISS *Orpheus*. Identify yourself immediately."

There was silence for several seconds. Finally someone on the other end cleared their throat. "This is the *Charlemagne*, out of Vesta," a tired voice said. "What can we do for you?"

11

TO TALI'S DISAPPOINTMENT, Sanchez ordered them to wait nearby and keep the ship under observation. After about thirty minutes, Palmer arrived with a security team in the second patrol ship and landed next to the *Charlemagne*. Soon Lucas caught a glimpse of two men being escorted out of the mining ship.

"Did we really have to handcuff them?" he asked.

"It's standard procedure," Tali replied.

"We're heading out," Palmer called over. "Cadet Chen, can someone on your crew fly that thing back to the *Orpheus*?"

"Yes, sir," Tali radioed back. She looked around at the other cadets for a moment, and then sighed and turned to Lucas. "Come with me. Oliver, follow Lieutenant-Commander Palmer back to the hangar."

"Yes, ma'am," Oliver said, clearly relieved not to be

picked to fly the mining ship.

Tali depressurized the cabin and Lucas followed her out through the main hatch. The asteroid was too small to have a noticeable gravitational field, so they used their thruster packs to fly over to the *Charlemagne*.

"See you back home," Oliver radioed. "Don't get lost."

As soon as they were through the mining ship's airlock, Tali pulled off her helmet and wrinkled her nose. "Ugh."

Lucas had a similar reaction—after a month on a spotlessly clean Navy cruiser, the miner's ship seemed like it had been used to haul nothing but trash and sweaty bodies. But still, he didn't like the disgusted way she looked around the ship.

"The *Josey* isn't much cleaner than this," he pointed out.

"Believe me, I haven't forgotten," she said, heading into the cockpit.

Lucas eyed a shovel on the wall and briefly entertained the fantasy of bonking his sister over the head. Doing his best to keep his anger under control, he sat down next to her and looked around. The important controls were all familiar, and they weren't going to have any trouble flying the ship back. He helped Tali power everything up and sat back as she lifted them off the asteroid and accelerated off toward the waiting *Orpheus*. The two of them sat back in their seats, and soon a familiar calmness settled over them.

"So do you really like this whole command-training thing?" he asked. "I thought you always wanted to be a pilot, like me."

Tali shrugged. "Flying is fun on little ships. But when it comes to the bigger ones, I'd rather be in charge."

"Remember when Dad had that fever, and you and I had to fly us all the way back to Ceres?"

To Lucas's astonishment, the hint of a smile flickered across her face. "I was only eight, I think?" he went on. "I was so proud of you. When we got home I told everyone the story until they were sick of it."

"Dad laid in the course," Tali said. "All I did was watch the autopilot do the work."

Dad, she'd said. When was the last time she'd called him that, instead of saying "your father" or "Tomas"? Her face hardened a little as she realized her slipup. "And here I thought my days of flying rusty ore haulers were over. I guess everything you do comes back to haunt you, one way or the other."

"Was it really all that bad?" he asked. "Growing up on the *Josey Wales*?"

"Being stuck on a ship like this for months at a time? Having to make new friends almost every time you got back to port? Waking up every day to a future of mining stupid rocks, over and over, until finally you turn too old and gray to run an ore loader? Yeah, Lucas, it was really that bad."

"You didn't always hate it."

"Only because I didn't know there was something better," she said.

"Do you even enjoy being in the Navy?" he asked. "You don't seem to have any real friends here."

"I *can't* have friends, Lucas," she said. "What would I say when they asked about growing up on Mars? Or if they noticed how I know my way around the colonies better than the officers do?"

How would it feel, Lucas wondered, to be at the school you'd always dreamed of going to, on a ship filled with other cadets who'd grown up the way you wished you'd grown up—and yet still be so isolated? He was starting to understand some of the crazy stress she'd been under since he'd arrived. She didn't want him on the *Orpheus* because she was afraid people would find out she was really just a kid from the Belt like him. But at the same time, he was the only person she could actually talk to.

"There's something I still don't understand."

"There are a *million* things you don't understand," she said. "But please, if you've got a question, go ahead. Now is the time."

180

"Why did you plant that device on the sensor array?"

She looked startled for a moment, and then quickly regained her composure. "I don't know what you're talking about."

"I saw you out on the hull," he said. "The other day, right before the capture-the-flag game. And then later that night, I went outside and found it."

Tali was silent. Lucas tried to read her expression, but there were too many conflicting emotions for him to sort out. "That was you?" she said finally.

He nodded. "What was it? Why did you do it?"

"It doesn't matter."

Lucas's frustration with his sister over the last month suddenly all boiled up at once. "Of course it matters! Do you realize what they'd *do* to you?"

"Yes," she said simply.

"Then *why*?"

"Because I had to pay off a debt."

Lucas blinked in surprise. He wasn't sure what sort of explanation he'd been expecting, but this definitely wasn't it. "A debt? To who?"

"I can't tell you," she said, shaking her head. "But the important thing is that it's over. I've already told them I'm done."

"I don't understand. Why would you—"

181

"I don't *want* you to understand, Lucas. I don't want you to get anywhere near this. It's bad enough that you're here at all."

For the hundredth time he wondered how his sister kept finding ways to be so amazingly, indecipherably frustrating. How did it help to keep him in the dark? Being here was all he'd ever wanted, and she was making it sound as if it was some kind of prison sentence.

"I know you don't believe me," she said. "I wish I could persuade you that everything here isn't as great as you seem to think it is. Sometimes I think that if I could just find a way out . . ."

"A way out?" he asked. "What do you mean? Where would you go?"

"Someplace where I don't owe anyone anything," she said, squeezing the control stick with her fingers. "Like what if you and I just took off, right now, and headed for the outer planets? The Navy doesn't have any jurisdiction there. Nobody cares who you are or where you came from. We could go to Titan, maybe. Start a new life."

There was a wistful, longing tone in her voice that Lucas had never heard before. She was the strongest person he knew, but he could tell that the pressure she was under was almost too much, even for her. He put his hand over hers and squeezed it gently.

She turned her head and looked at him, and for a

moment he thought that maybe she was going to tell him something. Then she seemed to catch herself and sat up straighter. "It's just an idea, okay? All I'm saying is that there's more out there than just a stupid asteroid belt filled with miners and cadets."

She flipped on the radio and cleared her throat. "Cadet Chen to the *Orpheus*. Requesting permission to land."

"Permission granted," Sanchez called back.

Lucas sighed. "You have to promise me something, Tali. You have to promise me that whatever you were doing, it's all over."

"It's over," she replied.

"You promise?" he said. "If I'm going to keep all of this quiet, I have to know for sure."

She reached out toward him with her little finger extended. He hooked his own finger around hers, and they shook hands solemnly.

"I pinky swear, Lucas," she said. "It's over."

A small cluster of cadets was waiting for them at the back of the hangar. As soon as the mining ship's hatch opened, Rahul and Elena rushed forward. "That was awesome!" Rahul said.

"It was nicely done," Elena agreed. "The captain had all of the cadets watching in the rec room. Though I don't think she expected it to be quite that interesting."

183

"Someone tell me which one is the damn ship!" Rahul shouted, in a decent imitation of the captain.

"None of them!" Elena answered, doing her best to sound like Lucas. She and Rahul doubled over laughing.

Lucas smiled shyly. "It wasn't *that* big of a deal."

The three of them headed up the ladderway toward the front of the ship. Rahul paused at deck nineteen. "So what will happen to them?" he asked.

For a moment Lucas wasn't sure who he was talking about. Then he saw an armed guard outside the brig, where two grimy miners were sitting against a wall. In all the excitement, he'd practically forgotten that the crew of the *Charlemagne* would be arrested as a result of their mission. The two men stared blankly at the floor with dejected expressions, as if they'd just lost everything they had in the world. Which, Lucas thought, was probably true.

"Their cargo will be impounded, at least," Rahul said.

"More than that," Elena said. "Evading pursuit is a serious offense. They'll lose their ship, and probably get jail time too."

An ugly feeling settled in Lucas's stomach, pushing out the pride that he'd been feeling for the success of the mission. This wasn't a game or an exercise, he told himself. Those two men were now going to go to prison.

"Well, they shouldn't have tried to run," Rahul said.

"Come on," Elena said. "Afternoon classes are about to start."

She and Rahul headed up the ladderway, but Lucas stayed behind, watching the miners in the brig. Rahul was right. Why hadn't the crew of the *Charlemagne* just stayed where they were? Mining an unlicensed asteroid would only mean getting their cargo impounded. They'd made a stupid gamble, and they'd lost.

But still . . . who did it benefit to put them in prison? Was the only point of the Navy to arrest people like this? How did that help anyone?

"That's Hampton and Nichols," McKinley said quietly, coming up the ladderway from the hangar. "Good men. Families back on Vesta. This will hit them hard."

"It was all because of me," Lucas said in a monotone.

It was true. If it hadn't been for his bright idea, the two miners would still be out on that asteroid. The guilt he felt was harsh and stinging, but even so, it wasn't the worst part. The worst part was how even now he could feel the excitement of the chase and the thrill of doing his job. What was happening to him? How could he feel both proud and remorseful, all at the same time? Was this what his dad had been talking about when he'd asked Lucas to not become "like one of them"?

"I was listening, like everyone else on board," McKinley said. "Hampton and Nichols were too smart for their own good—and still not as smart as you. That's nothing to be ashamed of."

"I didn't want this," Lucas insisted. But at the same time came a thought that he couldn't push away. *This is exactly what I wanted.*

"I know," McKinley said. "But this is what serving on a Navy ship is. Someday you're going to have to decide which side you're on."

Sides. When he'd arrived, Lucas had insisted to himself that that there didn't need to be sides—that it was possible to be both a Belter and a Navy cadet at the same time. But was it? How could he do his job as a cadet when the job meant putting miners in prison? Maybe McKinley was right. Maybe he was going to have to choose one or the other. The thought made Lucas feel like he was being torn in two.

He watched Hampton and Nichols follow Palmer down the ladderway toward the rear of the ship. *Ships impounded. Families back on Vesta. This will hit them hard.*

And it was all because of him.

12

"WHAT'S THAT CRAZY pulling sensation?" Rahul asked as the patrol ship they were on with all the alpha and beta cadets settled into the hangar on Vesta.

"It's called gravity," Lucas said, rolling his eyes.

"*Gravity*, right," Rahul echoed, his face comically innocent. "I remember now. That's the thing that makes stuff fall downward."

"Barely, in this case," Elena said. She held out a small water bottle and let it go. It drifted lazily down to the cabin floor.

"Well, it's way better than nothing," Rahul said. He stretched his arms and leaned past Lucas to look out a side window. "I thought this was a Belter station? It looks just like the hangar on the *Orpheus*."

"This must be the Navy's part of the station," Lucas guessed, peering out. He'd been to the Belter side of the

Vesta colony lots of times, but he'd never been inside the naval base. Rahul was right; other than being a lot bigger, the hangar looked just like the hangar on the *Orpheus*.

Ten meters away, the gamma and delta cadets were climbing out of the other patrol ship. Willem jumped down and looked around with a bored expression and then ran off with Aaron and Katya. Lucas wondered what they were going to think of the Vesta bazaar—and what the bazaar was going to think of *them*.

"All right, listen up," Oliver said, standing up at the front of the cabin. "Shore leave is six hours, which means the last shuttle leaves seventeen hundred sharp. Mass allowance coming back is ten kilos, so don't buy any baby elephants."

"Do they really sell baby elephants?" Elena asked.

"'If you can buy it, you can buy it on Vesta,'" Lucas said. "That's the official motto here."

"Technically you're allowed anywhere in the naval base or the bazaar," Oliver continued. "But I recommend you stay on the high street. Things get much crazier the farther out you go. Not to mention dangerous—at least for your wallet."

"I want to see crazy and dangerous," Rahul whispered, his eyes gleaming.

"Until you get used to the gravity, stay close to the walls and pull yourself along on railings, just like you do in zero gee. Don't try to run, and for god's sake don't jump."

He opened the cabin door and hopped out onto the floor of the hangar. The rest of alpha section filed out behind him. Even the second- and third-year cadets had trouble moving—the gravity here was too much to ignore completely but not enough to be able to walk normally.

"It's easiest if you think about it like pulling yourself with the soles of your feet," Lucas explained to Rahul and Elena. He showed them how the floors were rough and slightly sticky. "Get traction with one foot and then propel yourself along. Like this."

He glided toward the wall of the hangar, brushing his feet against the floor to keep his momentum up. When Rahul tried to imitate his motion, he ended up launching himself in a high arc and crashing into the wall above Lucas's head. Lucas grabbed him and helped him back down to the floor.

"Thanks," Rahul gasped.

Elena watched the other cadets for a moment and then glided in three long strides to where Lucas and Rahul were standing.

"Show-off," Rahul muttered.

"Until you get used to it, just stay close to the railings," Lucas said. "So where do you want to go first?"

"I want to eat something that doesn't come in a pouch," said Elena.

"Yes," Rahul said, rubbing his stomach dramatically. *"That."*

Lucas pulled up a map on his wrist screen. He looked around the hangar and pointed toward a door on the far wall. "That way."

It would have been much faster for him to just walk across the hangar floor, but he stuck with Rahul and helped him use the waist-high railing to pull himself along. The hangar door led to a long, wide hallway that ran slightly downward. Officers and crew members passed by them in a steady stream in both directions.

After about thirty meters Lucas could hear whispering and giggling, along with the occasional thunk. They turned a corner and found Willem, Aaron, and Katya hanging from a wide doorway that led to the base's rec room.

"My turn," Willem said. "Make some room!" He swung himself back and forth for a moment like a trapeze artist and then launched himself down the corridor. Lucas, Rahul, and Elena moved aside to avoid being struck, cannonball-style, as Willem somersaulted along the hallway. After a few meters he collided with one of the walls and bounced up, wearing a who-cares-what-anyone-thinks grin.

"Maybe you should find a better place to do your acrobatics," Lucas said, a little irritably. He pointed at a small glass-covered box on the wall just above Willem's head. "That's an evacuation alarm you almost ran into."

Willem peered at the switch inside the box. "Oh, really? So if I pull it, an alarm goes off? A loud one, I'll bet."

"That, and every door in the base opens up," Rahul said. "Weren't you paying attention in Weber's class yesterday?"

"Every door? Even the bathrooms?" Katya asked.

"This sounds like fun," Willem said, reaching toward the box.

Elena grabbed his arm. "Are you really that stupid?"

"Come on, I was just kidding," he said. "I wouldn't actually set off a basewide alarm."

"Good." Elena pushed him toward his friends and stomped off down the hallway, though in the low gravity the effect was more comical than angry. Rahul gave Willem a withering look and followed her.

"At least, not unless I thought it would be *really* funny," Willem called after them, sending Aaron and Katya into fits of laughter.

"Sometimes I really wonder about the Navy's recruiting standards," Elena muttered to Lucas as they headed down the hallway.

Soon the corridor made a sharp turn to the right and ended in a wide archway with a sign that read YOU

ARE NOW LEAVING RIESCHLING NAVAL BASE. A bored-looking guard sat behind a small desk. Past the archway, the corridor opened onto a large plaza, ten meters wide and thirty meters tall.

"Welcome to the bazaar," Lucas said, waving his arm.

A large thoroughfare led off toward the center of the station, and a half-dozen small alleyways radiated out from the plaza in all directions. Shops and buildings of various sizes lined the streets, ranging from tiny metal shacks to massive concrete apartment buildings. The center of the plaza and the sides of the streets were packed with small kiosks, each nearly identical except for the merchandise. Long, rickety-looking catwalks crossed over the main street to connect some of the larger buildings. The ceiling, around twenty meters above their heads, displayed a gigantic image of Titan's swirling orange clouds.

Hundreds of people milled about on the street, buying, selling, and haggling. Small kids as young as three or four years old bounded along the streets, shouting at slower pedestrians to move out of their way. Some shoppers were officers or cadets in uniforms like them, but everyone else was dressed Belter-style in loose-fitting, multicolored jumpsuits.

"And this is still the not-so-crazy part?" Elena said.

"Come on," Rahul said, pushing forward through the crowd. "I want to see more."

Lucas led them off the high street and through a residential area. They passed a small grassy park with an artificial sun where a dozen people were stretched out on blankets and towels, and then the avenue they were on ended in an oddly shaped intersection with four other streets. At the center of the intersection was a tiny plaza with a bubbling stone fountain. Elena stood on her tip-toes next to the fountain and craned her neck to see what was offered along each side of the intersection.

"That shop is selling Earther clothes," she said, point-ing down a small street where a sign read SMYTHE'S HABERDASHERY. "Somehow that seems weirder than the store selling Titanian goat cheese."

A boy and a girl standing near the shop exchanged a look and walked over to the cadets with long, fluid strides. The boy was a little older than Lucas, while the girl was around nine or ten. Both of them had long hair tied in complex braids that hung down to their shoulders. The boy bowed deeply, sweeping his arm so low it almost brushed the pavement. "If you can buy it, you can buy it on Vesta."

"So we heard," Rahul said.

"I'm Jo Smythe," the boy said. "And this is my friend Mai."

Mai produced a stack of small glowing cards and passed them out to the cadets. Each card had a picture of a martial-arts ring with the caption "The Janusarium—Fine Low-Gee Combat Sports."

"*This* sounds good," Elena said, inspecting her card.

"First bout in twenty minutes," Mai said, curtsying with ridiculous sweetness. "Tell them I sent you."

Jo took Elena's arm and ushered her toward the store. "Twenty minutes will give you just enough time to examine a number of amazing, one-of-a-kind items—"

Lucas grabbed Elena and pulled her back. "She's not interested," he said to the boy in a low voice. "Find some other logs to sap."

Jo's eyes went wide, and then he snorted. "Are they teaching Belt-speak in the baby academy now?"

"No," Lucas said, irritated at the boy's tone. "They teach it on Ceres, where I was born."

"Oh, come on," Mai said. "You expect us to believe that you're from the Belt?"

"I don't care what you believe," Lucas said. "But I've been downstation enough times to know a pick-it-up when I see one. So like I said—find some other mark."

"We all gotta make eat, kid." Jo's voice was lower pitched than before, and not nearly so pleasant. "Apparently some of us even sign up with the muskrats."

"We all gotta make eat," Lucas agreed, staring levelly back at Jo.

Jo snorted again and shook his head. He and Mai

glided over to a group of older cadets from gamma section. "Greetings! Is there something I can help you find today?"

"What's a muskrat?" Elena asked.

"That's what Belters call a Navy officer," Lucas said, heading off across the intersection. "Come on."

"Why don't Belters like the Navy?"

Lucas sighed. Did he really have to explain all of this again? "Because our job is to arrest them."

"But we do a million other things too," she said. "And we only arrest people who mine illegally."

"Elena, every Belter who has ever *lived* has mined illegally," Lucas said.

"Hey, there's the Janusarium," Rahul said, pointing down a wide boulevard that dead-ended into a round building with a sign that read SEE GARTH XI—FIGHTS DAILY. "You wanted to see some low-gee judo, right?"

Elena's eyes gleamed. "Perfect."

"We can we buy food there, right?" Rahul asked Lucas.

"If you can buy it—"

"—you can buy it on Vesta," Rahul finished. "Got it."

The Janusarium was built to resemble an ancient stone amphitheater. The seats were plain stone benches carved out of the ground, encircling a rectangular stage about five meters long. A metal cage had been set up on the stage and a short, wiry man with a shaved head was prancing around inside, shouting challenges and insults to the small crowd. A blue-white hologram of a two-faced, bearded man floated high above the stage.

"I'm buying," Elena said. "Three tickets, please."

"Fifteen sols each," said a bored-looking attendant at the door.

"Oh . . . I'm supposed to tell you that Mai sent us," Elena said.

"Wow, that's great to hear," the attendant said in a sarcastic voice. "Fifteen sols each."

Unfazed, Elena pressed her thumb into her handheld screen and bounded down the stone steps into the amphitheater. As he followed along behind her, Lucas suddenly noticed McKinley sitting on the opposite side of the arena. Their eyes met for a brief moment, and then McKinley whispered something to his companions, a burly man with jet-black hair and a pale-skinned woman in a yellow bodysuit. Immediately they both craned their necks to look at Lucas.

What was McKinley doing here? And who were those people with him? The way they were watching Lucas made him feel like a lobster who was just about to be auctioned off. He grabbed Elena's arm.

"Come on. Let's go somewhere else."

"No way," she said, shaking him off. "I want to see this."

"Yeah," Rahul said, looking down one of the rows of spectators. "And I want one of those tofu burgers."

They found an empty row of seats near the front and sat down. Lucas kept his eyes on the back of the woman's head in front of him. Maybe McKinley hadn't really seen him? Maybe they'd all been looking at someone else?

Rahul went off to the concession stand and came back a few minutes later with a tray of food. "French fries for everyone."

"Wow," Elena said as she popped one into her mouth. "It feels nice to eat something that doesn't float away."

"Mmm," Rahul agreed through a mouthful of fries.

The first bout was more of an exhibition of gymnastics than actual fighting. Two men did backflips, somersaults, and flying kicks without ever touching each other. At the end of their 'fight' Elena stood up and clapped loudly, to Rahul's obvious embarrassment.

The second match was much more serious. The crowd cheered as a big man with tattoos that curled around his biceps climbed up onto the ropes. The lights dimmed and smoke bellowed out of hidden vents in the floor, and a wiry man pranced out of a doorway and vaulted into the ring, followed by Mai, the girl who had handed them the glowing cards. Mai walked around the outside of the ring holding up a sign that read GARTH XI, LOW-GEE JUDOKA.

Garth did a series of high, looping somersaults over the big man's head, shouting insults the entire time. The crowd loved it, cheering him on as if this was exactly what they had come for.

"Lucas!" a voice said. Lucas turned and saw McKinley standing in the aisle, smiling broadly. His mouth went dry.

"Hello," Rahul said. "You're from the *Orpheus*, aren't you?"

"I'm Abbott McKinley, bosun's mate and a good friend of Lucas's here." McKinley shook Rahul's hand and then paused as if an idea had just come to him. "Speaking of friends, there are a couple of old mining hands I'd like you to meet, if you've got a moment."

Lucas glanced at Rahul and Elena with a frantic, wide-eyed expression, but Elena patted him on the back, oblivious to what he was trying to signal. "Sure, of course he can. Go on, we're fine here."

Lucas tried to think of an excuse, but nothing came to mind. "Gee, thanks," he muttered to Elena. He exhaled slowly and followed McKinley around to where his friends were sitting. Maybe he could find some way to make this brief.

"Lucas, meet Stockton and Willis, two of the best uranium miners in the Belt," McKinley announced.

Stockton reached out and shook Lucas's hand. "Nice to meet you, son."

"It's a pleasure," Willis said with an unsettlingly wide smile. "You're a bit of a celebrity with us miners, you know. A Belter kid teaching the Navy how to fly! Even the ones who'd rather boot the muskrats straight back to Earth get a kick out of that."

"Thanks," Lucas mumbled, though the idea of being a "celebrity" with these particular miners made him feel uncomfortable. Something was not at all right about any of this, though he couldn't put his finger on what it was. He looked back at where Rahul and Elena were sitting. How long before he could make a polite exit?

Down in the cage, the tattooed man was taking haymaker swings at Garth, who danced out of the way, sticking out his tongue and shouting vulgar taunts.

"Were you there when they nicked the *Charlemagne*?" Willis asked. Without waiting for a response, she shook her head. "Hampton and Nichols were good."

Lucas looked at McKinley in surprise. Had he not told Willis and Stockton that Lucas was the one who'd figured out the trick of the decoys?

"We were there," McKinley said smoothly. "It was a real shame."

"Goddamn muskrats," Stockton growled. He glanced at Lucas. "No offense."

Willis shook her head. "Hampton had been bragging to everyone how his new decoy system would let him escape

199

any Navy ship. But they caught him anyway."

"So, Lucas," Stockton said, in a let's-change-the-subject tone. "How is it studying with the Navy? Are they letting you get some flight time in? Those patrol ships are little beauties."

"Sure," Lucas said. "I've done a bit of flying."

"And bridge simulations too, I'd guess?" Stockton said.

"Sometimes," Lucas said, a little guardedly. What was Stockton getting at?

"That reminds me," Willis said. She pulled a little data chip out of her pocket and handed it to Lucas. "A few of us put this together for you. Thought it might help you out."

"For me?" he asked in surprise. He held the chip up to the light to examine it, but she grabbed his hand and closed his fingers around it.

"Put it in your pocket now, and don't let anyone see it. We've put a lot of high-quality VR simulations in there. Stuff that's really hard to get."

"Sims for all the most advanced ships," Stockton put in.

"Nothing there is illegal, exactly, but the Navy probably wouldn't look too kindly on it, either," Willis went on. "But it'll give you a good leg up on the competition, so to speak."

Three different alarm bells went off in Lucas's head at the same time. Did they really think he was stupid enough to take a data chip from people he'd just met and bring it onto the *Orpheus*? Based on their expectant faces, this was exactly what they thought.

The safest thing to do, he figured, was to play dumb. "Oh, great," he said, with as much enthusiasm as he could muster. "Thanks!"

"Looks like the next bout is coming up," Stockton said. "Sit awhile and watch with us."

Lucas nodded, not really listening. Why were they giving him this chip? There had to be something more to it than VR simulations. He was still mulling it over when Mai jumped up onto the top rope of the ring with a microphone in her hand.

"Ladies and gentlemen! Our next challenger hails from a place called Peru, where the sun is always warm and the water is always cold. She has a black belt in judo and says her favorite animal is the Scottish terrier. Please give a warm Vestan welcome to Elena Pruitt!"

Lucas sat up so quickly he nearly fell out of his seat. He stared in shock as Elena climbed into the ring and held up her hands. The crowd roared its approval.

"I've got to go," Lucas gasped. He sprinted around to where Rahul was sitting, vaulting over rows of empty seats like an Olympic hurdler. As soon as Lucas ran up, Rahul raised his hands defensively.

"I tried to talk her out of it!"

"Is she crazy?" Lucas said. "Does she know what he's going to do to her?"

"He won't actually hurt her, will he?" Rahul asked. "This is all just for show?"

Garth bounced back onto the stage. The crowd screamed in delight. He grinned and did a high backflip.

"Let's have a good, clean fight," Mai said into her microphone. "Are you both ready?"

Elena nodded. Garth stuck out his hand toward her. She looked at him in confusion for a moment and then reached out to shake it.

"No!" Lucas screamed.

Garth grabbed her hand and twirled around, slinging her over his shoulder in one quick motion. She hit the mat with a loud thud. The crowd screamed in delight. Garth danced around the ring, shaking his hands above his head as if he'd already won the bout. Elena sprang to her feet and shouted at him angrily. Garth put his thumb on his nose and blew a raspberry at her.

"The girl has spunk, you have to give her that!" Mai said. "But she's down one throw to none."

Elena moved toward Garth, keeping her feet wide and her hands out, looking for a chance to grapple. He darted toward her and tried to knock her off-balance, but she turned to the side and grabbed his upper arm. Garth went flying toward the other end of the ring, but he executed

202

a graceful midair somersault and landed on his feet. He grinned and nodded at her in acknowledgment.

"A good throw! But the champion remains on his feet. The score is still one to zero."

Again Garth danced toward her. Elena shifted to one side and reached out for him, but Garth sidestepped and kicked at her leg. She stumbled, and before she could recover he hooked his arm around her elbow and threw her to the mat.

"Two for Garth!" Mai yelled over the roar of the crowd.

Garth shook his fists and bounced up into the air. Elena rolled toward him and swung her leg along the surface of the mat. Her foot caught his ankle just as he was landing and he toppled backward.

"A tricky, underhanded move!" Mai shouted, and in response the crowd booed her loudly. "But it's still two throws to one, and it's the last chance for the little girl!"

Garth shouted something at Elena. His maniacal expression had been replaced by a dark glower. In response, Elena wiped the sweat off her face and held up her fists.

"He didn't like that," Rahul said.

Garth strode quickly toward Elena. They grappled, and for a moment it looked like Elena might have gotten Garth off-balance. Then he brought his knee up into her gut, and she doubled over. Garth wrapped his arm around her waist and threw her to the mat.

Mai jumped up onto a corner of the ring and waved one arm above her head. "Our challenger has been defeated!"

The audience cheered and hooted. Elena rolled over onto her side, clutching her stomach. Garth stood in a corner of the ring, holding his clasped hands above his head and shouting to the crowd.

Lucas and Rahul ran down toward the ring. "We're with her!" Lucas shouted as a guard tried to stop them. The guard glanced back at Elena and let them by.

"Elena!" Rahul called, leaning into the ring. "Are you okay?"

Elena stood up and limped toward them, pressing her hand against her left side. "I've been better."

"Come on, let's get you to a medic," Lucas said.

She shook her head. "I want a rematch."

"A rematch?" Rahul said. "Are you serious?"

"Now that I know how he fights, I think I can beat him." She turned and glanced back at Garth.

"It's a trick," Lucas said. "There's no way you can throw him in this low gravity. He'll land on his feet every time."

"It was crazy enough to fight him once," Rahul said. "At least you're still in one piece. Who knows what he'll do if you fight him again?"

"I'm not giving up," she insisted. She straightened with a grimace and waved her hand at the announcer.

"Lucas, do something!" Rahul said.

"Elena, wait!" he called. Elena turned toward him. "There's only one way you're going to beat him."

She cocked her head. "What's that?"

"Can you make him mad?"

Elena nodded.

"Then here's what you do."

"Ladies and gentlemen, our spunky friend here is asking for a rematch. What do you think? Do you want to see her go up against our champion one more time?"

The crowd roared its approval, and Mai grinned. An older man walked over to Elena, who was still rubbing her rib cage. He handed her a towel and shook his head. "Be careful, sweetheart. That waiver you signed covers death and dismemberment, for good reason. Francis has a real temper."

"Francis?"

The man smiled sheepishly. "That's his real name. Francis Bonaforte doesn't have quite the same ring as Garth Xi, does it?"

Elena raised her eyebrows and glanced at Lucas. "No," she said thoughtfully. "It really doesn't, does it?"

She walked over to the center of the ring, where Garth was already waiting with his hands on his hips. The man who had given Elena the towel ushered Lucas and Rahul to a pair of empty seats in the first row.

"I'm not going to go easy on you this time, little girl," Garth said.

"Give it your best shot, *Francis*."

Garth clenched his jaw and waved his arm at Mai. "Readysetgo!"

He lunged toward Elena and grabbed her arm, lifting her in one quick motion and tossing her toward the side of the cage.

"Elena!" Rahul screamed.

But Elena pulled her legs in toward her body and did a quick somersault, landing on the balls of her feet. As nervous as he was, Lucas grinned proudly. Elena was a fast learner.

She raised her fists and waggled one finger at Garth. "You're going to have to do better than that, Francis."

Garth screamed and charged toward her. Elena ducked down low and bent her front knee. As he reached her, she grabbed his arm and pivoted. Garth tumbled over her shoulder. Immediately, he curled up his body and started to roll, preparing to land on his feet.

But Elena didn't let go. Instead of continuing with the throw, she reversed her motion, jerking him backward. The move caught Garth by surprise. He tried to straighten out, but it was too late. Elena held on tightly to his arm and let Garth's own rolling motion do the work.

There was a loud *pop*, and he tumbled onto the mat.

The crowd went silent. Even though he'd been expecting it, the sound of Garth's arm dislocating from his shoulder made Lucas wince. Garth grimaced and clutched his arm, which hung at an odd angle from his body. Mai ran over to him, waving frantically at a pair of assistants just outside the ring.

"Ladies and gentlemen," Mai said, scowling at Elena, "it appears our champion has been defeated by an ugly and dangerous trick! One that certainly does not deserve the payout of the thousand-sol purse."

The crowd booed.

"Pay her!" one man shouted.

"She won fair and square!" a woman called out.

"Keep it," Elena said. She vaulted out of the ring and down to the floor of the amphitheater. As soon as she landed, she grimaced and clutched her side. "Okay, that was a mistake."

13

"THAT WAS AMAZING," Rahul exulted as they helped Elena back through the bazaar toward the naval base. "Lucas, how did you know that would work?"

"Basic physics," Lucas said. "But also I saw someone do the same thing on Ceres."

"He's going to be okay, right?" Elena asked, looking back toward the Janusarium. "I didn't actually want to hurt him."

"He'll be fine," Lucas assured her. "Just a dislocated shoulder."

"Hey," Oliver called, jogging over to them. "Sanchez is looking for you."

"For us?" Rahul said anxiously. "Why? Did we do something?"

"Dunno." Oliver cocked his head to one side and looked at Elena. "You okay? What happened?"

"I was in a low-gee judo match," she said, wincing a little. "I think it's just bruises, but it's possible I cracked a rib. Lucas says I dislocated the other guy's shoulder but he'll be okay."

Oliver stared at her. "A quick word of advice. If anyone else asks you what happened, *don't* tell that story."

"She's a Truther," Rahul explained.

"Oh," Oliver said, as if this explained everything. "Well, then, just hope nobody asks. And get to medbay as soon as you get back to the ship."

When the three of them arrived at the hangar, Captain Sanchez was standing near one of the *Orpheus*'s patrol ships, talking to a few other officers. Elena straightened up with an almost imperceptible wince and strode confidently toward her, with Lucas and Rahul hurrying to catch up.

"Ah, cadets," Sanchez said, turning toward them. "I've got a job for you. Come with me."

They followed Sanchez through a wide door on the other side of the hangar and then down a long corridor as she explained. "There's a power unit that's failing in a radar station a few kilometers from the base. We need a repair party to go out and replace it. Normally the crew here would handle it, but I see this as the perfect chance for a training exercise. And Cadet Adebayo will be able to practice some cross-team leadership skills."

"Cross-team leadership?" Lucas asked.

Sanchez turned and headed through the doors of a large cargo airlock. "Indeed. This will be a multisection effort. The engineers here have already briefed the rest of your team on the details."

Lucas stopped short. Through the window in the outer doors of the airlock he could see a flatbed rover parked out on the surface. Its cargo area was taken up by a large, boxy device that Lucas guessed was the replacement power unit. Willem, Katya, and Aaron were sitting on the rover's tailgate, dangling their legs and talking among themselves.

"Them?" Rahul said, with obvious dismay. "Ma'am, you can't be serious."

"I gather you find them difficult to work with?"

Rahul nodded. *"Extremely."*

"Good. Find a way to overcome that." Sanchez turned to Lucas. "Remember our discussions about leadership."

Sanchez headed back out into the corridor, closing the inner airlock doors behind her. As soon as she was gone, Rahul groaned.

"She's serious about this?"

"Apparently," Elena said, grimacing at the three delta-section cadets through the window. In response, Willem waved with mock cheerfulness.

"If he never makes it back inside, will that be considered

a failure of the mission?" Rahul asked darkly.

"I'm guessing so," Lucas said. He took a suit off the wall and paused. "Hey, maybe you should both ask the captain to skip this one. Between star vertigo and a hurt rib—"

"I'll be fine," Rahul insisted. "There's gravity here. It's totally different than being in space."

"I'm not missing it," Elena said flatly.

Lucas's instinct told him that this wasn't a good idea. But Elena knew her limits, and it wasn't like Rahul would be in any danger, right? Worst-case scenario, he could just send them back on the rover.

"Okay," he said. "Just be careful. Both of you."

When they got outside, Willem, Aaron, and Katya jumped down off the tailgate. "We're ready, *sir*," Willem said.

Lucas ignored the mocking tone in Willem's voice and looked over the power unit. Even in the low gravity, it would take all six of them to get it installed. "So you guys know where we're supposed to be taking this?"

Katya saluted smartly and held up her screen. "Coordinates right here, *sir*."

Lucas sighed. Clearly this was going to be a long trip. Willem hopped into the cab of the rover and powered it up. Lucas shook his head. He didn't trust Willem anywhere *near* enough for that. "I'm driving."

"Oh, I can do it," Willem said breezily.

Whatever you do, don't lose your temper, Lucas told himself. He tried to think of how Sanchez would have handled the situation. "Maybe you could," he said. "But I'm driving. Move over."

Lucas waited for whatever snide comment or retort Willem had ready, but it didn't come. Instead, he just rolled his eyes and slid to the other side of the seat.

Lucas exhaled. His heart beat loudly as he climbed into the driver's seat. He'd made it through his first challenge, at least. And now all they had to do was complete the mission—preferably without killing each other.

Katya climbed in on the other side of Willem, and the other cadets squeezed into the back of the truck with the power unit. Katya checked her screen and entered the coordinates into the navigation computer. Lucas double-checked the route and pressed down on the accelerator. The rover lurched forward, kicking up a few small plumes of dust that settled back down quickly.

"Hey!" Elena called, clinging to the roll bar and grabbing her side. "Careful!"

As they climbed the small ridge that bordered the colony, the main dome of the bazaar came into view, glowing like a luminescent pearl. The nav computer's route took them around the south side of the dome and then down into a wide, flat crater.

"This is the old colony, right?" Aaron asked, pointing

at a few small concrete mounds that were half covered in gray dust.

"Right!" Katya said, her eyes gleaming. "Where the plague was!"

The story of the first Vestan colony was famous, having been made into a big-budget movie that even Lucas had seen. "It wasn't a plague," Lucas said. "Just a virus."

"What's the difference?" Elena asked. "Everyone died, right?"

"I heard everyone came back as zombies," Aaron said.

"Oh, don't be stupid," Rahul said irritably.

The radar station turned out to be farther than Lucas expected—it took them almost ten minutes to get there, even at the rover's top speed. When they arrived, everyone hopped out and stretched.

"Rahul and Katya, open up the station and disconnect the old unit," Lucas said, pointing at the base of the station. "Aaron will move it out of the way and get the new one in place."

Even in the low gravity, it took a while to get the replacement unit off the back of the rover and swap it with the old one. It was a tricky operation, even in low gravity, because although the power units didn't weigh much here, getting them to start moving—or, more important, to *stop* moving—would take the same amount of force as it would on Earth.

Lucas guided Aaron through the process and made sure he moved slowly and didn't let the power unit build up too much speed. The last thing Lucas wanted was for someone to end up with a crushed finger or a broken foot because they forgot that a kilogram of mass was the same anywhere in the universe.

Elena, who was still favoring her left side, saw what he was doing and stayed carefully out of the way. Lucas would have thought that Willem, who'd grown up under low gee on Luna, would be smart enough to do the same. Apparently he was wrong. Even though Willem was the smallest and skinniest cadet from the *Orpheus*, he seemed to think that he would somehow be of instrumental help in moving the power unit. After twice asking him to stand back and let Aaron do the lifting, Lucas finally lost his temper.

"Get out of the way before you get yourself hurt!" he barked.

Startled, Willem finally did the smart thing and backed up a few meters. When Aaron finally got the old power unit hoisted up onto the rover and slid the new one in place, Katya cheered.

"Nice job, big guy," she said, clapping Aaron on the back.

Willem glowered at her. "Well, lifting things is what he's good for," he said loudly. "Just don't expect much else. He's pretty much as dumb as a rock."

A furious look passed over Aaron's face, but then it was gone as quickly as it had appeared. This was new to Lucas—as far as he'd ever seen, Willem had just devoted himself to teasing kids outside his little crew. Apparently, though, he could be just as mean to his friends. Which raised the question of exactly *why* they would be his friends in the first place, but that was one Lucas didn't think he'd figure out anytime soon.

The teasing didn't stop at that dumb-as-a-rock comment, either. Willem slipped in a few more pointed comments about Aaron as they hooked up the new unit.

"You must have snored right through Mr. Clarke's basic electronics class," he said to Aaron at one point. And then later, to Katya: "Remember on the transport ship when he couldn't figure out how to use the bathroom? The instructions were printed right there on the *wall*."

"Oh, shut up," Katya said tiredly. In response, Willem glared at her and sat down on a nearby rock with his arms folded across his chest.

"Is this as weird to you as it is to me?" Rahul whispered over their private channel as he inspected the power unit's connections.

"Every bit," Elena said. "Though to be honest, it's kind of fun to watch."

"No kidding," Rahul said. He stood up and turned to

the others. "Okay, the last thing we need is the activation coupler."

"That little connector thing?" Aaron said. "Willem has it."

"No—I told you to bring it," Willem said.

"I don't remember that," Katya said. "You said you'd—"

"Are you really *both* that dumb?" Willem shouted. "I was still putting on my suit, so I said one of you needed to put the coupler into the rover."

"So it got left behind?" Elena said. "Wonderful."

"Apparently," Katya said, through gritted teeth. "I guess the only thing to do is for Aaron and me to go back and get it. Sound good?"

"Yeah," Willem said. "Hurry back, though."

"I was asking *Lucas*," she said pointedly. "He's commanding the mission."

Rahul stifled a laugh, which only made Willem angrier. "Sure," Lucas said. "Grab the coupler and bring it back. The rest of us will finish up the connections."

"You know," Rahul said thoughtfully as Aaron and Katya drove off, "I can probably pull the coupler from the old unit and update the identification codes. It's not like these things are engineered for security."

"Good idea," Willem said. "Let's get this done and go back inside."

While Rahul worked, Willem watched moodily as the

rover disappeared over the horizon, leaving only a faint gray dust cloud in its wake. Lucas was fascinated. Out of all the people on the *Orpheus*, Willem was the last one who Lucas would have expected to have any kind of difficulty with his friends. He seemed to always be in control of everything. But right now he looked just as lost and alone as Lucas had felt when he'd first arrived.

To his surprise, Lucas actually felt sorry for him. There was no doubt Willem *deserved* it—he'd been a complete brat to Aaron and Katya. But everyone made mistakes, and maybe in the end he wasn't all that different from the rest of them.

"Perfect," Rahul said, looking down at the ground with the unfocused stare that meant he was accessing his AI implant. "I found what I need. This will just take a minute."

"Fantastic," Willem said. "Aaron? Katya? Did you hear that? You can come back."

"You want us to come back?" Aaron asked. There was a pause, followed by what Lucas was pretty sure was a giggle from Katya. "Uh, we can't hear you very well," Aaron said, adding an unconvincing imitation of radio static. "Must be some interference."

"Stop kidding around," Willem snapped. "We're almost done here. Come back and get us."

There was another burst of fake static from Aaron,

followed by twin peals of laughter. Then the link went silent.

"Very funny, Aaron," Willem said. He laced his fingers over the top of the helmet and turned toward Lucas. "They'll be back. They wouldn't leave me."

Elena sighed. "I'm pretty sure they just did."

"Are you kidding me?" Rahul said, smacking the replacement power unit with his palm. "I mean, in hindsight, we totally should have seen this coming, but *still*."

"It's just a joke," Willem insisted.

"Great joke," Rahul said, closing up the access panel. "Super clever. When we get back I'm going to make sure to tell those two *exactly* how funny it is."

"How are we going to get back to the base?" Willem asked. "They took the rover!"

"We walk," Lucas said. "It's about five kilometers. Not too bad."

Willem stared at him as if he'd just suggested they flap their arms and fly home. "*Walk?* Are you serious?"

"Well, if you want, you can wait behind and see if they come back," Lucas said as he, Elena, and Rahul started off on foot. "Up to you."

Rahul crossed his fingers. "Please wait behind," he whispered. "Oh, please!"

Unsurprisingly, Willem didn't wait very long before hurrying after them. Apparently he wasn't all *that* convinced that his friends were going to come back for him.

In the low gravity, climbing down off the small ridge where the transmitter was located was frustratingly difficult. It was hard to find a pace that wasn't either glacially slow or too fast to control. The effort of running after them seemed to have exhausted Willem, and Lucas found he had to pause periodically to let him catch up.

Finally they reached a long, flat stretch. "Not much farther to the edge of the colony," Lucas said. "Then it's just another few kilometers to the hangar."

"Hang on," Rahul said, bending over with his hands on his knees. "I need a minute."

"Vertigo?" Elena asked worriedly.

"Yeah," Rahul said, grimacing. "It started a little while back. My implant is helping, but I didn't think we'd be out here this long."

Lucas motioned to Willem. "Put his arm over your shoulder. We'll help him walk."

"What about Elena?" Willem asked. "Can't she—"

"Elena cracked a rib in a fight with the local judo champion," Lucas said impatiently. "Now get over here and help me out."

To his surprise, Willem didn't argue any further. He and Lucas positioned themselves on either side of Rahul, and the three of them began to stumble along together.

"Thanks," Rahul mumbled, closing his eyes.

After half a kilometer, as they climbed over the edge of a small impact crater, Willem pointed at a cylindrical building about fifty meters away. "That's an airlock, right?"

"It's part of the old colony," Lucas said. "We should keep going until we get to the base."

"Do you think we can make it?" Elena asked doubtfully. "What's going to happen if he pukes in his suit?"

Lucas considered this. At this point, maybe the best thing to do would be to call for help. It wouldn't take too long for someone to get here in a rover, and then they could get inside quickly.

But calling for assistance would mean admitting that he'd lost control of a simple mission to replace a power unit. Enough things had gone wrong already. What was Sanchez going to say if Lucas couldn't even manage to get his team back inside without help?

"I think he's right," Rahul said, keeping his eyes tightly closed. "I don't know how much longer I've got before I blow chunks."

"All right," Lucas said. "We'll check it out."

When they reached the airlock, Lucas brushed dust off its control panel. He flipped a few switches experimentally, but nothing happened. There were no status lights or anything to indicate that it was actually functional.

Rahul sagged down to the ground. "It doesn't have power?"

"Look for a manual override," Lucas said, running his hands over the doorframe. "There's got to be a way to open it, even without power."

Willem and Elena got down on their knees and followed his example. After a few minutes, Willem yelped in excitement and opened a small metal door on the side of the airlock. "Here!"

Inside the panel was a circular hand crank about half a meter across. Lucas, Elena, and Willem each grabbed a section of the crank and started to turn. For several seconds the crank refused to budge. Then, with a deep shudder, it turned slightly. As it did, the airlock doors opened a fraction of a centimeter. "There we go!" Lucas gasped. "Keep turning!"

With agonizing slowness, the wheel rotated around once, twice, three times. As soon as the doors were open far enough, the four of them squeezed through into the airlock. It was pitch-black except for the glow from their wrist screens. Lucas turned on a light in the collar of his suit and looked around. The airlock was cramped, with barely enough room for them to move. Rahul leaned against the wall, breathing heavily but already looking better.

"There'll be another manual override somewhere," Lucas said.

"Here," Rahul said hoarsely. He opened up a panel next to him, exposing a hand crank identical to the one on the outside. They all grabbed on and turned it as the outer doors slowly sealed themselves shut. By the time they were finished, Lucas's arms felt like jelly.

"There's no power for the air pumps," he gasped. "So we need to look for a release valve. There's a mechanical fail-safe—as long as there's vacuum inside the airlock, we won't be able to open the inner doors."

They found the red emergency equalization switch behind a small pane of clear plastic. Lucas smashed the plastic with his fist and jerked the lever downward. At first, nothing seemed to be happening. Then, very slowly, the air pressure gauge on Lucas's wrist screen started to creep upward. One kilopascal, then two, then three.

"It's working!" Willem said.

Lucas frowned. Why wasn't the air flowing more quickly? After almost a minute, the pressure was only up to eight kilopascals. The pressure inside the colony would be almost ten times that. He stared at the display as if he could cause the numbers to climb by sheer force of will.

But instead of rising more quickly, the pressure seemed to be leveling off. Lucas bent down and pressed the side of his helmet against the panel. For a moment he caught the faint hissing of oxygen flowing into the airlock. Then the sound faded, until all he could hear was the sound of his own breathing.

He jerked the switch up and down several times, with no results. The pressure display on his screen stayed flat at fifty kilopascals. Would that be enough to turn off the fail-safe mechanism that sealed the airlock?

Lucas opened the manual override panel for the inner doors. But even with all of their combined strength, the crank wouldn't turn. It was still locked off by the fail-safe. "It's not going to work," Lucas panted. "Not without more air pressure."

"What do we do?" Willem asked.

"We'll have to find another airlock," Lucas said.

Exhausted, he grasped the hand crank that opened the outer doors and tried to turn it, but the wheel wouldn't move. Willem and Elena threw their weight into it without any luck.

"What's going on?" Elena asked. "It was just working a minute ago."

A chill ran down the back of Lucas's neck as he suddenly understood what the problem was. There was a fail-safe on the outer doors too. Except that instead of locking itself when the air pressure was too low, these doors would lock when the air pressure was too *high*, to prevent someone from accidentally opening the doors and venting the entire atmosphere of the colony into space. The emergency equalization mechanism had let just enough oxygen into the airlock so that *both* fail-safes were active. Unless they could either raise or lower the pressure, neither door would open.

They were trapped.

•

14

"WHAT'S HAPPENING?" RAHUL asked. "Why won't the doors open?"

Willem banged on the doors with his fists. "Someone help us!" he shouted. "We're trapped in here!"

"Calm down," Lucas said. "Take deep—"

"I'm not going to calm down!" Willem screamed, throwing his shoulder against the doors as if he could smash them open.

Lucas switched to the emergency radio channel. "Can anyone hear me? We're stuck in an old airlock on the south side of the colony. If you can hear me, please respond."

There was no answer. His wrist screen showed no connections to any uplink satellites in orbit around Vesta. The ancient, reinforced walls of the airlock were blocking radio signals. Somewhere in the ceiling there was probably a transmission repeater, but even the backup power to this part of the colony had been cut off a long time ago.

"It's okay," Lucas said. "We're going to be okay. I'll figure out a way to get us out of here."

He hoped he sounded more confident than he felt. How were they possibly going to get around the two failsafes? Their best hope was that someone would come looking for them. But how long would that take? Hours? Days?

He checked the reserve air on his suit. The small liquid oxygen tank on his back was eighty percent full. Combined with the air scrubber that would pull some of the oxygen back out of the carbon dioxide they exhaled, their suits had around four hours of air.

Would someone find them by then?

As he watched the pressure display on his wrist screen, something clicked in Lucas's mind. The liquid oxygen in their tanks was stored at high pressure. When it was converted to gas, it expanded to almost a thousand times its previous volume. Which meant that maybe there was a way out of here.

"How big is this airlock?" he asked, turning to Rahul. "Can your implant tell?"

Rahul glanced around. "About twenty cubic meters. Why?"

He pointed at the pressure gauge, which was hovering just above fifty kilopascals. "How much air do you think it would take to raise that to seventy-five?"

"Not *that* much, I guess," he admitted. "But where are you going to get it from? You'd need . . ."

He trailed off and closed his eyes. "Please tell me you're not thinking what I think you're thinking."

"It could work," he said. "If we have enough air."

"What are you talking about?" Elena asked. "What could work?"

"He's talking about venting our reserve air," Rahul said, pointing at the small tank on Lucas's back. "It's an enclosed space, so the pressure in here would rise."

"Which would disable the fail-safe and let the inner doors open," Lucas said.

"Sure," Rahul said. "But if it doesn't work, then we've just dumped our air for nothing."

Willem shook his head. "We're better off just waiting for someone to find us."

"Who's going to find us?" Lucas countered. "How long do you think it will take for Aaron and Katya to realize that we're not coming back?"

Willem considered for a moment. "A long time," he said finally.

"We've each got four hours of air," Lucas said. "A little more if we conserve it."

"I'm not sure it's worth the risk," Elena said. "But it's your decision, Lucas. You're the commander."

The first lesson of command, Sanchez had said: a leader is responsible for his crew. Up till now, Lucas had always thought of that responsibility in abstract terms. But right now, his decision could mean life or death for all three of them.

"We could wait a little while and see if anyone comes," Rahul suggested.

Lucas shook his head. "The longer we wait, the less air we have to vent. It's now or never."

He unclasped the outer seal on his collar, causing his suit to beep angrily at him. The inner seal was locked with a fail-safe similar to the ones on the door—as long as it detected low pressure outside the suit, it would refuse to open. He found the override command on his wrist screen and disabled the fail-safe.

There was a loud hissing sound as the air in his suit started to vent out into the airlock. Lucas's ears popped painfully as the pressure in his helmet dropped. His suit beeped again and pumped more oxygen out of the tank on his back. The reserve air display on his suit dropped to seventy percent, and then to sixty. He let out some more air, careful to not bleed it off too quickly.

Finally the hissing stopped, and he pulled his helmet off completely. The air was thin and had an unpleasant, metallic tang, but it was breathable—for now, at least. The pressure gauge on the wall showed a little less than sixty kilopascals. He tried the hand crank on the inner door, but it was still locked tight.

"How high do you think it needs to be?" Rahul asked.

"Seventy, I'd guess. That's usually the minimum safety pressure."

"So it didn't work?" Willem said.

"Not yet," Elena replied. "Show me how to do it."

"Me too," Rahul said.

"Are you sure?" Lucas asked.

"We're not letting *you* be the only one to try," Rahul said. "Come on, show us."

Lucas demonstrated how to open the collar seal and override the safety mechanism. "Be careful—don't let out too much air at once."

Elena nodded and unfastened the seal. There was a loud hissing sound, and she grimaced in pain. She adjusted the seal and worked her jaw back and forth to get the pressure in her ears to equalize. After a moment of fumbling with his collar, Rahul followed suit. Lucas watched the gauge on the wall settle at sixty-eight kilopascals.

"That's as much as we can spare," Elena said, pulling off her helmet. "We need more."

"Stupid," Willem said, pulling at the crank. "You all did that for nothing."

Rahul pointed at the pressure gauge. "Not for nothing. We're almost there."

"All you need is the air in *my* suit," Willem said. "Except that you don't know for sure that it will even work."

"We could tear that helmet off your head," Rahul said darkly.

"Just because the three of you were dumb enough to let out all of your air doesn't mean that *I* have to," Willem said.

Leadership was about persuasion and empathy, Lucas reminded himself. Willem was obviously scared—that was no surprise. And, Lucas guessed, he wasn't taking too well to the idea that anyone could order or force him to do something risky like vent all his air. But maybe there was another angle Lucas could try.

"Listen, we're going to get out of here," he said. "This is all going to be a funny story we'll tell a few years from now at our graduation dinner. 'Hey, remember the time we were all trapped in that airlock?'"

He hoped he sounded convincing and authoritative, especially since right now he desperately wished there was someone *else* here to be the authority. "But Willem, you're right. We don't know that dumping your air is going to make our situation any better. Which is why it's up to you."

Lucas looked pleadingly at Rahul. If this was going to work, he needed them all to be on the same side. Rahul sighed and folded his arms across his chest. "Okay, sure. We're not going to force you. But I swear, if I die, I'm going to haunt you for the rest of your life."

"Your ghost would be about as scary as a labradoodle," Willem said, rolling his eyes, but his voice had only the tiniest hint of its usual sarcasm. He looked at the gauge for a moment, and then he took a deep breath, disabled the fail-safe, and tugged open the seal at his collar.

The air hissed out of his suit, and he pulled off his helmet. "If that didn't work—" he began, but he was cut off by a faint but distinct click inside the airlock doors.

Rahul and Elena looked at each other for a moment, and then they simultaneously grabbed the hand crank and turned. The inner doors slid open a fraction of a centimeter, and a light gust of air rushed through the gap.

"It *did* work!" Rahul shouted. He grabbed Willem and hugged him tightly.

"Hey, watch it," Willem said, pushing him away. "We're not out of here yet."

They took turns on the hand crank, rotating it a little each time. It was much harder to turn than the one outside the airlock, though it wasn't clear whether there was corrosion or some mechanical problem. After a few minutes of grunting and straining, the gap was wide enough for them to slip through.

"I didn't think I would ever be so glad to breathe

forty-year-old air," Rahul said, leaning against a wall of the corridor outside the airlock. "Now let's get back to the base before the last shuttle leaves."

The short hallway they were in ended in a circular stairway that led down to a much longer passage with rows of doors on either side. The walls were metal, but the floor was rough concrete. Everything was covered in a fine layer of gray dust.

"This is the old colony?" Willem asked. He gave a wan smile. "I don't see any zombies, at least."

They poked their heads into a few of the rooms. An old metal bed frame had been left in one, and in another a faded family portrait hung at an angle on the wall.

Elena wrinkled her nose. "People really used to live underground like this?"

"They still do, on some of the smaller asteroids," Lucas said.

They reached a common room with passages leading away in four directions. In the middle of the room was a metal table with six neatly stacked chairs. A tall pyramid of plastic crates was piled up against one wall. Lucas shone his headlamp around, trying to figure out which way they needed to go to get back to the main colony.

"There," he said, pointing at a door on the far side. "I think."

As they headed across the room, the clang of metal on metal echoed from the hallway he'd chosen. Lucas froze, staring at the open door. Far down the corridor he could see the faint flicker of a flashlight or headlamp.

"What was that?" Willem whispered.

Lucas turned off his light and motioned for the others to do the same. Even as he did, part of him wondered what he was worried about. Shouldn't they be happy to find someone else down here? If nothing else, it would save them the trouble of wandering around until they found the bazaar.

But a much louder voice in his head told him that there was something very strange about running into other people here in the old colony. Maybe whoever it was had a good reason for being here—and maybe they didn't.

Lucas crept to the doorway and listened. After a moment he could make out footsteps and a rhythmic squeaking. Rahul, standing on the opposite side of the door, waved his hand to get Lucas's attention. "Someone's coming," he mouthed.

He was right—the sounds were getting louder. Lucas pointed to the space behind the stack of plastic crates. They huddled down and held their breath, listening to the approaching footsteps.

"This is it," a woman's voice said. Lucas's eyes went

wide. He recognized that voice—it was Willis, one of the Belters who McKinley had introduced him to back at the Janusarium.

Someone opened up one of the plastic crates. "Should be forty of them," Willis said.

"Looks like it," a man replied. "High-quality. Nice."

Lucas fought the temptation to peer around the side of the stack of crates. Why was Willis down here? What was inside the crates? Whatever the answers were, Lucas was now very certain that it would be a bad idea for the Belters to find them here.

For several minutes the cadets listened anxiously to the sounds of crates being opened and the contents loaded onto some kind of cart or truck. Every crate that was removed from the stack brought them closer to being found out.

"That's it," Willis said finally. "The rest of the boxes are just junk."

Lucas breathed a sigh of relief as the cart, now heavily loaded, rattled and squeaked down the hallway. He peeked out and risked a quick glance, but all he saw were the shadowy forms of Willis and her companion disappearing through the doorway. He waited until the sounds of the Belters' footsteps had died away completely and then crept out of his hiding place.

"Who was that?" Elena whispered.

"Nobody we want to run into," Lucas said, turning on his headlamp. "Let's get out of here in case they come back."

They followed the same hallway that Willis and the other Belter had gone down, moving quietly and pausing frequently to make sure there was nobody waiting for them ahead. The farther they went, the more signs of activity they could see: occasional boot prints leading into side rooms, indecipherable graffiti on the walls, bits of trash tossed into corners. After a few minutes they saw the steady gleam of an overhead light down a cross-corridor. They followed the light until they came out into a large storage room that was almost twenty meters across.

This area had clearly seen recent use, and not just from smugglers. Boxes and containers were stacked all around, stamped with labels like 64 Count Dinner Rations or 72 Emergency Suits. Colorful Belter clothing had been stuffed so tightly into a large metal rack in one corner that the whole thing looked like it was ready to topple over. At the far end of the room, a rusty ladder led to a metal hatchway in the ceiling.

After checking carefully to make sure that Willis and her friend weren't around, they climbed up the ladder. Lucas pushed the hatch open and stuck out his head. He found himself in a small side alley that was empty except for a pile of signs advertising sales, like ALL SARIS HALF

OFF. A small brown monkey wearing a gold collar sat on top of the signs, eating from a plastic bag filled with grapes. Through a window a few stories above them came the sounds of a talk show being played at high volume.

The monkey chattered at Lucas for a moment, apparently annoyed at the intrusion, and then scampered up the back wall of the alley with the grapes under one arm. Lucas helped the others climb through the hatch, and they jogged out into the street.

"Massage, sir?" a deep voice said.

They turned and saw a burly man standing in the front window of his shop; its sign advertised THE SOLAR SYSTEM'S BEST MASSAGES. The man flexed his fingers in what Lucas assumed was supposed to be a demonstration of his ability.

"No thanks," Lucas said.

They followed the street to a larger intersection. Lucas looked around, trying to get his bearings. Willem craned his neck and pointed through the crowd. "There's the base!"

They ran through the crowds and past the guards, who gave them only a brief glance. They headed directly for the hangar and sprinted past loader bots and stacks of transport containers until they reached the *Orpheus's* patrol boat. Palmer, standing in the hatchway with his arms folded, glared at them as they passed by.

236

"Get inside, *now*!" he roared.

"Yes, sir," they said in unison, vaulting up into the cabin. Only a few cadets had stayed for the last flight. Aaron and Katya were sitting by themselves, looking nervous and talking quietly. Aaron stopped mid-sentence and looked up at them.

"There you are," he said, sounding relieved.

"Worried about us?" Elena asked, sitting down across from them with a tiny grimace of pain.

"We went back to look for you," Katya said uneasily. "It was just a joke."

"Funny joke," Willem said. He leaned toward the two of them with an icy smile. "*Super* funny joke."

"So how did you make it back, anyway?" Aaron asked.

Willem sat back, folded his arms, and leaned his head against the seat as if he were going to take a nap. "All you need to know," he said, closing his eyes, "is that Lucas here isn't *nearly* as much of a punk as you guys think."

15

THE *ORPHEUS* **STARTED** accelerating away from Vesta almost as soon as the patrol ships landed. Lucas climbed up to their cabin in an exhausted, hazy stupor and fell asleep in his bunk fully dressed. When reveille sounded the next morning, he opened one eye blearily.

"Physical training this morning," Rahul said, sitting up in his sleep sack. He turned around his screen as proof. "I was sure they'd cancel it. Doesn't Palmer know we're under acceleration?"

"That's exactly *why* we're doing it," Elena said. She stretched and pressed her fingers against her rib cage experimentally.

"I'm sure Dr. Voorhaus would tell you to skip it," Lucas said.

"Probably," she said. "Which is why I'm not going to ask him."

Rahul rolled his eyes. "Elena Pruitt, ladies and gentlemen."

Any hopes that Lucas had for a thawing of alpha section's rivalry with Willem and his friends were dashed when they got to Palmer's class. The kids from delta section seemed to have completely forgotten about everything that had happened down on Vesta, and Willem was back in his role as the leader of their little trio.

"Hey, Lucas!" Aaron called. "Don't puke on the teacher today, all right?"

Katya and Willem dissolved into laughter and immediately started pretending to vomit all over each other.

"Looks like everything has returned to its rightful place in the world," Rahul said, watching the delta-section kids laughing and wrestling on a judo mat. "Too bad. Seeing the two of them rebel against Willem was almost worth getting stuck out there."

Was this really how it was going to be? Lucas didn't care much about the teasing, but he'd thought that maybe things were going to be a *little* different. He caught Willem's eye. "Seriously?" he mouthed.

Willem paused for just a moment. Was that regret on his face? Guilt? Or just irritation? Lucas wasn't sure. Willem gave a little noncommittal shrug and turned back to his friends.

"I should have just left him out there," Lucas

muttered to himself.

"You did the right thing," Elena said, elbowing him gently.

By the end of phys ed that morning, everyone was too exhausted to walk, much less speak. Palmer evidently had decided that today was the right day to introduce them to devil stands, which even Elena found difficult.

"My arms," Rahul moaned as they climbed slowly up toward their cabin. "My poor arms."

"I think this is the first time I've ever looked forward to zero gee," Elena said, massaging her shoulders.

When they reached alpha section's deck, Lucas headed to the showers to clean off and change into a fresh uniform. When he got to his cabin, he shoved his sweaty uniform into one of the drawers next to his bunk. As he closed the drawer, the data chip that Stockton and Willis had given him clattered onto the floor.

Rahul bent down and picked it up. "What's this?"

"Oh—nothing," Lucas said. With everything else that had happened down on Vesta, he'd actually forgotten about the chip entirely. "Just something McKinley's friends gave me."

"They gave you a data chip and you brought it back to the ship?" Elena asked. "Didn't you hear Jones's lecture about infosec? There could be megaviruses on that thing."

"I sure hope you weren't going to plug it in," Rahul

said, peering at the chip as if he could see inside. "At least, not into any of the ship's computers."

Lucas was pretty sure that megaviruses were *exactly* what was on the chip. "Of course not," he said, a little weakly. "I was going to throw it away."

"On the other hand, if someone happened to have their *own* forensic setup, that would be different," Rahul said. His eyes gleamed as he pulled a high-tech folding screen from one of the drawers next to his sleep sack. "Mind if I check it out?"

"You're going to plug it into your own computer?" Lucas asked doubtfully. "That seems kind of . . ."

"Idiotic," Elena said. "I believe the word you're looking for is 'idiotic.'"

"I was a founding member of the Mumbai Chaos Computer Club, remember? The tech I've got is *way* better than whatever nummer little virus might be on this chip." He sat down on the floor with his legs crossed and opened up the screen. "But just in case, I'll disconnect from the ship's network so we'll be air gapped."

Rahul tapped the screen, and a light on the side of the computer went dark. Lucas knelt down behind him, torn between wanting to find out what was on the chip and worrying about what would happen if Rahul plugged it in. "You're sure this is safe?"

"Totally safe," Rahul said, plugging the chip into a

port on his computer. "Now, let's see. Lots of VR data, looks like. Most of it is encrypted. But otherwise, nothing super interesting."

He typed a few commands and screenfuls of text scrolled by quickly. "Bingo. A hidden executable. Pretty lame, really. I'd hoped for something a little more advanced."

Rahul's computer trilled. "What was that?" Lucas asked.

"Okay, looks like that first file was just a decoy. Whoever did this was more advanced than I'd thought. Looks like . . ."

He trailed off and frowned. "Looks like what?" Elena prompted.

"There's multiple levels to this thing. I've found three so far, and I think there's more." There was a nervous tone in his voice that hadn't been there a moment ago. He typed quickly, hammering the keyboard with his fingers. "It's looking for an ID badge."

"Like, one of ours?" Elena asked. "Why?"

"I'm not sure."

Lucas was starting to think that this whole idea was a big mistake. "If it infected the badge—and then we used it on the ship's network . . ."

"That would be bad," Rahul said. He stared at his screen. "I take back everything I said. This thing is smart.

Looks like it's trying to reach out to our sensor grid. But I've got it contained."

A small green light on the side of his screen flickered on. "Did you connect to the network again?" Lucas asked nervously. "I thought you were going to keep it disconnected."

"Wait, what?" Rahul said, glancing at the light. "How did that happen?"

"Did the virus reactivate the connection?" Elena asked.

"There's no *way* it could do that," Rahul said, typing another command. "Except that yeah, I think it did."

"Shut it down," Elena said. "Now."

"I'm trying!" he said. "But something is blocking me. Maybe—"

Elena jerked the computer out of his hands. In one smooth motion, she lifted it up and swung it against the wall. The screen split from the keyboard with a splintering crack and it went dark. She examined it for a moment and then handed the pieces to Rahul, who stared at them mutely for a moment.

"I was going to say that maybe I could just unplug the power supply," he said accusingly.

"Well, maybe you should have done that sooner," Elena said.

"That was a really expensive computer!"

"Emphasis on *was*," Lucas said, looking at the mangled

wreckage in Rahul's hands. "Do you think the virus managed to do anything?"

"Other than to my computer, via Miss Judo Expert here?" Rahul said. "No. It was still trying to get through my outbound firewalls when she did her karate-chop maneuver."

"Are you sure?" Lucas pressed.

"I'm sure," Rahul said crossly.

He stuffed the remains of his computer into a drawer and slammed it shut. Elena picked up a few shattered pieces of plastic and handed them to him. "Here you go."

"Gee, thanks."

"We should tell Sanchez about this," Elena said, oblivious to Rahul's sarcastic tone. "What if someone else got one of these?"

"I'll do it," Lucas said, grabbing the chip from her hand. "I was the one who brought it."

"I could come," Elena offered.

"That's okay," Lucas said, backing out of the room. "No need."

He climbed up the ladderway toward the front of the ship. His arms and legs were still sore from Palmer's class, and it was achingly slow going compared with just floating along under zero gee. As he passed deck four, he saw McKinley standing in front of an open panel filled with circuits and wires. Lucas hurried upward, hoping

McKinley wouldn't notice him.

"Lucas, there," McKinley called. "Wait a minute."

Lucas paused on the ladder. "Oh . . . hi."

"Where are you hurrying off to?" McKinley asked, putting his hand on the ladder.

"Nowhere," Lucas said. "I mean, I just need to talk to the captain."

McKinley gave Lucas his usual toothy smile, but this time there didn't seem to be any humor behind it. "Now, talking to the captain isn't *nowhere*, is it? The way you're hurrying, someone might think that you were doing something stupid, like getting ready to tell Sanchez a few things that you'd best be keeping to yourself."

Lucas blanched. "No—of course not."

"Mmm," McKinley said. "I'm sure I can trust you. After all, we're friends, aren't we? But just to be sure, let me explain a few things that would happen if you *did* go talking to Sanchez."

He pulled Lucas over to the far corner of the deck and dropped his voice to just above a whisper. "First there would be an investigation. And that would find out quite a few things, wouldn't it? Do you really want those officers poking around in your business?"

"I don't—" Lucas began.

"Now, maybe you were thinking that you could just tell the captain a little bit, eh? Just the parts you want her to know? Except it doesn't work like that. You tell her anything, and she'll start asking questions. Soon she'll know *everything.*"

"I've got nothing to hide," Lucas insisted.

McKinley chuckled. "Everyone has something to hide, son. But I wasn't talking about just you. If you talk to the captain, it won't be long before she knows everything about your sister too. And Tali, bless her heart, has *lots* to hide."

Lucas froze. McKinley knew about his sister? Suddenly several pieces of this puzzle clicked into place. How had he not seen it before? Lucas had been trying to figure out what Tali was hiding, but the answer had been right in front of him the entire time.

"*You* gave her that device to plant on the hull."

"Might have been," McKinley said. "And *you* were the one who removed it, weren't you?"

Lucas shrugged. "Might have been."

"Either way, Tali is the one that's going to suffer. If you go talking to the captain, she'll be lucky if all they do is expel her. Me, I'd put my money on prison—at the *very* least."

"All she did—"

"You don't know the *half* of what she's done. Have you ever wondered how she came here in the first place? How she's managed to convince the Navy that she grew up on Mars?"

"You helped her," Lucas said, remembering what Tali had told him about needing to pay off a debt. "And then you blackmailed her."

McKinley held up his hands. "Oh, not me. None of this is my style. I'm more of a *facilitator*."

"Stockton and Willis, then."

"Now you're seeing it a little more clearly. Which brings me to my second point. If you go talking about what you know, my business partners will be *extremely* angry. They'll find people to hurt, and they won't stop at just you. There's your sister, for one. And those friends of yours back in your cabin. And of course your father, all alone out on his ship."

Lucas stared at him. Would McKinley and his friends really hurt his dad?

"Like I said, none of this is my style," McKinley said, reading his expression. "I'm just trying to make sure you understand exactly who you're dealing with. And that brings me to my third point, which is what happens if you *don't* say anything."

McKinley's genial smile returned and he spread his arms wide. "Nothing at all. Or at least, nothing worth worrying about. Some tariffs don't get paid. Some rich

Earthers don't get any richer. Some Belters—people a lot like your father—are a little less under the thumb of the planetsiders. Now, what's the harm in that?"

"You expect me to believe that?"

"It's the honest truth. You know what that program they gave you does? It lets certain ships hide from the Navy's sensors. That's it."

Lucas remembered what Rahul had said—that the virus had been trying to connect to the *Orpheus*'s sensor grid. Maybe McKinley was telling the truth?

"Now, I'm not telling you to go plugging that thing in. That's outright sabotage, isn't it? But turning a bit of a blind eye and letting bygones be bygones—well, that's just doing what's right for you and the people you care about."

McKinley patted him on the shoulder. "It's your decision, and it isn't an easy one. I'll leave you to it."

He climbed onto the ladder and descended toward the back of the ship, humming a weird little tune under his breath. Lucas leaned his head against the bulkhead and looked up at the ceiling.

As much as he didn't like it, McKinley was right. Lucas wasn't sure how much he trusted McKinley's story, but one thing he did believe was that Stockton and Willis would hurt people who got in their way. People like his friends and his family. How could he risk that just to stop some smuggling that would probably happen anyway?

Slowly he went up to deck two, just outside the captain's cabin and below the bridge. He floated there for a long time, looking out the window at the glow of the Milky Way. If Captain Sanchez came out of her cabin, he told himself, then he'd talk to her. If someone came down from the bridge and asked him what he was doing here, he'd go inside.

But nobody came out, and nobody asked him what he was doing. The ship was silent except for the laughter of some cadets down in the rec room. Finally Lucas headed back down to alpha section's deck, feeling sick to his stomach. Instead of going into his own cabin, though, he knocked on the door to the fourth-years' bunkroom.

Tali opened the door and regarded him with a carefully neutral expression. "Yes?"

"Can I talk to you for a minute?" Lucas asked. "It's important."

Clearly irritated, she moved aside so he could come in and then closed the door behind him quickly. "So what's so important?"

He showed her the data chip. "Someone down on Vesta gave me this."

"Someone?" she asked, taking the chip from him and inspecting it.

"Actually, I think you know him. His name is Stockton."

At the mention of Stockton's name, she looked up, startled. "He gave this to you?"

"Well, his friend, anyway. Willis."

"Please tell me you weren't stupid enough to plug it in," she said sharply.

Lucas shook his head. "No."

"What are you planning to do with it?" she asked. Was it his imagination, or was she trying hard to sound casual and disinterested?

"They're the ones who were blackmailing you, weren't they?" he asked. "Stockton and his friends. They're the ones who helped you get into this school."

"I told you—I'm finished with them."

"You're sure?" he pressed. "Because—"

"I'm sure," she said, putting the data chip in her pocket. "But listen to me, Lucas. Don't trust them. Don't talk to them. And whatever happens, don't do *anything* they ask you to do. Understand?"

She was telling him what he wanted to hear. But was she being honest, or just trying to push him away? "I can't tell the captain, can I?"

Tali was silent for a long moment. "No," she said finally. "You don't want Stockton as your friend, but you absolutely do not want him as your enemy. Just tell him you lost it or something."

"What are you going to do with the chip?"

"I'll take care of it," she said, opening the door and ushering him through. "It's all under control."

He crossed the deck toward his own cabin, wishing that he could believe her. He wanted there to be some way to make everything turn out all right. But the more he learned, the more he was sure that there weren't going to be any easy answers. When he opened the door to his cabin, Rahul and Elena looked up expectantly.

"You told the captain?" Elena asked. "Is everything okay?"

Lucas closed the door and looked at his friends for a moment. He really, really didn't want to do this. But he didn't have a choice. People might get hurt—*they* might get hurt—if he didn't.

"Yeah," he said. "It's all under control."

16

BY THE NEXT afternoon, Lucas had decided ten different times that he'd done the wrong thing by agreeing to not tell Sanchez. But every time, he came back around to one thought: that if he did the right thing, people he loved would suffer. No matter how hard he tried, he couldn't weigh anything against the possibility of Tali going to prison and his dad getting hurt.

He didn't even know what would happen if he kept quiet. What were Stockton and Willis trying to do? For all he knew, their plan was just going to involve smuggling soy milk without paying any import taxes. What was the harm in that?

After lunch, Chief Engineer Moskowitz and two of her assistants led all the first-year cadets out onto the hull to demonstrate how to check for and repair micro-meteroid impacts. On any other day, this would have intrigued Lucas, because he'd never been on a ship where the hull was repairable mid-flight. But today he found himself just staring out at the stars, unable to concentrate on Jones's demonstration.

"All right," Moskowitz said. "That's the process. Now fan out and see if you can find any impact spots."

Lucas headed out along the sunward side of the ship, looking down at the hull with unfocused eyes. It was good to be outside, at least. He always felt better when he could see the stars.

"Hey," Elena said over a private link, catching up to him. "You okay?"

"Yeah," he said. "Why?"

She pointed at a small circular dent in the hull just below him. "If it had been a snake, it would have bit you."

"Oh. Sorry."

They used one of Jones's repair kits to fill in the hole with a gray metallic goop and used a heat lamp to activate it. The patch slowly melded into the hull, and soon it was hard to tell there had been any damage at all.

"Are you worried about that virus?" Elena asked. "Did Captain Sanchez say what she was going to do about it?"

"No, not really," Lucas said. "Just that they would take care of it."

Elena nodded and looked at him silently. He knew her well enough by this point to know that there was something she wanted to ask him. "Go ahead," he said wearily. "What is it?"

"You said you're protecting someone."

He nodded.

"Are you sure you're doing the right thing?"

"I'm not even a little bit sure," he said. "I don't think I know what the right thing is anymore."

"My grandmother used to say that knowing the right thing is the easy part. The hard part is ignoring all of the voices that are shouting at you to do something else."

Lucas looked out at the outstretched arm of Orion, glittering blue and white and yellow. Maybe she was right. Maybe he was making it harder than it needed to be. If he stopped paying attention to all the voices that were trying to tell him how to feel, then maybe he knew what he ought to do.

They worked together for almost an hour, searching out and patching as many impact craters as they could find. It was relaxing work, in a way. Each little hole was a tiny, solvable problem. There was no question about what needed to be done. Just make the repairs and move on.

"All right, head back in," Moskowitz finally called out. "Whoever had the most patches gets to sit out next time we clean hydraulic feeds."

"I wish she'd told us that *beforehand*," Rahul said as the three of them cycled through the waist airlock. "I would have patched a hundred."

"Well, we've got bridge training next," Elena said. She looked at her wrist screen. "In less than ten minutes. *With* Hofstra, even. So let's hurry up and get inside."

They ended up being six minutes late getting to the backup bridge, but Lieutenant-Commander Hofstra wasn't very interested in their excuses. "Sit down and get ready," he said, waving his hand. "We're short on time."

They took their seats behind the consoles. "Today will be an exercise in fast decision-making," Hofstra said in his booming voice. "You're all getting used to your responsibilities in each area. But in the heat of a situation, you may not have much time to react."

"Bridge to the captain," Weber called over the intercom. "I'm seeing some odd activity on the secure network."

Hofstra cocked his head to one side and listened. "Odd?" Sanchez called back.

"I'm not sure what it is. It doesn't look like any of our normal traffic. Are we running a simulation on the backup bridge?"

Hofstra tapped the intercom button on the commander's console. "This is Hofstra. We were about to start a simulation run."

"Bridge, this is engineering," Moskowitz said. "Weber is right. Something is trying to get into the main sensor grid."

Lucas's skin went cold. *Sensor grid?* Elena and Rahul looked back at him with worried expressions. He knew what they were thinking—that this sounded just like the virus they'd found on the data chip.

"Can you block it?" Sanchez asked.

"Trying," Moskowitz said, sounding like she was about two steps from being completely frantic. "But it's already past our strongest firewalls. If we can't get it contained quickly we're going to have to start physically unplugging our server core."

"Lieutenant-Commander Hofstra—is there anything unusual on your end?" Weber said. "This is looking like it's coming from your part of the ship."

Hofstra frowned. He peered at each of the computer consoles, though it wasn't clear what he thought he might see. Elena and Rahul exchanged a look and leaned back to help him see better. "Nothing," Hofstra said. "Everything looks—"

He paused, looking past Lucas at the computer console on the back wall. With a quick motion he darted forward and pulled something out of a port. He held it up to the light and turned it back and forth.

Elena gasped, and suddenly Lucas felt dizzy. He recognized the chip in Hofstra's hands. It was the same one that Stockton had given him. The same one that Rahul had analyzed on his computer.

The same one he'd last seen his sister putting into her pocket.

Hofstra smacked the intercom button. "Captain—I've found something. A data chip was plugged into the secure network on the backup bridge."

There was a brief moment of silence. "Get those cadets out of there," Sanchez said. "Moskowitz, tell me what you need."

Hofstra pointed at the door. "You heard her. Up and out."

Lucas's heart pounded in his chest as he followed Elena and Rahul out into the hallway. There was only one explanation—Tali had planted the data chip. Like an idiot, he'd given it to her, and she'd gone and done the exact thing she'd told him not to do.

"How could you?" Rahul asked in a hoarse voice. His arms were wrapped around his chest as if he was shivering. "You knew what was on that chip. How could you plug it in?"

"I didn't," Lucas insisted. "I swear, it wasn't me."

"You said you gave it to the captain," Elena said.

Lucas opened his mouth to answer, but his throat had closed up. It was as if everything he cared about was being ripped apart in front of his eyes. After a moment he just shook his head mutely.

"You lied," she said incredulously. "You lied to us."

"You really expect us to believe that you didn't plug the chip in?" Rahul asked. "It was the exact same chip!"

"I got rid of it," Lucas said weakly. "I thought—I thought it was gone."

"Got rid of it how?" Elena asked.

In response, Lucas just closed his eyes.

"Let me guess," Rahul said. "You can't tell us. How amazingly convenient."

"Right now the only thing that matters is telling the captain," Elena said. "We have to get onto the bridge and explain. Maybe it will help if she knows where it came from."

Rahul and Elena darted up the ladder toward the front of the ship. When Lucas started to follow, Rahul stopped and glared down at him. "No way. You're not coming."

"Yes, he is," Elena said, grabbing Rahul by the arm. "He knows the most about what happened."

Rahul clenched his jaw and started up the ladderway again, muttering quietly to himself. They rushed straight past the NO CADETS ON THE BRIDGE sign and up through the hatchway.

"Hey!" Ensign Weber shouted. "What do you think you're doing?"

Elena turned to Captain Sanchez, who was huddled over a computer console with Palmer. "Captain! We need to speak to you."

"Cadets," Sanchez said in a tired voice, "you'd better have a *really* good reason for doing this. It takes a lot of paperwork to put all of you in the brig."

"That data chip Lieutenant-Commander Hofstra found—we know where it came from," Lucas said quickly.

Sanchez and Palmer exchanged a look. "Tell me everything you know," Sanchez said, folding her arms across her chest.

"Some miners on Vesta gave it to me," Lucas said. "It has a virus—the same one Moskowitz is fighting. I think it tries to put blind spots in our sensors."

"How do you know all that?" Palmer demanded. "And how did it get onto the backup bridge?"

Lucas swallowed. "They told me, sir. But I didn't plant it there. I swear."

"It just magically appeared," Rahul said sarcastically.

"I got rid of it," Lucas said. Which was true enough, he guessed. "Someone else must have plugged it in."

Palmer snorted. "There are so many holes in that story I don't even know where to start."

"That's going to have to wait till later," Sanchez said. "Right now—"

"Bridge, this is engineering!" Moskowitz called over the intercom. "Our patrol ships are picking up an unidentified ship approaching quickly."

"There's nothing on our main sensors," Lieutenant

259

Feinman said, looking down at her console.

Sanchez's face turned grim. She leaned down and smacked a button on the arm of the captain's seat. "All hands, prepare for emergency acceleration."

"It's matching speed!" Moskowitz called. "One of my crew got a visual—some kind of beefed-up courier ship. They're coming around to the waist airlock."

"Get ready for full emergency thrust," Sanchez barked. But even as she spoke, a faint clang echoed through the hull. "Belay that—it's too late."

She hit the shipwide intercom button again. "Attention! We have a hostile party attempting to board the ship. Cadets and crew, shelter in place and stay off the ladderways. This is not a drill."

Palmer opened up a locked storage bay at the back of the bridge and took out handheld pulse weapons for Sanchez, Weber, Feinman, and himself. "They'll be ready for us."

"You take Lieutenant Feinman," Sanchez said to him. "Secure the backup bridge and then head to engineering. Ensign Weber, with me."

"What about the main bridge?" Palmer asked.

"I guess it's time to see how well those simulations prepare our cadets," Sanchez said, turning to Lucas and his friends. "Stay here. Keep the door closed. Turn the ship around and head back to Vesta, and then get a message to Rieschling Base and let them know what's happening."

Lucas swallowed hard. "Yes, ma'am."

"Under no circumstances are you to open this door until a ranking officer gives the all clear."

"Understood, ma'am."

Sanchez led Weber, Palmer, and Feinman down the ladderway. She swung the hatch closed behind her and locked it with a loud clang.

"I can't believe she trusts you enough to leave you on the bridge," Rahul said harshly. "If it were up to me—"

"It's not," Elena said. "And right now isn't the time. We need all three of us to run the bridge."

Lucas's skin felt cold and clammy. This was the moment he'd been dreading. It felt like it was only yesterday that he'd discovered what it felt like to have real friends. Now he was finding out what it felt like to lose them.

"I don't blame you for hating me," he said, his voice trembling a little. "But Elena is right—we have orders to follow. Get a return course plotted and open a link to the naval base."

Rahul muttered something to himself and tapped out a few commands on the engineering console. "Link is up."

"Rieschling Base, this is Cadet Lucas Adebayo of the ISS *Orpheus*," Lucas said. "We have an emergency situation and need immediate assistance."

There was a brief crackle of static, and then silence.

"Are you sure you're using the right frequency?" Elena asked.

"I'm sure," Rahul snapped. "But nobody is responding."

"Rieschling Base, this is the *Orpheus*, please respond," Lucas said again.

Nothing.

"Bridge, this is the captain," Sanchez said over the intercom. She was breathing heavily and in the background Lucas could hear shouts and scuffling. "Shut off the hatchways at decks twelve and thirteen."

"On it," Elena said, leaning over her console.

"Have you heard from Vesta?"

"We can't raise anyone," Lucas said.

"Keep trying. If—"

But whatever Sanchez was going to say next was interrupted by a series of incoherent shouts. There was a loud screech of metal, and then the link went silent.

"Captain!" Lucas called. "Captain Sanchez, are you there?"

There was no response. Suddenly the lights on the bridge cut out, leaving them in darkness except for the faint gleam of starlight. All four of the crew consoles went black. After a moment, a pair of emergency lights turned on, bathing the entire bridge in a sickly red glow. The consoles flickered back on with four identical messages: *Emergency Power Activated.*

"Someone disabled the main power grid," Rahul said.

"Was it the captain? Or the intruders?" Elena asked, echoing the question in Lucas's own mind.

"Even on emergency power, we should still be able to get a message to Vesta," he said.

"We've still got a link up," Rahul said, checking his console. "But I'm getting nothing back."

Think, Lucas told himself. *There has to be something you can do besides sitting here.*

A sudden pounding on the bridge hatchway made him jump. "Open this door!" called a man's voice. The attackers had reached the bridge.

Lucas moved over to the hatchway and listened. He heard muffled voices, but he couldn't make out any of the words. Had the intruders secured the rest of the ship? Or were they all here at the bridge? Maybe if he gave the captain enough time, she and the other officers would be able to fight their way back.

"Lucas," called another voice from the other side of the hatchway. He recognized that voice: McKinley. "Lucas, I know you're in there. Open the door so we can sort all this out."

"We'll sort it out, all right," Elena muttered.

"Don't make this hard, Lucas," McKinley said. "We've won. It's over."

They might have taken over most of the ship, but with

the backup bridge locked down, they wouldn't have control of anything as long as Lucas could keep them on the other side of that hatch. He turned to Elena. "Turn back for Vesta. Increase power to two-thirds."

She nodded and bent over her console. After a few moments, the pitch of the engines increased and the ship swung around in a broad arc.

"That's not wise," McKinley said angrily from the other side of the door. "You're just making this harder."

A fist pounded on the hatch again. "Lucas, this is Stockton. You remember me, I'm sure. If you don't open this door, I'm going to start killing cadets, one by one. And first up is going to be someone that you know rather well."

There was a brief sound of struggle from the other side of the hatchway. "Lucas!" Tali shouted. "Don't open it! Do you hear me? Don't—"

Her voice was cut off, as if someone had put their hand over her mouth. Lucas froze. His skin went cold. They were lying. They had to be. They wouldn't kill her.

"In about ten seconds, there's going to be quite a mess out here," Stockton said. "Tali is a smart girl. It'll be a shame to have her clever brains splattered all over this hatchway."

Lucas closed his eyes and wrapped his arms around

his chest. He didn't think that McKinley would hurt Tali. But Stockton might.

A voice crackled over the radio. "This is Rieschling Base," a woman said. "We've received your message."

Lucas's heart leapt. Someone had heard them!

"Or, I should say, this is what used to be Rieschling Base," the woman said. "It's now part of the Free State of Vesta, along with everything in this sector. You're under our jurisdiction, and your ship is being impounded."

"The Free State of Vesta?" Rahul repeated incredulously.

McKinley pounded on the door. "You're not going to be getting any help from Vesta," he called. "Our friends there took it over about an hour ago."

Rieschling Base had been taken over? It wasn't possible—just like it wasn't possible for them to have boarded the *Orpheus*. Just like it wasn't possible for them to have taken over the entire ship in just a few minutes. None of it was possible, and all of it was happening anyway.

"You have five seconds, Lucas."

Lucas bowed his head and opened the bridge door.

17

"YOU'RE GOING TO have to talk to me at some point," Lucas said.

In response, Tali made a sound halfway between a snort and a cough. Though from the way she was floating at the far end of the captain's quarters with her legs folded and a book held neatly in her lap, it wasn't even clear that she actually was responding to him. She might have just been clearing her throat.

Truthfully, in the eighteen or so hours since McKinley had locked the two of them up here in Sanchez's room, she'd done a remarkable job of not talking to him. That coughing sound she'd just made was the closest she'd come to acknowledging his existence. She'd perused Sanchez's bookshelf for a while and pulled out an old hardcover book. At 2200 sharp, she'd closed the book, climbed into Sanchez's sleep sack, and turned off the lights without saying a word, leaving Lucas to sleep out in the middle of the room. Sometime in the middle of the night, the ship had turned off its main engines and entered free fall. Without a sleep sack to hold him in place, Lucas had floated around the room, buffeted by the air currents from the vents in the ceiling. At 0500, Tali had turned on the lights and gone back to her book.

"Remember the week you spent ignoring me when I was six? When I broke your robot project? You almost had me convinced I didn't actually exist."

"It was a *drone* project, not a robot," she said. "And I've already said everything I have to say."

The sound of Tali's voice made Lucas jump. It took him a moment to decide whether she'd actually spoken, or if maybe his sleep-deprived brain had just imagined it.

"You haven't said anything at all," Lucas protested.

"I've said plenty," she replied, with her eyes still locked on the book in her lap. "But for your dimwit brain, I'll repeat. *You. Shouldn't. Have. Opened. That. Door.*"

"What else was I supposed to do?" Lucas said. "They'd captured the ship and they'd taken over everything on Vesta. And they were going to kill you!"

Tali turned toward him angrily and ticked off her arguments one by one on her fingers. "First, they hadn't actually captured the ship until you let them onto the bridge. Second, for all you know, that person you talked to was a Belter on some ship who intercepted your transmission. Third, they weren't going to kill anyone. They were just bluffing."

"They weren't bluffing," Lucas said.

"And you knew that because of the vicious tone in their voice? The angry way they pounded on the bridge door? The murderous smell of their body odor?"

"I know them," Lucas insisted. "I met them on Vesta."

"You don't know anything about them, Lucas. Stockton was only threatening me because he knew you'd give in."

"How do you know that?"

"Because he's my uncle," she said in an exasperated voice.

Lucas stared at her. His sister couldn't have surprised him more if she'd told him she was really a four-armed alien. "Wait, what? That guy who just kidnapped us is your *uncle*?"

"Unfortunately."

"Stockton—the guy who—"

"*Lucas,*" she snapped. "Yes. Him."

Lucas exhaled in a long, low, whistling breath. "Okay, can you start at the beginning, or something? Because out of all the things I thought you might get around to telling me, 'Stockton is my uncle' was pretty far down on the list. Did he just call you up and say, 'Hey, I'm your long-lost uncle, how about you help me hijack your ship?'"

Tali pursed her lips. From her expression, Lucas knew that this was the part of the story she really didn't want to tell. He half expected to get her usual I-can't-tell-you answer, but to his surprise, she answered the question.

"It wasn't like that. I contacted *him*. This was back when I was ten or eleven years old, when I didn't really know anything about him. I just wanted to ask him questions about my parents and find out why he didn't become my guardian."

"Did he tell you?"

She shrugged. "He said he was in prison on Mars when they died. He told me he was innocent, and I believed him. He can be very charming when he wants something from you."

"What did he want from a ten-year-old kid from the Belt?"

"I guess at first I was just a curiosity," she said. "Or maybe he liked having someone to listen to him. Back then all I wanted was to be *anything* other than a miner, and I loved his romantic stories about smuggling diamonds and outrunning patrol ships. At some point he started telling me that I ought to join the Navy and learn to be a pilot. He said he could make it look like I grew up on Mars instead of in the Belt by bribing people to forge transcripts and write recommendations. He even planted a fake article about how I won second place in the Port Meridian colonywide science fair."

Now everything was starting to make some sense. "Dad knew, didn't he? That was why he was so angry?"

Tali nodded. "He told me it wasn't worth coming here if it meant I had to get Stockton's help and lie to everyone about where I'd grown up." She paused. "I can't believe he never told you. I was sure he would."

Lucas remembered all the times his dad had refused to talk about Tali and the academy. He'd thought it was because he didn't want to talk about *her*, but maybe he just didn't want Lucas to know how she had gotten accepted. He'd carried that secret for three years. No wonder he'd been so angry.

"I think it was why he didn't want you joining up," Tali went on. "He knew Stockton would want something from me in return for getting me into the school, and he was worried the same thing would happen to you. And he was right—as soon as I enrolled, all of Stockton's charm evaporated. He told me that if I didn't work off the debt I owed him, he would tell everyone that I was a fraud. The first year or two it was tiny little things—information, mostly. Stuff that he could sell to other smugglers. Later it started to get more serious."

"Why didn't you just tell him no?"

"You make it seem like that would be so easy," she said. "If the Navy found out about my forged papers, I would have gotten kicked out of the school—maybe even gone to prison. And if I helped him, I could keep everything the way it was. I told myself I wasn't hurting anyone, and that someday I could finish paying him back, and then I'd be free."

Lucas remembered thinking the exact same thing when McKinley had told him to keep quiet—that nobody was getting hurt and the people he loved would stay safe. "It doesn't work that way, does it?"

"No, it doesn't," she said. "After you came here—after I planted that device on the hull—I told them I was finished. I thought by that point I had enough information on them that they couldn't expose me without getting arrested themselves."

"What changed your mind? Why did you help them install the virus?"

"You really don't know?" she asked, staring at him. "It was because of *you*, Lucas. They told me that if I didn't help them, they'd force you to do it instead."

"Me?" he asked, blinking in surprise.

"Yes, *you*," she snapped. "Haven't you been listening? It wasn't a coincidence that your name came up when Sanchez started asking around about a Belter cadet who could fill that last spot. Somehow Stockton must have arranged for some glowing recommendations about how the perfect candidate was a kid named Lucas Adebayo, conveniently located right there on Ceres."

Lucas was stunned. Just like Tali, he was here on the *Orpheus* because of Stockton? "He wanted me here because he thought I would help him?"

"Or because it would give him more leverage over me," she said. "Either way, he knew he'd get what he wanted."

Slowly Lucas pieced all of this together in his mind. Had this been Stockton's plan all along, or had he just figured that having people on the inside would pay off somehow? It didn't matter. They were here now.

"This is all our fault," he said. "We have to fix it."

"They've taken over the ship, Lucas," she said. "What can we do?"

The door opened, revealing McKinley and a grubby-looking man holding a pulse rifle. The man's hair was shaved down to a stubble, and his scalp was pockmarked with scars.

"That's an easy one," McKinley said. "What you're going to do is come with me."

"Go with you where?" Lucas asked.

"Down to the Free State of Vesta," McKinley said. "There's going to be quite a celebration. I'm sure you'll both want to be there."

"We don't want to be at any celebrations," Tali said. "Let us go."

"That's exactly what I'm doing," McKinley said. "Once you're down on the surface, you'll be citizens of Vesta, free to do as you please."

"What about the *Orpheus?*" Lucas asked.

"This ship isn't the *Orpheus* anymore," the other Belter said. "It's now the VSS *Liberty*, the flagship of the Vestan Navy."

"Vestan Navy?" Tali said. She laughed derisively. "What's the rest of the fleet? Six cargo haulers and a garbage transport?"

The Belter grabbed Tali and pulled his arm back as if he was going to punch her, but McKinley held him back. "Easy, Jonah. They're on our side, remember?"

"They ought to be in with the other little muskrats," Jonah muttered, shoving Tali back toward Lucas. "I don't trust them."

"We've got enough hostages," McKinley said. "We owe these two a debt, and we're going to repay it."

"Hostages?" Tali asked. "So that's what you're doing with the other cadets?"

"We're sitting ducks without them," McKinley said, shrugging. "The Navy has us outgunned twenty to one. As soon as we get a signed peace treaty and a guarantee that we'll be left alone, everyone will be free to go."

"A peace treaty?" Tali said. "There's no war going on."

"There is now," Jonah said sharply.

"You told me this was all about avoiding some tariffs," Lucas said to McKinley. "Now you've started a war?"

"I don't *want* a war," McKinley said. "I said that we were trying to keep honest Belters from being under the thumb of those idiots back on Earth. If the Navy plays it smart, then nobody will get hurt."

"And if they don't," Jonah added, "we'll make sure they realize who they're dealing with. This isn't a game."

"Fortunately," McKinley said, "the two of you will be away from any of that nasty business. You'll be downside, enjoying the peace and quiet of the bazaar."

"We aren't going to—" Tali began, but Lucas grabbed her arm. Whatever happened, being down on Vesta was better than being here, and he wasn't going to let Tali's pride keep them locked up.

"Yes, we are," Lucas said. "We'll go with you."

To his relief, Tali closed her mouth and didn't argue. McKinley gave them a broad, genial smile, and Lucas had to restrain himself from punching it right off his face.

"I always knew you were the smart one, Lucas," he said. "Follow me."

McKinley and Jonah led them down the Broadway ladder toward the back of the ship. Lucas caught a brief glance of three women playing cards in the fourth-year alpha-section bunkroom. Behind him, Tali tensed but didn't say anything. When they reached the hub, they saw more Belters hanging out in the rec room, laughing and talking. Each one of them had a pulse weapon on their belt.

"Where are the officers?" Tali whispered to Lucas.

"I don't know," he whispered back.

They followed McKinley down to the hangar. A team of Belters was escorting a line of twenty or thirty Navy personnel off of a big dingy-gray transport.

"The crew from Rieschling Base," Tali whispered, nodding at the men and women emerging from the belly of the transport. "They've brought them all up here."

"Move," McKinley said. "No time to chitchat."

Tali and Lucas followed McKinley up into the cabin of a little mining ship, where Jonah was already strapping himself into the pilot's seat. He flew them quickly out through the hangar doors and past a small flotilla of cargo haulers with stubby pulse cannons and long, spindly looking mass drivers protruding from their hulls. As they passed over the bazaar, Lucas noticed that the commercial landing pads, which were normally overflowing with vessels of all sizes, were completely empty.

"You commandeered *every* ship?" Tali asked. "You've turned the bazaar into a prison."

Jonah clenched his jaw and glared at her. "Once this is all settled, they'll be free to go. Till then they need to remember who the enemy is."

The hangar they landed in was barren and empty. Ships, engines, parts, and supplies had all been looted and removed. Lucas, Tali, and Jonah followed McKinley through the base toward the entrance to the bazaar. With all the Navy personnel up on the *Orpheus*, the hallways were eerily silent, and it gave Lucas chills to see scorch marks from mining lasers on some of the walls. Whatever had happened here, it had been well coordinated and vicious.

They rounded a corner and found Willis and another Belter escorting a line of cadets into a large rec room. Lucas's heart leaped as he saw Elena and Rahul near the end of the line. They stopped short and stared at him in surprise. Lucas opened his mouth to call out to them, but Rahul's eyes narrowed and he marched into the rec room. Elena gave him a look that seemed to be a cross between disappointment, anger, and confusion, and then she followed Rahul into the room.

Lucas felt as if someone had stabbed a knife straight into his heart. He could see exactly what they were thinking. He was a Belter, a liar, and a traitor. And how could he even argue with that? Maybe he hadn't intended for the *Orpheus* to be hijacked, but he'd helped it happen all the same. He looked at Tali. She was staring at the floor with her hands in her pockets. Her face was empty, as if all the life had been sucked out of her.

"What are you going to do with these two?" Willis asked. "In with the others?"

"I'm taking them to the bazaar," McKinley replied.

"If you ask me—"

"I'm not asking you," McKinley growled. He jerked his head toward Jonah. "Or him. Or anyone else. Do your job, and I'll do mine."

"Fine," she said, shrugging. She locked the door to the rec room and pointed at the other Belter. "You stay here. Make sure they keep quiet."

"Come on," McKinley said, grabbing Tali and Lucas by the arms. He led them through empty hallways until they reached the entrance to the bazaar. The wide doors were closed, which was something Lucas had never seen before. Two Belter guards sat on the floor with pulse weapons on their laps. As they saw McKinley approaching, they stood up quickly.

"Open the doors," he said crossly.

The guards exchanged a brief look, and then one of them pulled a lever on the wall. The big metal doors started to rumble open. Immediately, the two guards placed themselves in the widening gap, their weapons held tightly in both hands.

A moment later, Lucas could see the reason for their concern. Twenty or thirty Belter citizens were gathered on the other side in a loose bunch. As soon as the doors were open, they turned and started to shout.

"When do we get our ships back?"

"You can't just keep us here!"

"I insist on speaking with whoever is in charge!" a tall, white-haired man roared. He moved forward as if to push his way into the base, but stopped when the two guards leveled their weapons at him. The man glared at them with a look of disgust and turned back around. He paused briefly, then bent over and pulled down his pants and waggled his bare bottom at the guards. The crowd of Belters roared their approval.

"Could you have messed this up any worse, Willis?" McKinley muttered. He stepped forward and raised his hands.

"Listen up!" he shouted. "Your ships will be returned to you as soon—"

"They're *our* ships!" someone yelled back. "What gives you the right to take them in the first place?"

"You'll get them back as soon as we know what the muskrats are going to do," McKinley said.

"We can't make a living if nobody can come or go," the white-haired man said.

"You can't make a living if this colony gets blown to

atoms, either," McKinley snapped.

"Why should we trust you?" the man said. "As far as we're concerned—"

"I don't care who you trust!" McKinley roared. "This is how it's going to be. So figure out how to live with it."

He grabbed Lucas and Tali and half dragged, half threw them out toward the crowed. Lucas stumbled, and Tali grabbed him quickly to keep him from falling. The doors slid shut, leaving Lucas and Tali alone with the crowd of merchants.

For a moment, there was stunned silence all around. The white-haired man strode toward Lucas and Tali and jabbed his finger at them.

"Who in the great black void are you?" he demanded.

18

LUCAS FROZE. HE looked at Tali, who had an equally shocked expression on her face.

"They're muskrats, Dad," a boy said, pushing his way through the crowd. Lucas recognized him as Jo, the kid who had tried to talk Elena into visiting his clothing shop. He was followed close behind by his friend Mai.

"We met that one during their last shore leave," Mai said, pointing at Lucas. "He said he was a Belter."

"I am," Lucas said. "My dad is an ore miner—"

A woman in the crowd jabbed her finger at Lucas. "He's one of those miners, Smythe. Throw him back or lock him up!"

"No!" Lucas said quickly. "My dad would never do something like that."

"So why did they let you go?" Smythe asked. "You might be a Belter, but you're wearing a muskrat uniform."

"I . . . don't know," Lucas stammered.

Smythe snorted. "You're a terrible liar. What about your friend here?"

"It's none of your business," Tali snapped.

"I think it is *exactly* my business, girl." Smythe turned to Mai and Jo. "Put them in the storage cellars. Maybe they can find themselves some real Belter clothes."

As Jo approached Tali, she launched a vicious kick at his knee that he barely dodged. Lucas took her arm and pulled her close to him. "Now isn't the time to fight," he whispered.

"Listen to your friend," Smythe said. "We can throw you in the warrens, or out an airlock. Whichever you prefer."

Tali glared at him but relaxed her posture and let Jo and Mai lead them into into Smythe's Haberdashery, which was filled with racks of brightly colored robes, shirts, pants, and belts. At the back of the store was a narrow hallway lined with shelves overflowing with clothes and shoes. Finally they reached a small office with a metal desk that was mostly covered by the leaves of a vinelike potted plant. A faded tourist poster on the wall touted Vesta as THE PERFECT DESTINATION.

Jo dragged the desk toward the back of the office, revealing an old-looking metal hatch built into the floor. He bent down and jerked the hatch open. There was a puff of dusty, acrid-smelling air. Mai wrinkled her nose.

"I'm guessing there's some old emergency rations down there somewhere," Jo said. "But since they'd be about ten years past their expiration date, I don't advise eating them."

"You're just going to lock us in there?" Tali demanded.

"It's better than what I had in mind," Jo said, shrugging. "Maybe later the council will let you argue your case. On the other hand, they might just decide to forget about you altogether."

Tali glared at him and pulled her arms away from Mai. She knelt down beside the hatch. "There's not even a ladder!"

"Nope," Jo said. "But it's not far down."

Tali peered into the darkness for a moment. She shot one last angry look at Jo and dropped down through the hatchway. There was a muffled "Oof!" and the sound of boxes being knocked over.

"Watch out for the merchandise," Jo called. "It's out of style, but what goes around, comes around."

Tali kicked over more boxes and replied with a long and rather detailed curse. Mai prodded Lucas in the small of his back. "Your turn."

Either intentionally or unintentionally, Tali had managed to clear away most of the boxes from the space immediately below the hatch. Lucas dropped through the hatchway and fell about three or four meters before landing on a bare metal floor. He climbed to his feet and looked around. Thick dust swirled in the light shining down from the room above. Boxes were stacked haphazardly all around. Most were sealed, but some had spilled open, revealing moldy fabric. An old three-dimensional printing machine sat against one wall, next to a teetering stack of jugs filled with tiny plastic balls. Behind the machine was what looked like a door to a closet or another room.

"The lights don't work," Tali called, flipping a switch on the wall repeatedly.

"Not guessing they would," Mai replied. "Nobody's been down there for at least a decade. But don't worry, we'll leave this hatch open. At least, as long as you behave."

Jo chuckled. A few moments later, Lucas heard the door to the office slide shut, and then everything was silent.

Tali kicked a box, scattering small cylindrical objects across the floor. "I'm trying to figure out a way we could have screwed this up more badly. But I'm not coming up with much."

Lucas bent down and opened the box that she had kicked. "At least you found the flashlights," he said, taking one and flicking it on.

Tali squinted in the sudden light. "Wonderful."

She sat down on one of the boxes and leaned her head back. Lucas watched her for a moment and then began to pace back and forth. He wasn't giving up. There had to be some way to fix everything before it got any worse.

If they were going to have any chance at all at winning this fight, he decided, then they needed more allies and fewer enemies. The merchants clearly weren't happy about being pulled into a war. If Lucas could get the people of the bazaar on his side, then the odds of success went up significantly.

But the merchants weren't the only potential ally. The rest of the cadets were locked inside the naval base, less than a kilometer away. If Lucas could find some way to rescue them, *and* persuade them that he and Tali weren't traitors, *and* convince the merchants to fight back against the miners, then maybe they could stop this rebellion and take back the *Orpheus*.

What if the cadets refused to trust them? What if the merchants decided the Navy was a bigger threat than the miners? What if, what if?

It didn't matter. He'd deal with those problems when they came. Right now, he had a plan. And the first step was getting out of this room.

He held the flashlight in his teeth and grabbed one leg

of the enormous 3D printing machine. Slowly he dragged it away from the wall until there was enough space to reach the door behind it.

"What are you doing?" Tali said irritably. "That's just a closet."

"I don't think so," Lucas said. He inspected the door more closely. It was an old-fashioned hinged door with a metal handle. He could turn the handle easily enough, but when he pulled, the door only moved a few centimeters before grinding to a stop.

"This must be part of the old colony, right?" Lucas said. "Back when it was all underground. So whatever this room was, it had to connect to everything else."

"Okay, probably," she admitted. "But what good is it going to do to go wandering around an abandoned underground colony?"

Lucas knew that if he explained his whole plan to her, she would immediately list, in great detail, all the reasons why it had zero chance of succeeding.

"Well, it's no worse than hanging out in *this* part of an abandoned underground colony, right?"

In demonstration, he pulled harder at the door. With a loud creak, it swung partly open, revealing a narrow corridor that led off into darkness.

Tali folded her arms and looked away. She muttered

something to herself, but the only words Lucas could catch were "idiotic" and "pointless." Finally she sighed and grabbed a flashlight from the floor. "All right. We'll check it out."

They squeezed through the door and walked slowly down the corridor. Dust covered the walls and hung in the air like a fog. Lucas breathed through his nose and tried not to cough. Doors on either side of the passage opened up into more rooms like the one they'd started in. They were all empty except for bits of paper, empty food pouches, and other discarded trash.

After a few meters, the hallway dead-ended into a larger passage that ran left and right. They shined their lights down each side.

"Which way?" Tali asked.

Lucas tried to picture the layout of the bazaar and the Navy base. When he'd been down here with Elena, Rahul, and Willem, they'd been coming back from the radar station on the south side. . . . he pointed down the hallway to their left. "That way."

"Any particular reason?"

"I've got a hunch," he said. "Let's see where it ends up."

They passed more empty rooms and a few closed doors. Tali paused briefly to inspect a torn poster that listed safety regulations like KEEP YOUR HELMET

NEARBY AT ALL TIMES and OPEN FLAMES ARE STRICTLY PROHIBITED. After about ten meters, they came out into a large circular area. A few tables were arranged at the center, surrounded by faded orange plastic chairs. At the far end of the room was a long counter and what looked like a kitchen area. Three hallways led off in different directions, all identical to the one they'd come in.

His hunch was getting stronger. This was all starting to feel familiar to him. He peered down the hallways and picked the center of the three. He jogged with long, loping strides, glancing only briefly into the rooms on either side of the passage. If he was right, then they just had a little farther to go.

Abruptly, the passage ended in a set of double doors. As soon as he pulled one of the doors open, he was greeted by a rush of cool, fresh air. Lucas grinned and looked around. He was standing in a large storage area filled with boxes, containers, and shelves. "This is it!"

"This is *what*?" Tali asked doubtfully, coming up behind him.

Lucas shone his light on a set of overlapping boot prints on the dusty floor, following them to a ladder at the other end of the room. "That goes out to the bazaar."

He traced the boot prints back to a passageway on the

opposite wall. "And that goes out to the surface."

Tali looked at him skeptically. "You've been here before?"

"It's a long story."

She shook her head and went over to the ladder. "We're going to have to find some other clothes before we get to the bazaar. With these uniforms on, we may as well have 'arrest us' painted on our backs."

"We're not going to the bazaar," Lucas said. He nodded at the passage that led up to the airlock that he'd come through with Elena, Rahul, and Willem. "We're going back to the base."

"Back to the *base*? Are you kidding me? Why would we possibly want to do that?"

"Because we're going to rescue the other cadets."

Tali laughed harshly. "I don't think any of our fellow cadets are going to trust us to rescue them from a stubbed toe. As far as they're concerned, we're best pals with the guys who took over our ship."

Lucas remembered the looks that the cadets had given them. She was right—it was going to be hard to persuade any of the cadets to trust them. But they had to try.

"I guess this is where we find out whether Captain Sanchez's lessons about leadership actually taught us anything," he said.

She looked at him for a moment with an inscrutable

expression, and then she sighed. "So even assuming we decided to try this stupid idea of yours—how are we going to get into the base? And if we do manage to find the other cadets, how are we going to get them all out?"

Lucas smiled. "Don't worry," he said. "For *that*, I've got a plan."

19

"YOU'RE REALLY GOING to put one of those on?" Tali asked as Lucas opened up one of the storage containers marked EMERGENCY VACUUM SUITS. "They're older than either of us."

She unfolded one of the suits and squinted at it dubiously. It wasn't much more than a flimsy-looking plastic bag with tube-shaped sections for arms and legs. At the top, a collar contained the air filter and electronics. "Even when they were new, these things were only rated for thirty minutes, tops."

"It'll only take us ten minutes to get to the base," Lucas said. "And they're light enough that we can carry enough for all the cadets."

Tali opened up a box labeled MEDICAL SUPPLIES and found two medium-sized backpacks filled with bandages. They dumped the bags out onto the floor and packed the suits inside. It took some effort to cinch the bags again, but after a minute they managed to get them closed up.

He shone his flashlight around. "We need to find the power controls for this section so we can get through the airlock."

After a few minutes of searching, they found a room with a small sign that read ELECTRICAL SYSTEMS. Inside was a rack with rows of fist-sized switches. Lucas wiped the dust from the labels and started trying to figure out what each one controlled, but Tali pushed him aside and smacked each of the switches upward. When she reached the end of the first row, the overhead lights flickered on.

They followed the boot prints back to the stairway that led to the airlock. Once the inner door was sealed, they pulled their helmets over their heads and sealed up their suits. A warning label on the collars said Only for Use in Vacuum, and Lucas could see why: the flimsy material puffed in and out as he breathed, making him feel as if he was continually about to suffocate. Tali wrinkled her nose.

"Ugh," she said. "It tastes like I'm breathing plastic."

To Lucas's relief, the airlock was now fully powered, and it ran through its normal cycle without any problems. As the pressure dropped, the helmets ballooned outward to their full size. Lucas listened carefully for any sign of an air leak, but everything seemed to be fine. It was a very strange feeling, being in a vacuum without an air tank, radios, or any kind of instrument whatsoever.

Well, that wasn't quite true. On the inside of the collar was a small green light marked Air Filter Capacity. No gauge or estimated time until his oxygen ran out: just that little light. But it was better than nothing.

The outer doors opened, and they walked out onto the surface. Lucas pointed in the direction of the naval base and Tali nodded. They jogged in long, bouncing strides over the surface and soon found themselves running along a small trail marked by the ruts of rover tires. Lucas alternated between scanning the horizon ahead of them and watching the air quality light on his collar. Was it his imagination, or was it already starting to turn yellow?

After almost ten minutes, Lucas finally saw the gray outline of the naval base. He followed the outer wall until he reached the airlock that he'd come through with Willem and the others on their mission to replace the radar station's power unit. As soon as they got inside, he and Tali tore off their helmets and took deep breaths.

"Remind me not to do that again unless my life depends on it," Tali said with a shudder.

Lucas declined to point out that their only way back to the colony was by the same way they'd just come. "So now all we have to do is find the rec room, break in, and then lead everyone back the way we came."

"That's it?" she asked.

"That's it."

"And here I was hoping you had some genius insight that was going to give us a chance of actually pulling it all off." She sighed and pointed down the hall. "If we take the second corridor on the left, we'll end up at the back entrance for the rec room. It's about fifty meters. Not much to do except hurry and hope that there aren't any Belters wandering around looking for the bathroom."

"Got it," he said. "Let's go."

They hid the emergency suits in the airlock and jogged carefully down the hallway, moving as quietly as they could. Tali stopped at the first intersection and glanced down both hallways. "Clear," she whispered.

As they continued down the passage, Lucas started to wonder whether Tali was right. Maybe this entire plan was absolutely crazy. It was hard enough getting the two of them into the naval base. How were they going to manage to get the entire class of cadets out without anyone noticing?

They ran silently around the corner of the second intersection and down the hall toward the rec room. Lucas waited for a hand on his shoulder or a shout that would give everything away. But nothing came.

Tali pointed at a wide set of doors on the left side of the hall. A small placard read REC ROOM. The doors were closed, and the panel on the wall nearby glowed a dull red. Tali jabbed the button with her thumb several times.

"No good," she whispered. "They must have locked it off via the central computer."

"How do we get it open?"

Tali thought for a moment. "This isn't a prison. It's not designed for security. If I can find a computer console, I can get the doors open." She paused. "Probably."

"How are we going to do that?" Lucas asked.

"*We* aren't going to do anything," she replied. "You're going to stay here. Get inside as soon as the panel for the door resets. I'll meet you and the other cadets back at the airlock."

Lucas opened his mouth to protest, but she was already heading down the corridor. He crouched down and pressed himself into the small space between the door and the hallway. It was one thing sneaking into the base with Tali, but it was very different being here alone. The thought of being caught suddenly seemed much more real. If they found him, the best he could hope for was to be thrown in with the other cadets. At worst, they'd shoot him on sight.

After ten minutes he began to fidget. Where was Tali?

It shouldn't be taking her this long to find a console. Had she been captured? He was trying to decide whether he was better off waiting here or going out in search of his sister when he heard footsteps coming down the hall. He froze.

". . . and the sooner the better," Willis was saying. "This place is already starting to drive me crazy."

"You spend ten months out of the year in a ship that's barely big enough to turn around in," Stockton said. "At least here you get hot food and showers."

"Yeah, but that ship's *mine*," Willis replied. "I like it. Down here, I can't stop thinking there's a muskrat around every corner."

They were only a few meters away. Lucas looked around, but there were no better hiding places than the one he was in. He was trapped. As soon as the Belters reached the doorway to the rec room, they would find him.

"You'll have your rotation on one of the ships, just like everyone else," Stockton said. "If you—"

Without any warning, the overhead lights flicked off, leaving the hallway in complete blackness. "Great," Willis said. "*Now* what's going on?"

Stockton swore. "How are we going to fight a war if we can't even manage to keep the power on?"

After only a few seconds of darkness, the lights

flickered back on. The panel on the wall next to the door flashed red for a few moments and then turned to green. Lucas pressed it quickly. The door opened and he tumbled inside. He smacked the inner panel with his hand and the door slid shut.

Lucas tensed, expecting that at any moment the door would open and Stockton would find him. After a few seconds he relaxed a little and took a deep breath. Apparently they hadn't seen him.

He turned around and saw the rest of the *Orpheus*'s cadets watching him with expressions that ranged from shock to disbelief to complete confusion. He stood up and brushed himself off.

"Hi," he said, and stopped. Somehow, after all his planning, he hadn't put any thought into what he'd actually say when he found his classmates again.

Maria strode toward him with a furious expression, followed close behind by Oliver and Hanako. Lucas tried to back away, but she grabbed him and pushed him up against the wall with her forearm across his throat.

"You've got five seconds to convince me why I shouldn't just kill you now."

"I can explain!" Lucas started to say, but his voice was cut off as Maria pushed her forearm harder against his throat.

"Please do," she said. "Start with explaining why you and Tali are walking around free when the rest of us are locked up in here."

"We didn't know—we didn't mean to—"

Maria grabbed his face, squeezing his cheekbones with her fingers. "You mean you didn't mean to let a dozen roaches with pulse weapons onto our ship? It just kind of *happened*?"

"No!" he gasped. "I mean, yes. We didn't know what they were planning to do."

"Let him go!" Rahul said, pushing his way through the crowd of cadets, with Elena just behind him.

"He's a traitor!" Maria shouted.

"Maybe," Elena said. "But he's also our friend. He deserves a chance to explain himself."

Maria pushed Lucas away and faced Elena with her arms folded. Despite the fact that Maria was three years older and ten kilos heavier, Elena refused to budge. "You really think you're that tough?" Maria demanded.

"Stop!" Lucas said. "We don't have time to fight. We have to get back to the bazaar."

"Get back to the bazaar?"

"That's why we're here," he said. "Tali and I are trying to rescue you."

"So Tali is here too?" Oliver asked. "Where is she?"

"She unlocked the rec room door so I could get in here," Lucas said. "She's going to meet us at the airlock."

"Don't believe him!" Maria said to the others. "This is some kind of trick."

"He's here, isn't he?" Oliver pointed out. "Why would he have come back if he's not telling the truth?"

Hanako turned to Elena and Rahul. "You guys know him best," she said. "What do you think?"

In response, Elena just pursed her lips. Rahul shoved his hands in his pockets and looked down at the floor silently. Lucas's heart ached with a feeling that was getting all too familiar: that he'd betrayed the people he cared about. Maybe Tali was right—maybe it had been stupid to come here. Some mistakes were just impossible to fix.

"He lied to us," Elena said finally. "Multiple times."

Rahul nodded, still not looking at Lucas. "And he helped Tali plant a virus in the ship's computer—or at least, he covered up what she did so nobody would know."

Maria clenched her fists. "Like I said. He's a traitor."

"But I think that whatever he did, he was doing it for a good reason," Elena said. "When he says he didn't mean for this to happen, I believe him."

"Yeah," Rahul said quietly. "I believe him too."

Lucas's breath caught in his throat. Had he just heard that right?

298

"Are you kidding me?" Maria asked incredulously. "After everything he did?"

"I'm a truth-sayer," Elena said. "I don't lie. And when I choose to trust someone, then I trust them, even when they make mistakes."

Oliver nodded. "I've screwed up enough times to recognize when someone is trying to fix something. And right now I don't think we're in a position to reject help, no matter who it comes from."

"I agree," Hanako said. "When this is all over, the two of them are going to have to answer a lot of questions. But it'll be up to Captain Sanchez to decide what happens to them, not us. Till then, I think we have to trust them."

"So," Oliver said, turning back to Lucas. "What's your plan?"

Lucas blinked and looked at the expectant faces surrounding him. His mind was still trying to wrap his head around what had just happened. Rahul and Elena still trusted him, even after everything that had happened? And except for Maria, the rest of the cadets were at least ready to listen to him—that was a start. Now all he had to do was persuade them that he could get them back to the bazaar safely. He cleared his throat.

"There's an airlock not far from here. We've got emergency suits for everyone. Once we get outside, there's a tunnel a few kilometers away that leads back into the old colony underneath the bazaar."

"That's it?" Hanako asked. "What do we do if we run into those miners?"

"We take them down," Oliver said darkly. "This time, no peaceful surrender. If we have to fight, we fight."

The thought of unarmed cadets fighting adults with pulse weapons made Lucas queasy. Was this really what he'd gotten everyone into? Nervously he turned to the door and pushed on the manual release, but it didn't open. He tried again, pressing his shoulder against the door to try to unstick it.

"Please don't say it's locked again," Katya said.

Maria pushed Lucas out of the way and tried the door. "It's locked, all right."

"Brilliant," Aaron muttered. "Nice rescue plan, Lucas."

"Hey, at least he's here," Rahul said, glaring at him. "At least he's trying."

"What we need right now is more than just *trying*," Maria said. She banged her palm against the door and stomped off. "We need a plan that will actually work!"

Lucas slumped down against the wall, staring at the locked door. Maria was right. He'd been a complete idiot. How had he not planned for this? He watched as the other cadets slowly dispersed, leaving him alone with Elena and

Rahul. *So much for being a leader,* he thought.

"So I just want to be clear about something," Elena said, folding her arms. "Which is that I still *really* want to punch you."

"Got it," Lucas said glumly. "Looks like you'll have plenty of time."

"Hey, you did a million things right just getting here," Rahul said. "Now all we need to do is find a way to unlock that door."

Willem, hovering nearby, cleared his throat. "Actually, I think I have a solution for that."

The three of them turned to him in surprise. "You're telling us you can unlock that door?" Elena asked.

Willem pointed at a tiny ventilation shaft in the ceiling. "If you can get me up there, I can get out to the hallway and flip that emergency evacuation alarm. You said it would open every door in the base, right?"

Lucas looked up at the ventilation duct. It was a tiny opening, but maybe Willem would be able to fit. Certainly nobody *other* than Willem was going to get through.

"What if you get out there and decide that you're better off on your own?" Rahul asked. "It would be much safer for you to just leave us all in here."

"I guess you'll have to trust me."

Rahul snorted. "Fat chance of *that.*"

Willem pursed his lips and looked away. Rahul's words had clearly hurt him. It was definitely true that Willem hadn't shown a whole lot of reason for them to trust him. But Lucas had made too many of his own mistakes to judge anyone for *that*.

"It's a good plan," he said. "Let's try it."

"Are you serious?" Rahul asked, wide-eyed. "What makes you think he's not going to just let us rot in here?"

Lucas shrugged. "If he does, we're no worse off than we are right now."

Rahul turned to Elena. "What about you?"

"I agree with Lucas," Elena said. "Right now it's our best option."

Rahul scowled. "Fine. But don't say I didn't warn you."

Lucas and Willem went over to a table in the corner where Maria and Oliver were deep in conversation. "Hey," Lucas said. "Willem has a plan for getting us out of here."

Maria and Oliver stopped and turned toward him. "If you're thinking about getting into the door's circuitry, we've already tried that," Oliver said.

Willem shook his head and pointed at the ventilation duct. "Get me up there and I can open the door from the outside."

Maria considered this for a moment. "That might work," she said.

302

"Worth a try," Oliver said, peering skeptically at the air duct. "I just hope you're not claustrophobic."

"I guess I'll find out," Willem said with a bleak smile.

Oliver quickly organized the other cadets to help them, forming an unsteady human pyramid with Willem at the top. After a few aborted attempts, Willem managed to pull off the cover of the air duct and pull himself inside.

"How much do you want to bet he just runs off?" Rahul said as Willem disappeared through the tiny opening.

"Oh, stuff it," Katya said. "He wouldn't do that."

"That's funny," Rahul said. "He said the exact thing about *you*, right before you drove off and abandoned us out on the surface."

It gave Lucas some satisfaction to see how *that* shut her up, even though he fervently hoped that Rahul was wrong in this particular case.

"Is everyone ready?" he called out to the room. "As soon as Willem hits the alarm, we go."

There were a few murmurs of assent, though most of the kids just regarded him silently. They were scared, and who could blame them?

"This is going to be dangerous," he said. "But we've got some advantages. The miners are spread thin and there aren't many of them left in the base. That's our first advantage."

"Still, they have guns, and we don't," someone pointed out.

"Right, but we have the element of surprise," Lucas said. "That's our second advantage. If we do this right, we can be halfway to the bazaar before they even react."

"Any more advantages?" Britta asked. "Because I feel like we could use as many as we can get."

"One more," Lucas said, smiling thinly. "We're kids. That means they're going to underestimate us. And now we're going to show them what it means to be a naval cadet."

He looked around the room. Was it his imagination, or were they all standing a little straighter? They were still scared, but they weren't backing down, even though they knew the consequences. He didn't know how much he'd managed to encourage them, but he did know that no matter what happened, he was proud to be a part of this group of cadets.

He turned back toward the door. What was taking so long?

"Willem should have hit that alarm by now," Elena whispered. "What are we going to do if Rahul is right?"

"He'll do it," Lucas said.

A minute ticked by, and then another. Lucas's

nervousness grew. Some of the other kids started to mutter quietly to each other.

"Maybe it's time to start talking about alternative plans," Elena said.

Rahul strode over to the door and slammed it with his fist. "Willem, I swear, if you really did leave us here—"

He was interrupted by a piercing alarm. The doors slid open and the overhead lights flashed warningly. "Evacuation," a recorded voice said. "Please proceed to the nearest airlock. Evacuation."

Even though this was exactly what Lucas had been waiting for, the suddenness of it surprised him so much that he was briefly frozen in place. Maria lunged past Rahul and out into the corridor, followed by Oliver and Hanako. Elena pushed Lucas forward. "Go!"

Lucas's first thought, as his brain began to function again, was that they needed to find Willem and take care of any guards. But as he followed Maria and the other cadets out into the hallway, he found that wasn't going to be an issue. Oliver and Elena had a Belter pinned on the ground in a complicated-looking arrangement that had one arm over his windpipe and a hand over his mouth. Nearby, Willem was leaning over, breathing heavily.

"Sorry it took so long," he gasped.

"You did great," Lucas said, helping him stand upright. "Are you okay?"

Willem nodded. Elena and Oliver dragged the unconscious guard into the rec room. "He'll be out for a minute or two," Elena said, jogging back to them.

"Then let's hurry," Maria said. She led the cadets down the hallway at a quick pace, stopping briefly to look around the corner of each intersection. The alarm was still blaring, but so far there was no sign of the miners. How long would it take them to search the base and find them?

When Lucas reached the airlock, Maria, Oliver, and Elena were already passing out emergency suits. He did some quick math. With ten people at a time in the airlock, it would take five groups. It took around thirty seconds to cycle the airlock. They should all be outside in three minutes, if everything went well.

Lucas saw Rahul putting on a suit. He grabbed his arm. "The airlock we went through," he said. "It's powered now. Do you remember where it is? Follow the rover tracks and keep the crater on your left."

"I remember," Rahul said. He turned to the airlock and almost bumped into Willem, who was still putting on his suit. There was a brief moment of silence.

"Sorry," Rahul said gruffly. "I guess I should have trusted you."

Willem cocked his head to one side and gave a lopsided grin. "Hey, I don't know if *I* would have trusted me."

306

Rahul snorted a little laugh and squeezed into the air-lock with the first group of cadets. Lucas went around, helping some of the other kids with their emergency suits and ushering them into the airlock, packing them in as tightly as possible. When the last group had gone through, Maria turned to Lucas, Elena, and Oliver. "Our turn."

"Any sign of Tali?" Lucas asked.

"Not yet," Elena said.

"We're not leaving without her," Oliver said.

Maria shook her head. "We can't wait around any longer. She can take care of herself."

"We're not leaving her behind!" Oliver insisted. "I'll stay here by myself if I have to."

"I'll stay too," Lucas said.

"The rest of the cadets are waiting out there," Maria said. "They need us."

"You go," Oliver said. "Make sure they—"

He stopped suddenly as Jonah and Stockton rounded a corner at a dead run about twenty meters away. "There!" Jonah shouted, pointing at them.

Maria slapped the button to close the inner airlock door, but Jonah already had his pulse weapon leveled. There was a bright flash of light, and Oliver let out a quiet gasp. The door slid shut, and he sagged to his knees.

"Oliver!" Maria screamed, grabbing him by the

shoulders. A blackish-red dot had appeared on his chest, as if someone had jabbed him with a permanent marker. He looked up at Maria in confusion, and then he collapsed on the floor of the airlock.

20

MARIA DROPPED TO the floor and put her hand over the wound in Oliver's chest. The smell of burned flesh filled the airlock. Oliver's mouth moved as if he was trying to speak, but no sound came out.

"No, no, no," Maria moaned. "Oliver! Stay with us!"

Lucas knelt down beside them. He pushed Maria's hands away and probed the suit material with his fingers. He couldn't feel any holes or tears. Did these suits automatically reseal? There wasn't time to find out.

"They're coming!" Elena said, looking through the window in the inner door.

Lucas fastened Oliver's helmet and then pulled on his own. When everyone was ready, Maria grabbed the airlock cycle switch and jerked it downward. The pumps roared and their suits ballooned. Lucas checked quickly to make sure that Oliver's suit wasn't leaking, and then he opened the outer doors and helped Maria and Elena carry him outside and lay him down.

Stockton banged his fists on the inner airlock window and shouted inaudibly. Lucas grabbed a rock and set it down in the outer doorway, jamming the airlock open. Without an airtight seal, the airlock's fail-safes would refuse to let the inner doors open. The Belters would have to find another way out onto the surface. It wasn't much, but it would at least give them some time.

Maria grabbed him and pulled him away from the airlock. Elena was holding Oliver under the shoulders. His eyes were half open and he was breathing, but barely. Would he last long enough to get him back inside the colony?

The three of them lifted Oliver up and carried him along the trail. He was bigger than any of them, and even in the low gravity Lucas's arms soon started to feel as if they were being dragged out of their sockets. His lungs wheezed with the exertion, and beads of sweat rolled down his forehead. After a few minutes the air quality indicator in his suit faded from green to amber. He was using too much oxygen. If he'd been smart, he would have put on a fresh suit back at the naval base, but there was no helping it now. Either his air was going to last, or it wasn't.

A splitting pain built up in his head, as if someone were sawing his skull open, millimeter by millimeter. His vision went blurry. He squinted and tried to get his eyes to focus. Oliver's legs slid through his fingers, and he stumbled in one of the ruts in the trail. He collapsed hard on the ground, but the impact barely registered. All he could see was the faint red glow of the status light in his suit.

Someone picked him up under his arms and dragged him forward. He tried to open his eyes to see who it was, but everything was gray. His lungs sucked in air, but there was no oxygen left in his suit.

He was dropped unceremoniously on a smooth metal floor. The impact jolted him awake, and he sat up. A pair of hands ripped the flimsy plastic helmet off his head. Fresh air flooded over him, and he gasped.

"Oliver, can you hear me?" Maria was saying. "Breathe!"

My name isn't Oliver, Lucas was about to say, but then he remembered what had happened. He blinked his eyes and looked around. They were back in the airlock in the old colony. Oliver was lying on his back next to Lucas, with his blood-smeared emergency suit torn down to his waist. Maria was kneeling over him, pressing her hands over the wound.

Lucas stood up slowly and leaned against the wall. His lungs ached with every breath. Elena ran into the airlock carrying an armload of old Belter T-shirts from a nearby storeroom. Maria grabbed one and wadded it up to use as a bandage.

"Where's Tali?" Oliver mumbled.

"She's fine," Maria said. "Just relax and breathe."

Oliver tried to push her away. "We need to go back."

"Oliver, you have to relax," Lucas said hoarsely. "If you don't—"

"You're lying!" Oliver said, thrashing his legs wildly. "We have to help her!"

Maria tried to keep the bandage on his wound, but his agitation was making it difficult. They needed to calm him down. Lucas grabbed Elena and pulled her into the corridor. "Talk to him. Tell him Tali is okay. He'll believe you."

Elena looked at Oliver, who was still struggling on the floor. "But—"

"You have to," he insisted. "You're the one he'll listen to. If Maria can't keep pressure on that wound, he's going to die."

She closed her eyes for a moment, and then she nodded and headed back into the airlock. "Oliver, listen to me," she said, sitting down on the floor next to him. "Tali is fine."

Oliver turned his head to look at her. He looked confused for a moment, but then he relaxed a little. Quickly

Maria grabbed a second T-shirt and switched it with the first, which was already soaked with blood. "You're sure?" Oliver croaked.

Elena put her hand on his forehead. "I promise," she said, her voice tremulous. "I saw her just a minute ago. She went ahead . . . she went ahead to help the others. We all got out safe."

"Safe," he whispered. "All of us?"

Lucas knelt down next to him and held his hand. "All of us, Oliver. We did it."

Oliver's muscles went limp, and he turned his head toward Elena. His breathing was still unsteady, and it was getting slower. "That's it," Elena said, stroking his temple. "You're going to be okay. I promise."

He nodded and he closed his eyes. Maria adjusted her makeshift bandage and looked at Elena and Lucas with an anguished expression. The bleeding wasn't stopping. They were doing everything they could, and it wasn't enough.

Oliver coughed and gasped as if he was trying to say something, and then his body went rigid. Lucas held his breath, waiting for Oliver to inhale again. *Please,* he thought. *Please.*

"Breathe!" Maria begged. "Breathe, Oliver!"

But Oliver lay completely still, and Lucas knew that he wasn't resting, or sleeping, or pretending. He was dead, and nothing was going to bring him back.

Maria started to sob. Tears were already running down Elena's cheeks. Lucas closed his eyes and clutched Oliver's hand tightly, wanting more than anything in the world for his friend to squeeze back one last time.

The three of them sat with Oliver for a long time, as if they all knew that as soon as they stood up, his death would be final and irrevocable. Lucas kept his eyes down, afraid to look at Oliver's face. This was his fault. If he had had a better plan—if he'd stopped Tali from sabotaging the ship, if he had gotten the cadets out more quickly, if he had done something differently—Oliver would still be alive.

"We need to find the others," Maria said in a raspy voice.

Elena and Lucas folded Oliver's hands across his chest. They pulled the flimsy plastic emergency suit off his legs and left it in a corner of the airlock, and then the three of them carried his body down the stairs and along the hallway that led back to the storage room.

When they arrived, the other cadets were clustered in a few small groups, talking quietly. Everyone fell silent and turned toward them as they carried Oliver's body into the room. They set him down on a small pallet of boxes. Lucas found a thin white blanket on a shelf and spread it over him.

Elena grabbed Lucas and hugged him tightly, burying her face against his shoulder. Her body shook as she wept. He wrapped his arms around her and tried to think of something to say. But what could he tell her? Oliver was dead. There was nothing that was going to change that.

"I lied to him," she said, her forehead still pressed against him. "I lied to him, and he's still dead."

"Maybe it was a lie," Lucas said. "But it was the right thing to do."

"I'm going to make them pay," Elena said, wiping the tears away from her face. "They're going to regret this. I promise."

Maria jabbed her finger at Lucas. "This is your fault!"

"What are you talking about?" Rahul said. "He rescued us. If it weren't for him—"

"He's a traitor!" she shouted. "If it weren't for him, Oliver would still be alive!"

"That's not fair!" Elena said.

"Fair?" Maria snorted. "Tell Oliver what's *fair.*" She shoved Lucas hard in the chest, and he stumbled backward into a stack of plastic boxes. "When this is all over—"

Somewhere in the next room over, a door slammed shut. All the cadets froze.

"As you can see, there's nothing here," came Smythe's voice from the other room. "And now that I've indulged your curiosity, I'm going to have to ask you to leave."

"They're here," Stockton growled. "All of them. They're here somewhere."

Lucas moved quietly to the wall next to the doorway so he could hear better. Was Stockton alone? Or had he brought enough Belters to force their way in?

"The only muskrat children in the bazaar are the ones you yourself turned over to us a few hours ago," Smythe said. "Unfortunately, they seem to have run off. We're not very good babysitters, I'm afraid."

"I saw them," Stockton insisted. "They ran back here. Find them!"

"Find them yourself," Smythe replied coolly. "You may be in charge of that base, but here in the bazaar, you're just another citizen."

There was a brief moment of silence, and then Stockton grunted. "You're choosing the wrong side in this fight, friend."

"I don't usually choose sides, *friend*," Smythe said. "It's not good for business. But you're making me reconsider that position."

The door leading into the store slammed again. After a moment, Smythe's son, Jo, and his friend Mai unlocked the storeroom door and came inside. Jo looked around and folded his arms.

"Last we looked, there were two muskrats cadets in here," he said, glaring at Lucas. "Can someone please explain how we've now got an entire school?"

"These are my friends—" Lucas began.

"We know who they are," Mai said. "And those idiot miners know who they are too, which means they'll be back. With guns."

"So what happens now?" Elena asked.

"If it were up to me, we'd just turn you over," Jo said. "But this is all something for the merchants' council to decide. In a little while they'll be meeting to talk about it."

Maria stepped forward. "If you're going to be discussing what to do with us, it's only fair that we have a representative who can make our case."

"So everyone seems to think," Mai said. She sighed and nodded at Lucas. "Which is why they're inviting him to speak."

Lucas blinked in surprise. The merchants wanted *him* to speak at this council meeting?

"Lucas?" Maria asked. "Are you serious? He's just a little kid."

"Maybe," Jo said. "But he's a Belter. Which you should be glad for, because it means there's a chance the council will believe what he says."

"They shouldn't," Maria said darkly. "He's a liar and a—"

Hanako put her hand on Maria's shoulder and squeezed. "Stop."

"We'll come get all of you in thirty minutes," Mai said. She turned toward Lucas. "I suggest you spend that time coming up with an argument for why we shouldn't just turn you over."

21

LUCAS SAT AGAINST the wall with his arms folded and stared blankly at the floor in front of him. The other cadets gave him a wide berth. Once in a while one of them would glance at him, but mostly they just pretended he wasn't there. That was fine with him. He wasn't in a mood to talk to anyone right now.

Oliver was dead. This wasn't a game of capture the flag where he'd be back in sixty seconds. He was gone forever. And now it was up to Lucas to make sure that the rest of the cadets didn't end up stretched out under white sheets.

It was too much. How was he supposed to convince the merchants not to hand them right back to Stockton and the miners? What would he even say? Part of him wanted to tell everyone that this wasn't his responsibility. He was just a kid from the Belt. Some of the cadets and officers on the *Orpheus* hadn't even wanted him to be there. Why was it his job to try to save them all now?

He could hear Sanchez's voice in his head. *Because you are a leader now, whether you like it or not.* Jo was right. Belter merchants weren't going to listen to a kid from the inner planets. But maybe they would listen to Lucas—if he could figure out what to say.

Out of the corner of his eye, he saw Elena and Rahul whispering to each other and looking in his direction. After a few minutes, they came over and sat down in a little semicircle around him. Elena cleared her throat.

"So, Lucas," she said. "What exactly happened back on the *Orpheus?*"

"You told Maria you didn't know what they were planning to do," Rahul said. "But that means you knew *something.*"

Lucas had been half expecting this conversation ever since they'd gotten back to the bazaar. He took a deep breath and explained how the miners had given him the data chip. "It wasn't until later that I found out they'd given Tali an identical chip."

"So she was the one who planted it on the backup bridge?" Elena asked. "Why didn't you turn her in?"

"Because she's his sister," Rahul said.

Lucas stared at him in shock. "You knew?"

"Sure," Rahul said, waving his hand. "That wasn't too

hard to work out. The records are all public if you know what to look for. Didn't anyone else notice how they were always off talking by themselves?"

"So she's the person you were protecting," Elena said to Lucas.

Lucas nodded. "I thought I could stop her before she did any harm. I didn't expect . . . any of *this*."

"It did kind of come out of left field," Rahul agreed. "The question is, what did *she* expect? And why did she help them? Was it blackmail?"

"Or maybe she got something she wanted out of it," Elena said.

"It was a little of both," Lucas said. "She was paying off a debt. Stockton—the leader of those miners—helped her get into the Navy. But then once she was here, they started threatening to expose her."

"So she let them hijack the ship just so she wouldn't get expelled?" Elena asked.

"She didn't know what they were going to do," Lucas insisted.

"Maybe. Or maybe she's not as noble as you think she is. Isn't it kind of convenient that she disappeared when you rescued us? She could have decided that it was better to be in with the miners after all."

Rahul frowned. "Elena!"

"He's blinded by the fact that Tali is his sister," Elena

said, shrugging. "But just because someone is family doesn't mean they can't betray you."

"No," Lucas said. He could feel his temper rising. "She didn't run away, and she didn't join up with the Belters. If she didn't come back, it was because she was captured. And I'm going to find a way to rescue her."

"How?" Rahul asked. "Getting into the base through an airlock isn't going to work a second time. They'll have every entrance guarded from now on. And even if you're right, you don't have any idea where she's being kept."

"I don't know," Lucas said. "I'll think of something."

He jumped up and strode off toward the other side of the room. Maybe Elena meant well, but she was wrong. He knew his sister better than anyone else did. She'd made mistakes, and she was going to have to take responsibility for them. But he wasn't going to abandon her, no matter how many mistakes she made.

As he came around the corner of a large stack of boxes, he nearly ran into Britta coming the other way. "Oh . . . hi, Lucas," she said.

"Hi," he mumbled.

"I was kind of looking for you, actually," she said. "I wanted to thank you for coming back for all of us. It was pretty amazing, rescuing us like that."

Lucas glanced at where Oliver still lay under a white blanket. "I didn't rescue all of you."

Britta was quiet for a moment. "I already miss him . . . even though at the same time I'm expecting him to pop around the corner at any minute and tell one of his stupid jokes."

A lump formed in Lucas's throat. "Yeah," he said hoarsely.

"You know, after we won that capture-the-flag game, he talked for *days* about what a great match it was. He thought your plan was absolute genius. I think if he could, he'd tell that story all over again, right now."

"I guess," Lucas said.

"But he'd also tell you that it wasn't your fault he was killed. Because if you hadn't done what you did, the rest of us would still be locked up, and we'd have no chance at all of freeing the colony or taking back the *Orpheus*. It was heroic."

Lucas didn't feel at all like a hero. He felt like someone who had broken something priceless and was now trying to fit all the pieces back together. Except that some pieces could never be repaired.

The door to the storage room opened, revealing Smythe, Jo, and Mai, all wearing colorful Belter robes. "Follow us," Smythe said to the assembled cadets. "The council wants all of you there. Keep your mouths shut and stay in line."

Britta reached out and squeezed Lucas's hand. "You

323

can do this. You got all of us out of there. Compared to that, a bunch of Belter merchants is nothing. Right?"

She leaned toward him and kissed him lightly on the cheek, and then she jogged off toward her friends before he could react. He reached up and touched his cheek, replaying the moment in his mind. Had that really just happened? Or had it just been his imagination?

Rahul came over and grabbed his arm. "Come on, let's go," he said, pulling Lucas toward the exit. "You're the star attraction."

"Did you see that?" Lucas asked.

"See what?"

Lucas sighed. "Nothing . . . forget it."

They followed along behind the other cadets as Smythe, Jo, and Mai led them out of the warehouse and into an alley. Instead of turning toward the main boulevard that ran down the center of the bazaar, they followed a side street that curved along the edge of the dome. On one side of the street, two-story houses had been built directly against the dome so that the residents had views of the Vestan surface outside. Opposite the houses was a series of tall tenement buildings dotted with small fake-granite balconies. Men, women, and a few children stood on some of the balconies, looking down at the long line of cadets being led down the street. A young kid at a first-floor window stared openmouthed at Lucas as he passed. As soon as he saw Lucas looking back at him, he ducked down as if he was afraid.

Smythe led them into the back entrance of a large building. They followed a narrow tunnel that sloped down and then back up again before coming out into an oval-shaped amphitheater. About a quarter of the seats were filled with Belters talking quietly with each other. As soon as the cadets entered, a buzz went through the audience, and the men and women leaned forward and craned their necks to get a better view.

"It's the Janusarium," Elena whispered, looking around.

She was right, Lucas realized. He hadn't recognized it without the stylized lighting and hazy smoke. Someone had removed the mat and ring where the judo bouts had taken place, leaving a wide-open space at the center of the amphitheater. Smythe led the cadets up to an empty section of seats. Jo and Mai sat down at a control panel a few rows in front of them.

"Last time I was here, this place looked a lot different," Elena remarked.

Mai turned and glared at her. "Maybe when this is all over, we can settle that score."

"I'd be happy to," Elena said politely.

Smythe stood at the center of the floor and held up his hands. "Ladies and gentlemen," he said. He glanced at Jo, who flipped a switch on the control panel. This time, when he spoke, hidden acoustic sensors picked up his voice and amplified it through speakers in the walls.

"Ladies and gentlemen. We are here to decide what we will do with these naval cadets who, either through chance or design, have ended up in our custody—"

A tall woman in a red robe stood up in her seat. "Last I heard it was two cadets we had to worry about!" she shouted. "How'd we end up with the whole damn crew?"

"That's an excellent question," Smythe said smoothly. "One that I'm sure the cadets themselves will answer when it's time. However, we will first hear testimony from one of the miners who have occupied the Vestan naval base."

Smythe turned toward a tunnel opposite the one that the cadets had entered through. Lucas froze as he saw McKinley leaning against the wall, half hidden in shadows.

"Him," Rahul muttered.

McKinley gave a broad smile and stepped out into the light. "Hello and greetings, my fellow Belters," he said in a loud voice that barely needed any amplification. "My name is Abbott McKinley. I've made my living same as all of you, makin' eat as best I could. I've been a miner, a pilot, and an engineer, on everything from dusters to freighters."

"Don't forget bosun's mate on the *Orpheus*," Maria shouted.

McKinley's smile faltered, but only for a moment. "That's true! I can't forget that. When times got particularly hard, I took a job in the Navy, where every day I saw how the muskrats treat hardworking people like yourselves."

He waved his arms at the audience. "Some of them treated me like dirt, just like you'd expect. But what was worse was how they treated all of *you*. Time and time again I saw fine, upstanding citizens thrown in jail for the tiniest of offenses. Permits hours out of date: locked up. One measly item missing an import stamp: locked up. Men, women, and children of all types: locked up, locked up, locked up!"

"Baloney," Maria said from the row behind Lucas. "That's pure baloney."

But true or not, McKinley's words were having an effect on the Belter audience. The crowd was nodding in agreement, and people were muttering under their breath.

"We don't want to hurt anyone," McKinley said. "We took those children hostage for our protection. For *your* protection. Because when the muskrat admirals come calling, with their cruisers and destroyers, the first thing they're going to want to do is bomb this whole place until it's nothing more than a black hole in space. If we have those cadets, we can negotiate. We can convince Earth that all the Free State of Vesta wants is to be left in peace."

McKinley looked around at the audience. "I want what you want, friends. I want your safety. And that's why I need you to turn over those cadets."

He bowed deeply. There were cheers and scattered clapping from the audience. Smythe stood up and raised his arms. "Before we decide, we're going to hear from one of the naval cadets."

Smythe nodded at Lucas. Elena squeezed his shoulder. "Good luck," she whispered.

Lucas walked to the center of the arena floor. Everyone in the amphitheater was looking at him expectantly. He wiped his palms on his uniform jacket and took a deep breath to try to slow his racing heartbeat. How was he supposed to do this? He was barely comfortable talking to a few people at once, and now he was here in front of a hundred. And he still hadn't even figured out what he was going to say.

You can't persuade someone if you don't know how they see things, Sanchez had told him. He looked around at the colonists. He'd grown up with these people. He recognized more than a few of them. If anyone in the Navy understood their perspective, it was him.

Then you make them understand what you need them to understand. That was the hard part. But he'd started out where they were now, hadn't he? Being on the *Orpheus* had taught him a lot. And now his job was to somehow distill two months of experience into a two-minute speech.

"Hello," he said, and cleared his throat. His voice, amplified through the speakers, echoed around the room. "My name is Lucas Adebayo. I'm a Belter, like all of you. I can run an ore loader. For three years in a row, I spent a month here learning to code at Magus Finney's camp. My favorite flavor of ice treat at Roja's is indigo dream."

"Bollocks," a woman called. "Cherry incarnate is far superior."

The crowd laughed, and Lucas relaxed a little. "But I'm *also* a Navy cadet. I joined up just a couple of months ago. I've seen the way they do things. I've watched intercepts and investigations."

"Ambushes, more like it!" someone shouted.

"Yes," Lucas said, nodding as if the woman had just agreed with him. "Not everything I saw was fair. But the people I worked with were all good people, trying to do a job that they thought was right."

The crowd muttered and he raised his hands, palms upward. "Something has to change! Something is broken. I know why McKinley and his miners did what they did. But this isn't the right way to do it. Fighting isn't the answer.

"The Navy doesn't understand Belters. But when

someone doesn't understand you, do you punch them in the face? Or do you talk to them?"

Lucas looked around the room. There were a few nods of agreement, but they were outnumbered by the skeptical expressions. On the other hand, at least nobody was shouting at him.

"Ever since I joined up as a cadet, everyone has seemed to want me to choose: am I a Belter kid or a Navy cadet? But that whole *question* is wrong. As soon as you believe you have to be on one side or another, then you've already cut yourself off. The entire reason for this fight is because all everyone sees are divisions and separations and differences.

"Well, I'm Navy, and I'm Belter. I'm both. I'm not giving up on either one."

Lucas paused. The crowd was listening intently. His words were having some effect—but would it be enough? He took a deep breath and tried to keep his momentum going.

"I'm not asking you to like the Navy. Maybe it's hard for you to trust them right now. But I'm asking you to work with them. Figure out a solution that doesn't involve hurting people, and say no to people who tell you that the only way to fix problems is with violence. Because—"

"This meeting is over!" a voice shouted. Lucas turned

and saw Stockton standing in front of the tunnel on the other side of the amphitheater floor, pointing a mining laser up into the air. "We're taking the kids."

He waved his hand, and a dozen miners with weapons appeared at the top level of the amphitheater. They moved carefully down the steps, swiveling their weapons around as if they were afraid of being attacked at any moment. The audience muttered in anger.

"Stockton, you idiot," McKinley said. "I told you to wait!"

"I'm done waiting," Stockton snarled. "We tried it your way. Now we're taking the kids, like we should have done from the start."

Instinctively, Lucas backed up until he was standing next to the control panel. Stockton waved his weapon at Lucas. "Don't move. Or come to think of it, please *do* move. It'd be a pleasure to blast that smirk off your face, just like I did with that little—"

Before he could finish, Maria howled in fury and leaped down from her seat to the amphitheater floor. Startled, Stockton turned toward her, but Maria crossed the distance between them before he could fire. She bent her shoulder and tackled him at waist level, driving him to the floor.

All at once, the cadets from the *Orpheus* jumped to

their feet and surged after Maria. Rahul vaulted toward the miners, screaming at the top of his lungs, with Elena right behind him.

For a moment the Belters didn't seem to understand what was going on. A few of them raised their weapons, but before they could fire, four enormous pillars of smoke burst out from the floor, swallowing both the miners and the cadets. A moment later, the entire amphitheater went dark except for the faint yellow glow of emergency lamps on the stairs. Lucas looked around in confusion and saw Mai and Jo bent over the control board, flipping switches rapidly.

"Get them!" Stockton screamed. Mining lasers flashed in the haze, and someone cried out in pain. Through the swirling smoke, Lucas caught a glimpse of Stockton pulling away from Maria and struggling to his feet. Lucas rushed at him and grabbed his arm as he raised his laser to fire. Stockton slugged Lucas in the gut with his free hand, but Lucas kept his grip on his arm. Maria grabbed at the weapon and twisted it away from Stockton. In response, Stockton kicked savagely at Maria's knee. She cried out in pain and collapsed on the ground.

Stockton backpedaled and collided with Mai at the control panel. He wrapped his arm around her waist and lifted her up like a sack of potatoes. Jo grabbed his other arm, but Stockton swatted him away. Ignoring Mai's kicks and screams, Stockton staggered off into the tunnel that the cadets had come through.

Lucas knelt down by Maria. She grimaced in pain and clutched her knee with one hand. With the other, she pressed Stockton's mining laser into Lucas's hand. "I'm fine," she gasped. "Get him!"

Lucas sprinted into the tunnel. The emergency lights on the walls were dim, leaving giant pools of blackness everywhere. He looked around, certain that at any moment Stockton was going to spring out from the darkness to attack him. But there was no sign of either Stockton or Mai.

He heard a muffled cry from up ahead and saw a flicker of movement at the top of a long concrete ramp. Lucas vaulted over a railing onto the ramp and ran upward. He reached the top just in time to see Stockton disappear through a door at the other end of a narrow hall. He raced down the corridor and skidded to a halt in the doorway.

Stockton was standing on a long catwalk suspended over an enormous storage room. On the floor, ten meters below, old rovers and other bits of machinery had been jammed together and covered with tarps. The only light came from a dusty, flickering light bar in the ceiling. Stockton turned and held Mai in front of him, brandishing a knife in his free hand.

Lucas raised his arm and pointed the laser at Stockton. "Let her go."

Stockton snorted. "You don't have the guts to shoot me."

"Let her go," Lucas repeated, "and you can walk out of here."

"Ten to one you hit her instead," Stockton said, lifting the girl up a little higher and pressing the knife against her throat.

Lucas looked levelly back at him. "Try to run, and we'll find out."

Stockton's eyes narrowed. "I should have killed you when I had the chance," he growled.

In reply, Lucas held the mining laser a little higher, his hands trembling only slightly.

"You want the kid?" Stockton asked. "Take her!"

With a grunt, Stockton lifted Mai up over the side of the catwalk. For a moment, the girl was suspended, kicking and flailing her arms. Then, with one last sneering look, Stockton dropped her over the side.

22

"NO!" LUCAS SHOUTED.

Time seemed to stop. For a moment Mai was suspended in midair, an astonished look on her face. She thrashed her legs and reached out for the catwalk railing, missing it by centimeters. With a wordless cry, she disappeared into the shadows.

Stockton turned and sprinted away down the catwalk. Lucas leaped forward, covering the distance to where Mai had fallen in three giant steps. He bent over the railing and squinted at the darkness.

Mai was hanging by one hand from a horizontal support that ran along the bottom of the catwalk. She looked up at Lucas with a terrified expression. Lucas gave Stockton one last look, and then shoved the pulse weapon into his belt.

"Hold on!" he called.

"Help me!" Mai gasped. "My hand is slipping!"

Lucas lay on his stomach and reached down. He wrapped the fingers of one hand around her wrist and reached down with the other. "It's okay. I've got you. Grab my hand."

Mai reached up with her free hand but couldn't get it high enough. She grunted and tried again. The effort made her fingers slip free from the catwalk, and Lucas had to grab her wrist with both hands.

Lucas clenched his jaw and held on as tightly as he could. "One more time!" he said. "I need both your hands to pull you up!"

Mai swung herself upward, and Lucas managed to snag her free hand. His hands were sweaty and he could feel his grip already starting to give way. He pulled her up a few centimeters at a time. When Mai's head and shoulders were above the catwalk floor, Lucas heaved with all of his strength. Her legs scrabbled against the corrugated metal for a moment, and then she collapsed on the catwalk floor, panting for air.

Lucas pushed himself to his feet and helped her up. "Thank you," she gasped.

"You were the one who activated the smoke, weren't you?" Lucas asked.

"Didn't seem fair, a bunch of grown-ups with weapons. I figured that might even it out a bit."

"Well, I guess now we're even," Lucas said, grinning. "Come on. Let's see if anyone needs our help."

As it turned out, the cadets and merchants had everything well in hand by the time Lucas and Mai arrived back at the Janusarium. The lights had been turned on, and only a few wispy clouds of smoke hung in the air. Five surly looking miners sat in the center of the amphitheater floor, with a group of the older cadets standing guard. Only five, Lucas realized, which meant that most of the miners had escaped with Stockton. Elena, standing with Britta near a small crowd of cadets and merchants, waved at Lucas as he entered. He jogged over to her and saw Rahul and another cadet being lifted up onto floating stretchers.

"Are they okay?" Lucas asked, craning his neck to see better. "What happened?"

Rahul was holding a blood-soaked T-shirt against his arm. The other boy—Samir, Lucas saw—had his eyes closed, and his leg was heavily bandaged. A man was holding a bag of clear fluid over his head. A thin tube led from the bag to the skin under the bandages.

"They both took a blast at short range," Elena said. "Rahul's was a near miss, but Samir took it bad."

"We've got them now," the man with the bag said. He was wearing a shiny vest marked with a large red cross over his Vestan robes. "Just have to move them over to the clinic."

When he saw Lucas, Rahul sat up. "Did you see?" he asked. "Wasn't it awesome?" Another paramedic pushed him gently back down onto the stretcher, and they lifted him up the steps toward the exit. Rahul leaned out to one side of the stretcher and waved at Lucas. "It was awesome," he called.

"He's been talking nonstop like that," Britta said. "I think if he hadn't been hurt, he'd actually be disappointed."

"It was just a little second-degree burn," Elena said. "There's nothing heroic about getting hurt."

"Well, don't tell him that," Britta said. "And he *was* one of the first ones out of his seat."

"I still can't believe that everyone charged at the miners like that," Lucas said. "One second they were standing here waving their weapons around, and the next they're getting swarmed by cadets."

"Speaking of which, where were you during all of this?" Elena asked Lucas. "I don't remember seeing you in the fight."

"I was—"

"There's no shame in hiding," she interrupted in a teasing voice. "You were quite the target, standing out there. I suppose not all of us can be heroes."

338

Lucas was opening his mouth to respond when Garth pushed his way through the crowd of cadets, followed close behind by Mai. "This is him, Dad," Mai said.

Garth grabbed Lucas's hand and pumped it up and down like a piston engine. "I can't tell you how grateful I am for rescuing my daughter from that lunatic. You have my full support, no questions asked. Anything I can do, just say the word, understand?"

"Sure," Lucas said. "Of course. Thanks."

"Thank you, sir." Garth let go of Lucas's hand and turned to Britta and Elena. "You should be proud—your friend is quite the hero."

"Hero?" Elena repeated, dumbfounded.

Garth grinned and gave her a broad wink. "Next time you're downstation, we should have a friendly spar."

As Garth led Mai back into one of the tunnels, Lucas gave a long, dramatic stretch of his arms. "Like you said—not all of us can be heroes."

"Whatever," Elena grumbled, crossing her arms over her chest. "Just don't let it go to your head."

"What happened to McKinley?" Lucas asked, looking around. "Did he get away?"

"Smythe and some of the other merchants took him that way," Britta said, pointing at a set of stairs that led between two sections of the amphitheater. "They seemed pretty angry."

"Come on," Lucas said, dragging Elena away from the other cadets. "I need to ask him some questions. And I may need your help."

He ran up the steps to the very top of the stadium. Behind the last row of seats was a darkened grandstand area with a row of empty concession stands. A thin line of light was visible underneath a door in the back wall marked EMPLOYEES ONLY. Lucas opened the door and stuck his head through. Inside was a small office with a square table and a grimy desk covered with flyers and boxes. A pair of dusty boxing gloves hung from a hook next to a picture of a young man holding an enormous gold belt. In the far corner of the room, McKinley sat on a folding metal chair with a tired expression on his face. Smythe leaned against the wall next to the door with his arms folded.

"Hey, kid," Smythe said. "What do you need?"

"Lucas," McKinley said eagerly, leaning forward. "Maybe you'd be so kind as to explain to this gentleman how none of this was my fault."

Elena pushed past Lucas. "Not your fault? Of course it's—"

"Hold on," Lucas said, putting his hand on Elena's shoulder. "I want to hear this."

McKinley leaned back and spread his hands wide. "Sure, I went along with their plans. Didn't have much choice, did I? Would have gotten my throat slit and my body tossed out the airlock if I didn't."

He pulled his finger across his neck dramatically. "It was all Stockton and Willis. The whole thing. They're the real scoundrels. Right, Lucas? Tell them."

"They couldn't have taken over the *Orpheus* without your help," Elena countered.

"Probably not," McKinley said. He raised his eyebrow and looked at Lucas. "But I wasn't the only one. Stockton and Willis needed someone with access to the bridge."

"You mean the girl?" Smythe asked. "Tali?"

"She didn't know what she was doing," Lucas protested. "And you blackmailed her!"

"I wouldn't call it blackmail," McKinley said mildly. "Just an agreement. Quid pro quo."

"Where is she now?" Lucas asked. "Locked up in the naval base?"

McKinley laughed. "Locked up? No, sir. Willis and Stockton offered her a deal. A spot on their crew, so to speak. She's going to help them fly the *Orpheus*."

Lucas blinked in surprise. Tali helping them? After everything that had happened? It wasn't possible. "You're lying!"

"Why would I lie?" McKinley asked, holding out his hands. "It doesn't buy me anything."

"If she's up on the *Orpheus*, then she's a hostage or a

prisoner," Lucas insisted, turning to Elena. "Just like the officers. We have to rescue them and take back the ship."

"Well, maybe I can help you out with that," McKinley said breezily. "Give me a ship and I'll fly you right up to the *Orpheus*. Stockton and Willis will let me dock, no questions asked. Of course, rehijacking your hijacked ship will be your problem, not mine."

"And what do you get out of that deal?" Elena asked. "Because I don't get the impression you're going to do it out of the goodness of your heart."

McKinley smiled. "Well, certainly, miss, I'd expect to be compensated for my trouble. Meaning that after I get you to the *Orpheus*, you let me go my own way."

"Go free?" Elena said with a snort. "After everything you've done?"

"It's up to you. You can have me, or the *Orpheus*. Can't have both, I'm afraid."

There was a moment of silence. "It's a deal," a voice said from behind them.

Everyone turned to see Maria, who was standing in the doorway with her arms folded. Her face was tight with fury. "If you help us get our ship back, you can go. Though I can't promise we won't be chasing after you as soon as we get things settled here."

"I'll take my chances there," McKinley said. "The solar system is a big place."

"So what's the plan?" Elena asked. "Fly up there, board the ship. Then what?"

"Then we fight to get it back," Maria said. "Free the officers, take over the bridge. It's a big ship, and they'll be spread thin."

"It's going to be dangerous," Elena pointed out. "We can't force cadets to come."

Maria shook her head. "Volunteers only. But after what I just saw in that fight out there, I don't think that will be a problem."

Maria was right—once she presented her plan to the other cadets, virtually every one of them volunteered to go. The stirring speech she gave while standing on the floor of the Janusarium, with wisps of smoke still floating around her, certainly didn't hurt. Thinking back to his own attempts to instill confidence when they were locked up in the rec room, Lucas decided that there was clearly still a lot for him to learn about leadership.

The miners had raided or stolen almost every ship on Vesta to supplement their fleet, and the only ship left in the hangar that was big enough to carry everyone was an old ore hauler. Hanako and some of the cadets with engineering training worked to make sure the ship was ready to fly, while the others collected enough working suits for all the cadets. When they were nearly finished, McKinley grabbed Lucas and pulled him aside.

"Are you really sure you want to go through with this?" he asked in a low voice. "Think about what you're risking your neck for. Is it really worth all this to take back a Navy ship?"

"It's *my* ship," Lucas said. "It's my fault it was hijacked in the first place. And even if I didn't care about any of that, my sister is still on board."

"Your sister," McKinley said, and sighed. "You might not want to get your hopes up about that."

In response, Lucas just stared at him silently.

"All right," McKinley said, holding up his hands. "Just be careful. Stockton is dangerous. Willis and Jonah and the others are only fighting because they want independence. Stockton *wants* a war, and he'll do anything to start one."

Lucas nodded. "Thanks."

As he headed back to the other cadets, Elena cocked her head to one side. "What was that about?"

Lucas looked back at McKinley. "I'll tell you later. Are we all ready?"

"Almost!" Rahul said, jogging up to them. "Just need to put on a suit."

"Are you kidding me?" Elena said. "You should be in medbay."

"I'm totally fine!" In demonstration, he flexed his right

344

arm, which was wrapped in a gauzy white bandage. He winced. "Well . . . almost fine."

"Rahul, this is idiotic," Elena said.

"I'm not missing out on this," he insisted. "Don't even try to stop me."

Maria ushered them into the cargo hold of the ship along with all the other cadets, ignoring Elena's protests that Rahul should stay behind. "We need anyone who can move," she said, sliding the doors closed.

They found a spot near the back wall and sat down. The light bars in the ceiling turned off, leaving them in darkness except for the glow of their helmet lights.

"What do you think our chances of pulling this off are?" Willem asked.

"I'd guess one in ten," Elena said.

"That's reassuring," Willem said, leaning his head back. "I was beginning to think this was a bad idea."

23

"*ORPHEUS*, **THIS IS** Abbott McKinley. Requesting permission to land."

McKinley's voice, scratchy and far-off, came in through a speaker somewhere in the ceiling of the cargo hold. Lucas, floating gently against his harness, looked upward and listened carefully.

"Abbott? What happened to you?" Stockton asked over the radio link.

"Took me a little while to get away from the brats. My thanks for leaving me a ship. Now, can you please open the hangar doors?"

"Don't thank me," Stockton replied. "If we'd had more time we would have taken all of them."

"They don't trust him," Rahul whispered.

"I don't blame them," Elena said.

"You're welcome to join the fleet," Stockton went on.

"Until we get some reinforcements, everything but the flagship is on autopilot. But I'm afraid I'm going to have to decline your request to board the *Liberty*. Especially since you can't seem to remember that it isn't a Navy ship anymore."

Lucas winced. "Come on, McKinley, don't screw it up," Rahul muttered.

"I just need to meet with you for a few—"

"By all means, keep coming closer," Stockton interrupted. "In a few minutes we'll have control of our weapon systems, and we'll need something to test them on. I'll leave it entirely up to you. *Liberty* out."

McKinley held his course for a few more seconds and then slowed down, forcing the cadets to grab on to whatever they could to keep from drifting into the wall. The cargo bay doors opened up, revealing the gray surface of Vesta and a bright swath of stars. The glowing circle of the bazaar dome was already far off, barely visible at the edge of the horizon. The *Orpheus* itself was at least a kilometer away, possibly more, with a dozen ships spread out around her in a broad cluster.

"Looks like this is as close as I can get you," McKinley said from the cockpit.

"How are we supposed to get there?" Katya asked.

"We'll have to fly," Maria said. "Everyone remember their thruster-belt training?"

Rahul groaned. "I was worried you were going to say that."

"They'll see us coming if we try to do it in one jump. We'll have to make three separate hops." With her finger, Maria traced an imaginary line that connected two of the closer ships and ended with the *Orpheus*. "Buddy up with your bunkroom and stay in formation with the flight leaders I assigned. Once we get there, each team will carry out its part of the plan. Transponders off and short-range comms only. Any questions?"

The cadets gathered into twelve groups, one for each bunkroom. Maria pushed off from the cargo hold and led a ragged formation of the older kids toward a nearby mining skiff. Everyone else watched silently as the first wave landed on the hull of the Belter ship and then flew off on the next hop.

"Second group, with me," Hanako said, and led another dozen kids along the same path as Maria.

Lucas watched the *Orpheus*, glittering a beautiful pearly white against the blackness of space. How many miners would be on board? Were he and Maria leading everyone into a trap?

"When we get there, I'm going after Tali," he told Elena and Rahul.

"That's not the plan," Elena objected. "Maria said—"

"I know what Maria said. But she's my sister. I have to find her."

"Do you even know where she'll be?" Elena asked. "What if she's on the bridge, helping them?"

"I guess I'll worry about that when the time comes," Lucas said.

"Wait—Tali is your sister?" Katya asked.

Lucas nodded, and Willem gave a low whistle. "Well, that complicates things, doesn't it?"

The third group took off, led by a delta-section second-year. Lucas looked around at the remaining first-year cadets. "All right—stick close to me. The tighter the formation, the less chance we'll be seen."

He pushed off as hard as he could and used a few pulses of thrust from his belt to straighten out his course. The cockpit of the closest mining ship was dark and empty. Apparently Stockton had been telling the truth when he'd said the fleet was on autopilot. Lucas braced himself and landed on the hull near the engine cowling. A few seconds later, the rest of the first-year kids arrived. It was nicely done, he thought with some pride—especially since most of them had barely seen space until a few months ago.

Rahul was the last one to arrive. His face was pale, though there was a glint of determination in his eyes that

Lucas had never seen before. "You okay?" he asked.

"No," Rahul said hoarsely. "Not even a little bit. But I'll make it."

Lucas gave them all a moment to rest, and then he led them on the next hop. This one was longer, and it gave him more time to study the *Orpheus* and the little Belter flotilla. Did Stockton really think that one hijacked cruiser and a bunch of ore haulers would be much protection once the Navy got here? It seemed stupid and suicidal—which worried Lucas, since Stockton was neither of those. Did he have some other plan in mind?

As soon as he landed on the next ship, Elena grabbed him by the arm. "Where are Rahul and Willem?"

Lucas looked around. She was right—everyone was present except for the two of them. His mind had been so wrapped up with Stockton that he'd forgotten to keep an eye on all the cadets in his group. He scanned the sky frantically. Where could they be?

"Can we radio them?" one of the delta-section kids asked.

Katya scrunched up her face. "Didn't Maria say short-range transmissions only?"

Lucas looked out anxiously at the deep black field of stars. Katya was right. Anything other than the close-proximity comms they were using now might get picked up by the *Orpheus*. But they couldn't leave Rahul

350

and Willem out there by themselves. What if something had happened to them?

Five minutes, he decided. If there was no sign of them in five minutes, he would have to use the radio. Maria would be furious, but he wasn't going to abandon his friends, even if it meant risking their mission.

"We shouldn't have let him come," Elena muttered.

Maybe she was right, Lucas thought. Maybe he should have refused to let Rahul join the mission. Some leader he was turning out to be. It had barely been twenty minutes, and he'd already lost two of his team.

"There!" Aaron said, pointing.

Everyone turned toward the spot he was indicating. For a moment Lucas thought Aaron was wrong—there was nothing there that he could see. Then a tiny point of light that he'd been sure was just a star shifted slightly, accompanied by the telltale blue burst of a thruster pack.

"It's them!" Katya said excitedly.

Lucas shielded his eyes from the sun and squinted at the tiny light, which slowly grew bigger and bigger until it resolved into two small suited figures. Relieved, Lucas moved everyone out of the way to give Rahul and Willem a place to land. He had a million questions, but right now the only thing that mattered was that they were safe.

As soon as they touched down, Elena grabbed Rahul. "Are you okay?"

"I'm fine," Rahul gasped. "I got off course. Willem came after me."

"But then we lost our bearings," Willem added. "Had no idea which ship to go toward. Rahul finally figured it out. Pretty brilliant."

"Never would have gotten back without him," Rahul said, still catching his breath. "Once we started moving, I could barely tell up from down."

The two of them weren't scared, Lucas realized. They were excited—almost triumphant. He and Elena exchanged a look, and he could see that she was thinking the same thing: anyone who didn't know the two of them would have thought they were best friends. Apparently Sanchez was right—some things could change, even in the Navy.

The last hop was the longest of all. Lucas kept a close eye on Rahul, insisting to himself that whatever happened he wasn't going to lose anyone again. But this time Rahul kept on course and had no trouble staying with the others—helped, perhaps, by Willem, who stayed within a few meters of him the entire time.

They finally reached the *Orpheus* and joined Maria and the others near the engineering bay. As soon as she'd verified that everyone had arrived, Maria repeated the plan she'd gone over with them down on Vesta.

"Hanako's going to enter through the emergency

access hatch on deck seven. Lucas, take a small group to the brig so we know what we're dealing with. The rest of you, come with me through the hangar. The interference from the hull will make suit radios spotty, and we can't use the intercom system, so each group will be on their own. Got it?"

Everyone nodded. Lucas looked around at the determined expressions on the cadets' faces. Were they all as brave as they looked? Or did they just know that there was no backing out? Maybe there wasn't much difference. Maybe that's all bravery was—committing yourself to something that you knew might end badly. Whichever it was, though, the miners on the *Orpheus* were about to get a rude surprise.

He tapped Elena and Rahul on the shoulders and led them toward the waist airlock. This was the most obvious entry point on the ship, which was why the plan involved them waiting until the other teams had drawn attention to themselves. Rahul crouched down and opened the airlock control panel.

"Can you open it without alerting the bridge?" Lucas asked, remembering how Rahul had disabled the alarm on their trip outside in the middle of the night.

Rahul nodded as he poked through a mess of multicolored wires. "When I jimmied it that night we came out onto the hull, I left a way back in, just in case. It's standard procedure for situations like this."

"Have you ever *been* in a situation like this?" Elena asked.

"Well, no," Rahul admitted. "But you have to admit, it paid off."

He found a diagnostic switch deep inside the panel and flipped it on and off rhythmically. After a moment, the airlock doors slid open. "Voilà," Rahul said, waving his hand dramatically.

A tremor ran through the hull. "Maria just blew open the engineering airlock," Lucas guessed. "That's our signal."

They cycled the airlock and opened the inner doors quietly. From the back of the ship came more shouts and the distinctive ping of mining lasers. So far, though, it appeared that Maria's group was the only one that had been found—which meant maybe the others had a chance of accomplishing their missions.

He tapped on a wall screen and brought up a schematic of the ship. They wouldn't be able to use the main corridors to move, which meant finding a way through the ventilation system. . . .

There was a sudden burst of movement, followed by a thud and an unpleasant-sounding grunt. Lucas turned and saw Elena in the prep room holding Jonah with her arm around his neck and her hand over his mouth. A few droplets of blood welled up from a cut on Elena's temple and floated away.

"Help me get him tied up before—"

Suddenly Jonah jerked out of Elena's grasp. "Help!" he shouted, reaching for a mining laser that was clamped to the wall. "Muskrats!"

He didn't get any further. Elena swung her knee into Jonah's gut and slammed him against the floor. She and Rahul held him down while Lucas used suit-repair tape to gag him and tie his ankles and wrists. Elena let him go and grabbed the mining laser off the wall.

"I ought to just shoot you," she said, in a voice that was terrifyingly matter-of-fact. In response, Jonah's eyes went wide and he mumbled something inaudible through his gag.

"Elena, don't," Lucas said. He reached toward her, but she pushed him away.

"It's what he deserves," Elena insisted. "He killed Oliver."

"I know. But hurting him isn't going to help anything."

Elena held the laser against Jonah's chest. Her hand was trembling. "This is where you shot him," she said. "Do you remember? He was just a kid."

Jonah quivered with fear as she pressed the muzzle

355

of the laser harder and harder against his chest. "Oliver didn't deserve to die. He wasn't like you. He wasn't a killer."

Abruptly she threw the mining laser into the airlock and mashed the button with her fist. The doors closed and the airlock vented, blasting the laser out into space.

"You're lucky I'm not, either," she said hoarsely.

Lucas breathed a sigh of relief and put his hand gently on Elena's shoulder. In response she pursed her lips and nodded without meeting his eye.

"We have to hurry," Rahul said.

Lucas turned and pointed at a ventilation shaft in the ceiling of the hallway. "That way."

He led them through a series of air shafts down toward the brig on deck nineteen. The ductwork was narrow, and he had to pull himself forward using the palms of his hands. It was true, more or less, that Belters didn't get claustrophobic—at least not the ones who survived. Lucas hoped the same was true for his friends.

As soon as they reached the air shaft for deck nineteen, they heard voices arguing. Lucas, Elena, and Rahul crammed themselves in around a small ventilation grate. Directly below him, two guards were talking on radios and watching security videos on a wall screen. The brig itself was a few meters away. Through the barred doors,

356

Lucas could see a dozen officers watching the guards and the security feeds.

"The air shafts for the brig are separate," Elena whispered. "We can't get them out that way."

Rahul nodded. "I don't see Sanchez. Where is she?"

Lucas pulled a small flashlight out of his pocket. He shielded it as best he could from the guards below him and clicked it on and off a few times. *Come on*, he thought. *Pay attention.*

After a dozen flashes, Randall Clarke glanced up at the air grate. His eyes went wide. Carefully he leaned toward Novak and whispered something in her ear. Her eyes flicked toward the cadets for a fraction of an instant and then back down at the guards. Carefully she and Randall went around to the other officers and talked quietly with each of them.

Novak cleared her throat and turned toward Randall. "So from what we understand, most of the miners are in engineering or on the bridge. Is that right?"

"Apart from the ones guarding us here, yes," Randall replied.

"But none on deck twelve?"

"That's right. None on deck twelve."

"Hey!" shouted one of the guards. "Quiet in there!"

"What's on deck twelve?" Rahul whispered.

Lucas tried to visualize the layout of the ship, but everything was a jumbled blur. "I can't remember."

"Well, whatever it is, that's where they want us to go," Elena said. "Come on."

She led them forward, past the brig, until the vent dead-ended at one of the circular hallways that went around the outside of this part of the ship. She peered through a grate to make sure there was nobody around, and then she opened it carefully and floated down into the hallway. They found a cross-passage that led to the Park Place ladderway. Elena checked to make sure there was nobody above or below who might see them, then started downward.

"I'm not coming," Lucas said. "I'm going to find Tali."

Elena paused and looked back at him. After a moment she nodded.

"Good luck," Rahul said. "And be careful."

He nodded and moved quickly up the ladder toward the front of the ship. He was terrified that at any moment some miner with a laser might come around a corner and see him, but the officers seemed to be right—there weren't enough Belters to man anything but the most essential parts of the ship. The corridors and accessways were unnervingly quiet.

When he reached the Broadway ladder, he stopped. At the far end, through the hatch that led to the bridge, he could see Stockton. The Belter was floating with his arms crossed in an expression of frustration. His voice echoed down the ladderway.

"It can't be that hard. You told me you'd flown ships this size before!"

Stockton moved away from the hatch, pointing angrily at something Lucas couldn't see. Lucas raced up the ladderway as quickly as he could. Just as he reached alpha section's deck, a shadow appeared in the bridge hatchway. Lucas darted off the ladder and pressed himself against a bulkhead. His heart hammered. He was certain that at any moment, Stockton was going to come down the ladder and see him.

He counted ten slow breaths. Above him, he heard the miners arguing. The longer he waited, the more likely it was that he would be caught. He raced toward the fourth-year bunkroom, opened the door, and slipped inside.

Tali, floating near the window with her arms folded, turned toward him in surprise. "Lucas?"

"Shh!" Lucas whispered.

"What are you *doing* here?" she said. "Are you crazy? You're going to get yourself killed!"

"I'm here to rescue you," Lucas said. "Hurry. We need to go."

She gave a harsh, bitter laugh. "Rescue me? So that the Navy can put me in prison for the rest of my life? The deal Stockton offered me is better than *that*."

So McKinley was right—Tali wasn't a hostage or a prisoner. She'd agreed to help them. Lucas sagged back against the wall, feeling as if she'd just punched him in the gut.

Seeing his expression, Tali shook her head. "Don't look like that. I haven't made a decision yet."

"How can you even think about trusting him, after everything that's happened?"

"I don't trust him," she said. "Not even a little. But I can't let anyone else get hurt, Lucas. Stockton says that they'll let everyone else go if I help them fly the ship."

"Do you really believe him? Tali, they didn't hijack a Navy cruiser just to fly around in circles. They killed Oliver—did you know that?"

"Oliver is dead?" Tali said. Her face darkened.

Lucas nodded. Unbidden, the image of Oliver dying on the floor of the airlock appeared in his mind, so real it felt as if it was happening all over again. Grief and guilt and anger welled up inside him. "We have to do something about it. We can't just—"

"There is no *we*, Lucas," Tali said. "No matter what happens, I'm not a part of the Navy anymore. They don't just forgive stuff like this."

"You don't know that," he insisted. "Do the right thing. Help us take back the ship."

She looked down at the floor. From the back of the ship they could hear voices shouting and the clang of a bulkhead door being slammed shut.

"They really killed Oliver?"

Lucas nodded. Her lip trembled for a moment, but he couldn't tell if it was from anger or grief or both.

"Then let's find Stockton and—"

The door slid open. Stockton, floating just outside the bunkroom with a mining laser in his hand, grinned at them.

"No need to find me, girl. I'm right here."

24

TALI PUSHED HERSELF in front of Lucas. She squared her shoulders and glared defiantly at Stockton. "Let him go! He's not a part of this."

Stockton grunted. "He most certainly is. A bigger and bigger part, I'm beginning to realize."

Lucas looked around for some sort of weapon he could use. What would Elena do? Maybe if he could disarm Stockton, then he and Tali could—

"But I think he's worth more to me alive than dead, at least for the moment. Up to the bridge, both of you." When he saw Lucas's hesitation, Stockton aimed the laser directly at his chest. "Or we can end this now now. Honestly, I'm fine either way."

Tali put her hand on Lucas's arm. "Come on," she said quietly.

He followed her up to the bridge, with Stockton so

close behind him he could smell the Belter's breath. Willis was bent over the pilot's station, apparently still trying to work out some of the details of the ship's operation. Captain Sanchez was at the back of the bridge, watching him with a grim expression. Her hands were tied at the wrists, and her leg was burned from a close-range blast from a mining laser.

"Now, Ms. Sanchez," Stockton said smoothly. "You were saying something about how you aren't going to unlock the weapon systems for this ship, even if I were to kill every one of your officers?"

He waved his laser at Lucas. "So instead, I'll start with this brat. Believe me, I'm positively giddy about the prospect of blasting a hole in his skull, so please don't think I'm bluffing."

Sanchez's eyes met Lucas's. He could see the anguish on her face. But the weapon systems of the *Orpheus* were far too dangerous to turn over to the Belters. There was no way she could agree to their demands.

Out of the corner of his eye, Lucas saw a small light flash on the captain's console. Something clicked in his mind, and he realized what Randall and the other officers had been trying to tell them. Now he had to find a way to make Sanchez understand without giving everything away to Stockton.

"If I persuade the others to surrender, do you promise

not to hurt anyone?" Lucas asked.

"Of course," Stockton said, spreading his arms wide. "Violence is always a last resort."

Lucas tapped the intercom button on the captain's console and cleared his throat. "Attention—this is Lucas Adebayo on the bridge, with a message for all the cadets in engineering, the hangar, and deck twelve. To ensure nobody gets hurt, please stand down and get to a safe location. Repeat, to all cadets in engineering, the hangar, and deck twelve: stand down and get to a safe location."

Lucas saw Sanchez's eyes widen a fraction of a centimeter. He glanced at Tali, but her face was impassive. Had Elena, Maria, and the other cadets heard what he was trying to tell them?

"All right, Ms. Sanchez," Stockton said, aiming his laser at Lucas. "Turn over the weapon systems. You've got ten seconds."

"You win," Sanchez said. "The unlock code is G, nine, H, A, eight, one."

Lucas held his breath as Willis typed the command into the captain's console. As soon as she hit the final key, the overhead lights dimmed and turned red. Lucas smacked the intercom button.

"Elena, now!" Lucas shouted. "Full emergency power!"

For a brief, terrifying moment, nothing happened. Had his friends not understood? If they weren't ready, then he'd just given them away for nothing.

Then, with a deafening roar, the *Orpheus*'s main engines ran all the way up to their maximum thrust. Even though he'd known it was coming, the force of the acceleration still caught Lucas off guard. He barely managed to get his legs underneath him before he crashed against the back wall of the bridge. Sanchez grabbed on to the back of the navigator's seat and hung there, while Tali slid herself into the captain's acceleration couch and let it absorb the force.

The miners weren't so lucky. Willis toppled out of the pilot's seat and crumpled against the back wall of the bridge. Stockton almost managed to twist himself upright in time to brace himself against the acceleration, but he couldn't get his legs under him before he hit the edge of the hatchway. He dangled over the ladderway for a moment, and then he slid down out of sight.

"The brig is open," Elena said from the backup bridge on deck twelve, where Sanchez's emergency transfer code had given her and Rahul control of the ship. "Engineering is locked down."

Sanchez dropped to the floor next to Lucas, grimacing in pain. She took a step toward the hatchway, but her injured leg collapsed under her.

"Go after him!" she gasped. "Quickly! There's not much time!"

Tali climbed out of the captain's console and lowered herself to the back wall. The floor shuddered under the force of the *Orpheus*'s engines, and Lucas strained to keep himself upright. How fast were they accelerating? A full gee—maybe more?

He crouched over the hatchway and looked down. Six decks below, the rec room entrance was closed. But there was no sign of Stockton. He and Tali climbed down the ladder carefully. Had Stockton somehow managed to survive that ten-meter drop?

"Elena," Lucas called over the intercom. "Reduce thrust. Vector us away from the rest of the fleet."

A few moments later, the roar of the engines faded and the crushing acceleration died down to a manageable level. Lucas and Tali climbed quickly down the ladderway. As they turned a corner to head into one of the side passages that led past the rec room, they nearly ran into Maria leading a group of twenty cadets. Startled, she raised a pulse weapon and aimed it at them.

"It's us!" Lucas said quickly, putting up his hands.

Maria clenched her jaw and locked her eyes with Tali's. "So I see."

"I'm on your side, Maria," Tali said.

"How convenient," Maria said. "I guess we'll see how long *that* lasts."

"Thanks for that warning," Hanako said to Lucas. "We

managed to avoid any serious injuries. Are we running the ship from the backup bridge?"

Lucas nodded. "Elena and Rahul are there."

"Next step is to fan out and find the rest of the miners," Maria said. "Hopefully none of them knew what was coming."

"We locked six of them in a cargo hold," Hanako said. "Four cadets and two miners are in medbay being treated for burns."

"Stockton is still here somewhere," Tali said. "You didn't see him?"

"He wouldn't be alive if we had," Maria said grimly. She turned to the cadets behind her. "I'll take a squad to the brig and find the officers. The rest of you, search the ship top to bottom. Be careful."

As the cadets dispersed, Lucas used a wall console to open up a link to the backup bridge. "Rahul—any sign of Stockton?"

"No. But someone just opened up all of the outer doors in the hangar."

"That must be him," Lucas said to Tali. "Come on!"

"Be careful!" Rahul shouted over the console. "He's disabled the cameras in the hangar. It could be a trap."

They reached the Park Place ladderway and scrambled down the last few decks to the hangar. All three of the doorways were closed and locked. Tali looked through the window in one of the doors and pounded her fists against it in frustration. Inside, Stockton was already at the controls of one of the patrol ships.

"He can't get far," Lucas said.

Tali glowered at Stockton through the window. "Far enough that I can't wring his ugly little neck."

Stockton looked up at them and grinned. He climbed out of the ship and scrambled away. A moment later, the patroller's engines ignited, and it sped out of the hangar. Stockton jumped up into the only other ship in the hangar—a powerful-looking long-haul cargo ship. He closed the ship's hatch and powered up the engines. A moment later, he lifted off and darted out through the hangar's outer doors. Despite himself, Lucas felt a brief moment of admiration for Stockton's piloting skills— flying out of a larger ship while it was under acceleration was no easy feat.

Lucas tapped on the wall console next to the hangar doors. "Rahul, Stockton is in that cargo ship. Where is he going?"

"Tracking now," Rahul said. "Looks like he's making a fast burn and leaving orbit."

The intercom crackled, and Stockton's voice interrupted Rahul. "There's a war coming, little muskrats. What are you going to do when every Belter in the solar system rises up against you?"

368

"What is he talking about?" Tali asked.

Lucas had a sudden, sickening thought as he remembered what McKinley had told him. *Stockton wants a war, and he'll do anything to start one.* "Rahul—what about the patroller?"

"It's on autopilot, heading back down toward Vesta."

"Down to the surface?" Tali asked. "There's nobody on board. How is it going to land?"

"It's heading right for the colony," Elena said. "You're sure there's nobody on board?"

Lucas closed his eyes. He knew exactly what Stockton was planning. "It's not going to land. Stockton programmed it to crash into the colony dome. He's going to blame the Navy for destroying the bazaar."

"Oh, my god," Elena said.

"Shoot it!" Tali said. "Do something!"

"That won't work," Rahul said. "The debris would still hit the colony. We have to find some way to change its trajectory."

"Rahul, how long until impact?" Lucas asked.

There was a brief pause. "Ten minutes."

"I'll get word to the colony!" Elena said. "Maybe they can evacuate."

"They won't have enough time," Lucas said. He started climbing back up the ladderway toward the front of the ship.

"What are you doing?" Tali asked.

"I'm going after that patrol ship."

He scrambled up the ladder and around to the waist airlock. Tali followed close behind. "Lucas, this is insane!"

Lucas dug through the thruster packs in the back of the airlock prep room, searching for one with a full fuel tank. Tali watched him for a moment, and then she quickly began putting on a pressure suit.

"Tali—" he began.

"I'm coming with you," she said flatly.

Lucas paused. It was obvious there was nothing he could say to dissuade her. He picked out two thruster packs and handed one to her. They each slid one on and grabbed a helmet, and then Lucas followed Tali into the airlock. She cycled it and opened the outer doors.

"Remind me to tell you what a monumentally stupid idea this is." She bent her knees and jumped out, disappearing quickly as the *Orpheus*'s acceleration left her behind. Lucas took a deep breath and leaped out after her.

His stomach turned over as he was suddenly plunged into free fall. There was a brief flash as he passed by the ship's engines, and then he was floating in a silent sea of stars high above the gray bulk of Vesta. He activated his thruster pack and aimed himself down toward the surface of the asteroid. After a few moments he saw the glow of Tali's thrusters. He adjusted his angle and slid in alongside her. She pointed toward the surface.

"About a kilometer ahead. We have to hurry."

Lucas nodded, and they both increased their thrusters to full power. At first it seemed like they were making no progress at all. What if they couldn't catch up to the patrol ship before it hit? They needed to preserve enough fuel to get themselves back into a stable orbit, or else they would crash right alongside it.

They came out onto the sunlit side of the asteroid and the patroller appeared in front of them, about fifty meters closer to the surface. They aimed straight for it and then reduced thrust to match its course. Lucas grabbed the patrol ship's hatch and slid inside, and Tali climbed in after him.

Lucas sat down at the pilot's console. He pulled back on the control stick to activate the attitude rockets. Nothing happened.

"The controls aren't working!"

"Try the main engine," Tali said, huddling close over his shoulder. "Maybe we can at least change its course."

Lucas pressed the button sequence to kill their thrust. The control panel displayed an error, and the faint rumble of the main engine persisted. He tried again with the same result.

"He's done something to sabotage the controls," Tali said, smacking the screen with the palm of her hand.

"What do you mean?" Elena asked, her transmission crackling slightly. "You can't fly it?"

Lucas leaned back in his seat and stared at the controls. "No main engines, no attitude rockets, no controls at all. We can't change course."

"Three minutes to impact. You need to get out of there!" Rahul said. "There's nothing you can do."

Tali put her hand on Lucas's arm. "He's right," she said. "We've got no thrust and no control."

Thrust. Lucas suddenly remembered how they'd won the capture-the-flag game, ages ago. "Yes, we do! How much delta-vee would it take to miss the colony and hit the surface instead?"

"It wouldn't take much," Rahul said. "Just nudge the ship by a few meters per second, and it would land far enough away to not cause damage."

"How much fuel is in these thruster packs?"

There was a moment of silence as everyone realized what Lucas was suggesting, and then they all spoke at once.

"Lucas—" Tali began.

"After what you've already used—there might be enough," Rahul said.

"No!" Elena said. "That's not an option."

"We have to try," Lucas insisted.

"If you use all of your fuel, you won't be able to get

yourselves back into orbit," Elena said. "You'll crash along with the ship."

Tali pursed her lips. Lucas recognized the anguished look on her face, because it mirrored exactly what he was feeling right now himself. But there was something else too: a determination that saving their own lives and letting an entire colony of innocent people die wasn't an option they could accept.

She nodded. Without saying a word, they climbed back outside. The enormous bulk of Vesta took up almost their entire field of view. They positioned themselves on either side of the cabin door with their hands pressed against the hull, and then they fired their backpacks at maximum thrust.

The force was enough to make Lucas's arms buckle. He gritted his teeth and straightened them back out again. He glanced over at Tali. Her face was locked in concentration as she tried to keep herself steady.

"A quarter of a meter per second," Rahul said. "Point five. Almost one, now."

"It's not going to be enough!" Elena said. "Lucas, you don't have enough fuel!"

Lucas tried to look down at the gauge on his chest, but he couldn't make out the numbers. How much longer could they keep this up?

"One point five. One point eight. Two."

Lucas's thruster pack sputtered and died. A moment later, Tali's did the same. They pulled themselves against the hull of the ship and looked down at the approaching surface. The adrenaline that had been flooding through Lucas's body was gone, and he was suddenly more tired than he'd ever been in his life.

"We're out of fuel," Tali said. Her voice was exhausted too. "What's our course?"

There was a brief pause. "Projecting impact fifty meters from the colony," Rahul said. "That's enough!"

"Somebody do something!" Elena shouted. "They're going to die!"

"There's nothing left to do," Lucas said quietly.

The surface of the asteroid was all they could see. Craters and hills sped by so quickly they were almost a blur. Tali reached out and took his hand. He squeezed it wordlessly.

"Another ship!" Rahul said. "Fast intercept course!"

Lucas looked up and saw a cargo ship braking hard as it tried to match the patroller's trajectory. Its engines flared, and he had to shield his eyes from the glare.

"Hold steady!" McKinley called over the radio. "This is going to be tight."

The cargo hold at the rear of his ship slid open. There wasn't time to dock or even match speed. In a few seconds, their only chance of making it would be gone. Simultaneously, Lucas and Tali leaped out toward McKinley's ship. Lucas managed to snag the edge of the cargo door, but Tali crashed into the rear of the ship, just in front of the engine cowling. She scrambled up, and he reached out and grabbed her wrist.

"Go!" he shouted.

McKinley fired the engines. Lucas wrapped his fingers around the edge of the cargo hold's doorframe and concentrated on keeping his grip on Tali's arm. The gray surface of Vesta whizzed past them, seemingly close enough to touch.

"I've got you!" Lucas said to Tali, locking his eyes with hers.

He pulled her upward and into the cargo hold. They held themselves against the doorframe, breathing heavily. There was a sudden bright flash on the surface a few kilometers behind them. A massive cloud of dust burst skyward and then slowly drifted back down. When the dust had settled, Lucas could see the lights of the bazaar still glowing steadily.

Slowly the surface receded, until a halo of stars surrounded the planet. McKinley cut the engines and looked back at them through the cockpit entrance.

"Remind me not to hang around the two of you in the future, eh?"

* * *

On the ride back to the *Orpheus*, part of Lucas's mind wanted to worry about Stockton, the other Belters, and whatever they were planning next, but the rest of him was too exhausted to care. Tali sat quietly against the wall of the cargo hold with her arms wrapped around her knees. She looked . . . resigned? Content? Lucas couldn't tell.

When they landed, he helped her up, and they joined McKinley out on the hangar deck.

"Thank you," Lucas said. "You saved our lives."

Tali nodded and shook McKinley's hand. "Thanks."

"Well, there's good people down there," McKinley said, clearly embarrassed. "And what you did was brave. And stupid. Maybe the bravest and stupidest thing I've ever seen."

"Where are you going to go now?" Tali asked.

"Haven't really decided, to be honest. Someplace far from here. Maybe if I keep my head down, the Navy won't try too hard to find me."

"We'll tell them how you helped us," Lucas said.

"You could come too," McKinley said to Tali. "I could use a good copilot."

Tali shook her head. "I'm done with hiding."

"You've got more guts than me," McKinley said, smiling sadly. "Good luck."

McKinley climbed back up into the cargo ship's

cockpit. He started to close the hatch, and then he stopped. "You know, I think maybe you were right," he said to Lucas. "Maybe people can change. Even people as hard-headed as the Navy or us Belters. I hope we don't throw away the chance."

He closed the hatch. Tali pulled Lucas back to the rear wall of the hangar, and they watched McKinley lift off and disappear into the starry sky. *Was there a chance? Lucas wondered. And would anyone take it?*

As soon as they had repressurized the hangar, Elena and Rahul rushed in, followed by Maria and Hanako. Rahul collided with Lucas and hugged him tightly. "Ow! Hey!"

"That was the stupidest thing I've ever seen anyone do," Maria said, grabbing Tali and putting her into a mostly friendly headlock.

"She's right," Elena agreed. "But it was nicely executed."

"Don't let Ms. Calm and Collected fool you," Rahul said, elbowing Lucas. "She was more worried than any of us."

"Come on," Tali said. "Let's get to the bridge. We've got a lot of explaining to do."

25

LUCAS SAT IN his dress uniform on a bench in a long, empty hallway. The sounds of muted conversations and the clacking of heels on the granite floors echoed through the corridors of the naval base. The bench was hard and uncomfortable, and the tight-fitting dress uniform made his skin itch. It didn't help that after three days here on Ceres, he was already tired of gravity and ready to be back out in space.

The past month had been a whirlwind. The first thing Sanchez had done, once she was sure the immediate threat was over, had been to take Lucas and Tali into her cabin and have them explain absolutely everything that had happened. That had been easier than Lucas had expected, and to his surprise, Tali showed no hesitation or reluctance. She seemed relieved to finally be able to tell the truth. When they were done, Sanchez had asked them to write it all up so that they wouldn't forget any details.

When they'd gotten to Ceres, Lucas's dad had already been there waiting for them. As soon as they'd climbed out of the transport, Tomas had grabbed him in a hug so tight Lucas thought his ribs might crack.

"I'm fine, Dad," Lucas managed to say.

Tomas let Lucas go and turned to Tali. She put her hands in her pockets and looked down at the hangar floor. "It's good to—"

Their dad pulled her toward him and wrapped his arms around her. He held her that way for a long moment and then finally let go. Tali cleared her throat and looked at Lucas. "I know you two haven't seen each other in a while," she said. "But if you don't mind . . ."

Lucas nodded. This was a conversation he wanted desperately to hear, but they deserved their privacy. As he watched them head over to the other end of the hangar, talking quietly, he decided that seeing them together again, even for just a moment, was worth more to him than almost anything else in the world.

But since that brief reunion in the hangar, Lucas had hardly had five minutes alone with either Tali or his dad. The Navy had insisted on a full medical screen and multiple debriefings, where he'd had to repeat his story in agonizing detail. But whenever he asked what was going to happen to him, all anyone would tell him was that he'd have to wait for the tribunal.

Waiting, apparently, was what tribunals were all about. He'd been sitting out here on this bench for over an hour while Tali gave her testimony. He was starting to wonder if he had time to find a bathroom when the door opened and Tali walked out.

"How did it go?" Lucas asked, jumping off the bench to meet her.

"Well, I'm expelled from the academy and barred from the Navy. But at least they're not going to put me in prison. The captain put in a recommendation. I think that was what persuaded them."

A wave of relief flooded over Lucas. He'd tried not to think about what the tribunal might decide to do to Tali. But this was as good an outcome as he could possibly have hoped.

"Have you thought about what you'll do next?"

Tali shrugged. "I'll probably head out into the Belt. As a private citizen this time. I've got an open offer to be a copilot."

"Wait," Lucas said. "Do you mean—"

"No, not McKinley," she said, waving her hand. "This one's different. Very legitimate."

"That sounds great," Lucas said. "So maybe I'll see you out there?"

"Oh, you will," she said, punching him lightly on the shoulder. "Count on it."

"Ready?" Sanchez said from the doorway.

Lucas took a deep breath and followed her inside. The room was large and imposing, with decorative paneling made to look like real wood. Two men and one woman sat behind a long table at the far end. A smaller table with two chairs faced them. The rest of the room was taken up by rows and rows of chairs, as if for an audience that hadn't arrived yet. The three admirals watched him with expressions ranging from intense curiosity to bored indifference. Sanchez led him to the smaller desk and sat down next to him.

"You are Lucas Adebayo?" asked the woman. She was tall and imposing, even from her seat at the table. Lucas was pretty sure he wouldn't ever want to make her angry.

"Yes, ma'am," Lucas said.

The woman looked around at the other admirals. "We have a full accounting of the events near Vesta, both written and verbal. Are there any questions for the cadet?"

The younger of the two men leaned forward. He had black hair and a short, old-fashioned-looking beard. "No questions," he said. "But I would like to point out that by my count the cadet violated at least five different major regulations and about fifty minor ones. Under normal circumstances—"

"But these aren't normal circumstances," the woman said smoothly. "It's clear that without Cadet Adebayo's intervention, a great many civilians would have died and the *Orpheus* might still be in enemy hands."

"That's true," the man said, "but—"

"Unless there is further objection, I move that we close this portion of the case."

The man paused for a moment, and then nodded reluctantly. Lucas let out a quiet sigh of relief. At least *that* was over.

"I believe we have another matter to attend to," the other man said. He was much older than the others, and spoke with a slow drawl. "That being his performance as a cadet. We had serious questions about his suitability when Captain Sanchez made her original proposal to bring him on board."

Lucas's mouth slid open. They still hadn't decided whether he was good enough to stay on the *Orpheus*?

Sanchez stood up. "I believe you have the results of our initial evaluations, along with the reports of his performance during the term so far."

"Yes," the man said, peering down at a screen on the table in front of him. "I'll admit, none of it is quite what I expected."

"I'd like to hear the cadet's views before we decide,"

the woman said. She turned to Lucas. "Do *you* feel you belong in the academy?"

Lucas remembered Sanchez asking him that same question in her cabin once. How long ago had that been? A month? Six weeks? It felt like ages.

"No, ma'am," he said. "I don't."

The woman raised her eyebrows. "Oh?"

"I *want* to belong. I want that more than almost anything. My sister did too. She told me that I ought to pretend to be someone I wasn't, because there was no other way it was going to work."

"It doesn't seem like you took her advice," the older man said.

"Sometimes I wanted to," Lucas admitted. "But it's hard to hide when you stick out as much as I do."

"Are you saying you don't want to go back to the *Orpheus*?"

"No, sir," Lucas said. "I still want to be a cadet. More than ever, actually. But I guess it's up to you."

He took a deep breath. There was no point in stopping now—and after all, they'd asked for his opinion, hadn't they?

"But the real question isn't whether I belong at the academy. I'm just one kid, right? You can let me stay or you can kick me out now, and either way, it's not going to change much. The real question is whether you're going to do what it takes to make all the *other* kids in the Belt belong. There are thousands of them out there who could learn how to be great pilots and engineers and navigators and commanders. They deserve a chance to fit in without needing to pretend like they're somebody else. If you really want to make things better out in the Belt, then you need to make *them* belong."

He shrugged. "Like I said—it's up to you."

It took thirty-five agonizing minutes for the admirals to decide what they were going to do with him. Lucas paced up and down the hallway, keeping his eyes on the clock on the wall the entire time. How long could this last? What could they possibly be discussing? From the skeptical expressions on the admirals' faces, it had seemed pretty clear what they wanted to do. Couldn't they just get it over with?

He looked down at his sleeves. He still hated the way they clung to his forearms. Who would design a uniform like that? He tugged nervously at the material, trying to get it to relax. With a slight tearing sound, the seam on his sleeve tore open a few centimeters. He stared at it for a moment. *That* wasn't what he'd expected.

Impulsively he opened the seam even further and

rolled the sleeve up to his elbow. He repeated the process on the other sleeve and looked at his arms in satisfaction. There. *That* was how a Belter cadet wore his uniform. He leaned back against the wall and waited.

After several more minutes Captain Sanchez came out into the hallway and escorted him back inside. The three admirals watched him with—what? Curiosity at his appearance? Irritation at his lack of respect for his uniform? Lucas didn't know, and he didn't care anymore. He sat down and laced his fingers together, with his arms on the table. Finally the woman cleared her throat and spoke.

"We've been put into something of an odd position. According to all of our standard mechanisms for evaluating potential cadets, you are entirely unsuited for our training schools."

Boy, that's the truth, Lucas thought.

"When you arrived on the *Orpheus*, you had an inadequate educational background in several key subjects. But in other areas, you immediately demonstrated a mastery we don't often see even in fourth-year cadets."

The white-haired man nodded. "There's also the matter of your actions during the hijacking and insurrection. The traditions of the Navy don't appear to have an appropriate response for a situation like this."

Lucas nodded, though he didn't quite understand what the man was saying. *Response? As in some kind of punishment?*

"However, after a decision-making process that was about as fast as I've ever seen in this Navy, we've come up with an answer that I believe is quite suitable."

"Cadet Adebayo, at attention," Sanchez said.

Lucas fumbled out of his chair and stood up. He was still trying to figure out what was going on when Sanchez pinned a medal on his uniform.

"It is my honor to award you the naval medal for conspicuous bravery and heroism. You are the very first cadet to receive this award."

Lucas stared down at the red-and-gold medal on his chest. His mouth opened, but he couldn't think of anything to say. *Conspicuous bravery and heroism?*

"Thank you, ma'am," he said finally, and then turned to the admirals. "Thank you."

The woman nodded. "I sincerely hope that other cadets—from all parts of the solar system—will follow your example."

"Captain Sanchez, it is our recommendation that Cadet Adebayo return to the *Orpheus* to complete his training," the younger of the two men said. "Do you concur?"

"Yes, sir," Sanchez said. "Without question."

"Then I believe these proceedings are complete," the man said. "Cadet Adebayo, Captain Sanchez, you are dismissed."

Sanchez took Lucas gently by the arm and led him back into the hall. His mind was still spinning with everything that had happened. He kept looking down at his chest to convince himself that he hadn't just been daydreaming.

"Congratulations, Cadet," Sanchez said.

"Thank you," Lucas said. "And thank you too, for helping Tali."

"I did what I thought was right," Sanchez said. "No more, and no less."

She led him down to the hangar, where a half-dozen ships were being loaded, unloaded, or repaired in a row of berths. In between two gleaming white Navy shuttles was the *Josey Wales*. She was as awkwardly shaped as ever, and she was still stained with years of mining dust, but to Lucas's eyes, she was utterly beautiful.

His dad jumped up from his seat on the gangway and rushed over to them. He stopped abruptly and then reached out to shake Lucas's hand with an embarrassed smile. Lucas grabbed him and hugged him tightly.

"It's good to know heroes still hug their dads," Tomas said, kissing Lucas's forehead. He stepped back and inspected the medal on Lucas's chest. "Seems like it could be a bit bigger, under the circumstances. But it's pretty enough."

"I wish you could have been there," Lucas said.

"The Navy likes to keep some things private, I guess," Tomas said. He tapped on the hull of the *Josey Wales*. "Anyway, it gave me a chance to polish her up a bit."

"She's a fine ship," Sanchez said.

"Have you found a copilot yet?" Lucas asked.

"As a matter of fact, yes," his dad said. "And I think she's going to work out beautifully."

Lucas craned his neck to see into the cockpit. His heart swelled as he recognized who was sitting in the copilot's seat.

Natali Adebayo saw him watching her and smiled. How long had it been since Lucas had seen that smile? She looked as if an invisible weight had been lifted from her, one that she'd almost forgotten was there. He saluted, and she straightened up in her seat and returned the salute emphatically. "Good luck," she mouthed.

"I'll see you out there," Lucas said to his dad.

"Every chance we get," Tomas said. He leaned down and kissed Lucas's forehead. "Take care of yourself."

He hopped into the *Josey Wales* and closed the cabin door. Lucas ran up a flight of stairs to a small observation deck. The *Josey Wales* emerged from its berth and rose up into the dark sky. Lucas followed it with his eyes until the lights from its engines were just a tiny white star among thousands.

"Now, Cadet, I believe we still have the rest of your term to finish," Sanchez said. "Are you ready?"

Lucas smiled. "Yes, ma'am."

ACKNOWLEDGMENTS

One of the best parts about publishing a novel is that you get to work with fantastic people whose profession and passion is making your story better than it ever could have been on your own. It's been a joy working with Sarah Homer, Tara Weikum, Laaren Brown, Renée Cafiero, and everyone at HarperCollins. I hope they all found the experience to be as positive as I did.

Literary agents these days are about much more than contracts and sales, and I'm lucky to have Bridget Smith of JABberwocky as my partner in publishing. I'm frequently amazed by the combination of skills that it takes to be an agent, and I'm grateful that there are people like Bridget who can pivot so neatly between all the different parts of the job.

Shirin Bridges and her wonderful troupe of Bay Area writers have kept me grounded, connected, and inspired for almost ten years now. I'd like to thank Amanda Conran, Cady Owens, Cameron Lund, Carole Stivers, Cassia Brill, Chris Hall, Debbie DeVoe, Jenn Siebert, Julie Sullivan, Leata Holloway, Robyn Murphy, and especially Shirin herself for their feedback and friendship. I know I'll always be The Other Chris, but it's a spot I wouldn't give up for anything.

When you're growing up, you need family and friends who can help you discover the kind of person you want to be. Looking back, I know that I would have been much more lost if I hadn't had people like Casey McCann and Jonathan Malko alongside me. Both of them are immensely talented and creative, but even more important, they have strong internal compasses that have always helped guide me in my own life.

Almost exactly seventeen years ago, I sat outside a bar in Atlanta and talked for hours with a woman whose combination of warmth and wit made the rest of the world disappear. I remember very clearly the first time I reached out and held her hand, and I'm extraordinarily glad I never let it go. I love you, Kendra.

This book is dedicated to my children, Eleanor, Andrew, and Jack. I've never been given anything more precious than the opportunity to be their father. Each of them never ceases to amaze me, and I can't wait to see the worlds that they and their generation will build.